Delia Sherman was born ... City. Her 'New York Between' novels ... are *Changeling* and *The Magic Mirror of the Mermaid Queen*. Delia enjoys teaching writing workshops, most recently at the Hollins University Masters Degree Programme in Children's Literature. After many years in Boston, she once again lives in New York City, but travels at the drop of a hat.

Praise for *The Freedom Maze*:

An Andre Norton Award Winner

A Mythopoeic Fantasy Award for Children's Literature Winner

A *Kirkus Reviews* Best Children's Book

'This is an absolutely fascinating story. *The Freedom Maze* draws you into a world of danger and mystery, of daring and change, at the dawning of the Civil War. Sophie's adventures in the history of her family's Louisiana plantation feel real, and lead her to a real understanding of racial truths she would never have caught a glimpse of without magic. Beautifully imagined and told with satisfyingly matter-of-fact detail . . . *The Freedom Maze* is deep, meaningful fun.' Nisi Shawl, author of *Filter House*

'Vividly realized and saturated with feeling.' Elizabeth Knox, author of *Dreamhunter*

The FREEDOM MAZE

Delia Sherman

corsair

CORSAIR

First published in the United States of America in 2011 by Big Mouth House.

First published in Great Britain in 2015 by Corsair.

Copyright © Delia Sherman, 2011

The moral right of the author has been asserted.

A CIP catalogue record for this book
is available from the British Library.

ISBN 978-1-47211-752-6 (paperback)
ISBN 978-1-47211-793-9 (ebook)

Printed and bound in Great Britain by CPI Group (UK) Ltd, Croydon, CR0 4YY

Corsair
is an imprint of
Little, Brown
100 Victoria Embankment
London EC4Y 0DY

An Hachette UK Company
www.hachette.co.uk

www.littlebrown.co.uk

*For all the enslaved men and women whose names
in ledgers and newspaper advertisements,
and stories in slave narratives and memoirs,
inspired me to write this book.*

The
FREEDOM
MAZE

Chapter 1

Sophie Martineau looked out the window of her mother's 1954 Ford station wagon and watched her life slide behind her into the past.

It was raining. It rained a lot in May in Louisiana, but Sophie couldn't help feeling this rain was personal. It was bad enough to be saying good-bye to her friends and her school and the house she'd grown up in to spend the summer stuck out in the bayou with Grandmama and Aunt Enid, knowing she'd be coming back to a different neighborhood and a different school in the fall. Doing it in the rain was just rubbing her nose in it.

They drove past her best friend Diana Roget's house. In the wet, the big stucco house was grim and uninviting—just like Mrs. Roget after Papa up and moved to New York. Once the divorce was final, she hadn't even allowed Diana to come over any more, and Sophie wasn't invited to Galveston as she had been every summer since third grade. It was like Mrs. Roget thought divorce was catching, like cooties. Although she'd denied it, Sophie suspected Diana thought so, too.

They stopped at a red light and Mama glanced over. "You're very quiet. Are you thinking about your big adventure?"

"Yes, ma'am." The fib came automatically. Life was easier when Sophie told Mama what she wanted to hear.

"What a sad little voice! You're not nervous, are you? You used to love Oak Cottage when you were small."

"I'm afraid I don't remember very much."

This was beyond a fib and right on into a lie. Sophie had hated visiting Oak Cottage, even for a weekend. Even though she'd only been six at the time, she had very vivid memories of uncomfortable meals where Grandmama talked about how much better everything had been when she was a girl, Papa made silly jokes, and Mama radiated chill like an open refrigerator. There was no air-conditioning at Oak Cottage, and too many bugs. The idea of spending a whole summer there was hardly bearable. But with Mama working all day and going to Soule College at night so she could be a Certified Public Accountant, and no money for camp, there wasn't any other choice.

"Don't tell me you don't remember Aunt Enid's garden," Mama said. "All those beautiful roses! And Grandmama's snuff-box collection. You'd play with them by the hour, just as I did when I was a little girl. You haven't forgotten that, have you?

"No, ma'am." Another lie. "Of course not."

The light turned green, and they took off again.

Now she thought about it, Sophie did have a vague picture of herself sitting on a very high bed, making patterns with bright little boxes. Her memory of Oak Cottage itself was a lot more vivid. It looked like an ogre in a fairy tale, big and green, with two angry-looking windows sticking out of the roof for eyes and steep red steps up to the gallery that stretched across the front like a toothy mouth. She'd screamed blue murder the first time they visited, and Papa had had to carry her up from the car. He'd laughed when she told him why she was scared, but Mama had been too disgusted to speak to her.

As they reached the Huey P. Long Bridge over the Mississippi, the rain shut off like a faucet, the sun came out, and the Ford turned into a sticky steam bath. Sophie stood it as long as she could, then cranked the window down an inch.

"What on earth are you doing?" Mama asked.

"Letting in some air. My back's all sweaty."

"Horses sweat," Mama reminded her. "Ladies gently glow. I suppose you can open the window a crack. But put something over your hair, or the wind will blow it into a hooraw's nest."

Sophie's reflection in the window told her that her hair had already frizzed up like cotton candy. But she knew that arguing with that particular tone of voice was useless, so she tied a silk scarf around her head before rolling the window down all the way.

Hot air hit her face like a sponge soaked in gas fumes and swamp water. Sophie thought wistfully of Papa's Cadillac, which had air-conditioning and padded cloth seats that didn't stick to your back like the Ford's woven plastic. Papa liked to drive, and flew along the blacktop with his elbow cocked out the window, singing. He had a deep, clear voice and sang show tunes. "Oh, What a Beautiful Morning" was his favorite.

Mama, on the other hand, gripped the wheel with her hands at ten-to-two exactly and kept her eyes fixed grimly on the road. She never sang—she wouldn't even turn on the radio. Back when Sophie was little, Mama used to pass the time on long car trips telling stories about growing up at Oak Cottage and going to school with all the grades together in one room and reciting "The Wreck of the Hesperus" on Prize Day. It was her second-favorite topic, after The Good Old Days before the War of Northern Aggression, when the Fairchilds had raised sugarcane on Oak River Plantation.

Mama was very proud of being a Fairchild of Oak River. Sophie knew exactly how many acres the Fairchilds had owned at the outbreak of the War of Northern Aggression (nine hundred), how many slaves (one hundred and fifty), and when Mr. Charles Fairchild III had built his fancy brick plantation house (1850). She'd heard about Mammys (fat, fussy, and comical) and Beaux (dashing, polite, and handsome) and, most importantly, about Southern Belles, who had twenty-inch waists and huge frothy dresses and nothing to do all day but look pretty and decide who they'd dance with at the next ball.

In Sophie's mind, those Southern Belles looked just like Mama. Everybody said Mama was a beauty. Her chestnut hair was wavy and shiny like a Breck Shampoo Girl's, her skin was smooth and creamy, and her waist not much bigger than twenty inches around, even without a girdle. Sophie's puppy fat, frizzy, dishwater hair, imperfect skin, and thick glasses were a great trial to Mama, but she never gave up hope. She made Sophie brush her hair one hundred strokes and scrub her face with lemons every night. She'd even bought her a garter belt and nylons for her thirteenth birthday last year, along with a completely pointless bra that rode up Sophie's chest when she played volleyball. Sophie was wearing them all right now, under her blue seersucker suit and her first pair of high-heel pumps.

I bet those Belles were bored silly, she thought viciously. *I bet they didn't dare move because they might sweat and had a special slave to measure their waists and see how they were getting along with looking pretty. I can just hear it: "Why, Miss LolaBelle! I declare, child, you plain as puddin' this mornin'. You best stir yourself if you thinkin' of lookin' pretty today!"*

Past Bridge City, Route 90 plunged straight into swampland. Scrubby woods alternated with wide fields of young sugarcane and ponds of still, dark water spotted with neongreen duckweed. Sophie saw a heron standing stilt-legged in a culvert and a possum lying crushed at the side of the road. Every so often, a town would pop up—a handful of peeling clapboard houses, a general store, a church, a saloon bar, a filling station.

Mile after mile, Sophie watched it all scrolling past the window and wondered what she was going to do all summer out in the bayou. Unless things had changed, Grandmama and Aunt Enid didn't even have a TV. The nearest movie house was probably all the way up in New Iberia, or even Lafayette. Sophie had packed a suitcase full of her favorite books: *Alice in Wonderland, The Time Garden, The Witch of Blackbird Pond, Swiss Family Robinson, Great Expectations.* But she doubted they'd last the whole summer.

Sophie shifted uncomfortably on the seat, wincing as her garters pinched viciously at the flesh of her thighs. "Mama, can we stop soon?"

Mama considered a moment. "I might could stretch my legs. And a glass of ice tea would be welcome. We'll see if there's a nice drugstore in Morgan City."

Morgan City was a real town, with sidewalks and traffic lights and people and a drugstore with a brand-new neon sign in the window.

Inside, a couple of ceiling fans ruffled the pages of the magazines and comics on the revolving rack. Sophie looked around at the cracked Formica, the faded sign proclaiming Dr. Pepper to be "The Friendly Pepper-Upper!" and the three men in shirtsleeves slouching over the lunch counter, and wished she was back home in Metairie, where everything was nicer.

Mama asked the colored girl behind the counter where the restroom was, and disappeared. Sophie picked up *Little Lulu*. It was from March, 1960, two months old, and she'd read it already at the dentist's. But she pretended to be interested in Lulu's adventures until Mama returned, wiping her hands on her handkerchief.

"The restroom's nothing to write home about," she said. "But perfectly adequate. Remember to wash your hands with soap and use a paper towel to open the door. I'll order us some tea."

"Can I have a Coca-Cola? Please?"

"We'll see. Don't dawdle."

Above the bathroom door, a hand-lettered sign read Whites Only! Sophie locked the door, wincing at the strong smell of disinfectant, peeled off her nylons and garter belt, and stuffed them into her purse. With any luck Mama wouldn't notice, and if she did, maybe she'd pretend not to. Some battles were too small for even Mama to fight.

When Sophie came out, the men had left and Mama was sitting at the lunch counter, sipping ice tea and chatting with the colored girl like she'd known her all her life. A green bottle of Coca-Cola sat on the counter next to a glass of ice. Guiltily conscious of her stockingless legs, Sophie edged up on a stool and poured herself a glass. It tasted just like it looked, bright with bubbles and the sugar Mama said would rot her teeth.

Sipping and swinging on her stool, she caught sight of a Negro man tapping on the window. The counter girl glanced from him to Mama and shook her head just a little. Sophie was relieved. She didn't mind Negro women—Lily, the colored woman who did for Mama in Metairie, had practically raised her. But Negro men made her nervous. Mama had explained it to her over and over. Negro men, especially young ones, could be dangerous. They were lazy and dirty, and sometimes they drank. Never, under any circumstances, was Sophie to speak to any Negro man she didn't already know.

Well, the only Negro men Sophie knew were Lily's husband, Hector, and Mama's gardener, Sam. She didn't know about Hector—she only saw him when she went to church with Lily—but Sam was pretty much always busy and couldn't help being dirty, working in the garden all day. She sometimes wondered if Mama might be a little unfair—about Hector and Sam, anyway. Still, talking to strangers made Sophie nervous no matter what color they were, so it wasn't hard to obey.

Mama put down her empty glass and said, "Time to go, darling. We don't want to keep Grandmama waiting, do we?"

For all Sophie cared, Grandmama could wait forever.

Sitting out in the sun, the Ford had gone from steam bath to oven. Mama rolled down her window and handed Sophie a brown paper bag. "For a rainy day at Oak Cottage."

Sophie opened the bag and pulled out *The Secret of the Old Clock*, a Nancy Drew mystery. She looked up, surprised. Nancy Drew books were right on up there with comics on Mama's list of Things Young Ladies Don't Read. "Thank you, Mama."

"You're welcome. Now, close that window. I think it's going to rain again."

Sure enough, the heavens opened. Mama turned on the windshield wipers and slowed the car to a nervous crawl. Then they had to get gas, and then Mama saw an antique shop, and what with one thing and another it was almost four o'clock when they reached Oakwood.

Oakwood looked pretty much like every other town they'd driven through—sleepy, wet, all but deserted. Among the usual weathered clapboard houses, Sophie spotted two churches, a little restaurant called Cleo's Kitchen, a brick building with Trahan's Foundry, 1898 written on it, and a pink and white Victorian house with a sign out front: Iberia Parish Museum.

They drove out into cane fields again. "This used to be Fairchild land," Mama said. "It all belongs to a big commercial grower now, of course. Grandmama's hardly got twenty acres left, and that's all gone to scrub and weeds."

Rolling down the window, Sophie breathed damp, clean air and watched the cane flash by, pale green and graceful. Soon she'd be greeting Grandmama and Aunt Enid, curtsying like a perfect little lady and not speaking until she was spoken to. She wasn't looking forward to it.

A thick grove of oak and swamp maple appeared on the left. Mama turned onto a narrow dirt road, canopied with arcing branches. Sophie gasped as the heavy heat pressed down on her chest like a hand. The roaring of a million cicadas soared above the Ford's chugging. Great swags of Spanish moss hung everywhere like cobwebs in a haunted mansion.

"There's the old slave quarters," Mama exclaimed suddenly.

Beyond the dark, dark trees, Sophie caught a glimpse of a group of little silver-brown houses floating hazily in the sunlight, looking, if possible, even spookier than the oak grove. Despite the heat, Sophie shivered and turned her gaze back to the road, which opened into a weedy field scattered with trees. Down next to the bayou, she saw a shabby, deserted-looking house shaded by big old live oaks. Mama bumped the Ford across the field, pulled up in front of the house, put on the parking brake, and turned off the ignition.

"We're home," she said.

Chapter 2

Sophie got out of the car.

Oak Cottage didn't remind her of an ogre anymore. The angry eyes were just dormer windows, the toothy mouth just an old-fashioned gallery. The long tongue was just a stair, its red paint as chipped and faded as the green wooden siding. It was smaller than she remembered.

The screen door screeched. A sturdy woman in a cotton housedress appeared on the gallery, waved, and came down the steps. Sophie recognized her, more from her picture on the piano than memory—Mama's sister, Aunt Enid, as plain as a loaf of brown bread, with graying hair scraped back in a bun and a bony face. It was hard to believe she was Mama's sister, except for their noses: the Fairchild nose, Mama called it—straight and long, with delicate nostrils. Sophie had it, too.

The sisters touched cheeks. "You're looking well, Enid," Mama said. "I'm that glad to get here, I can't tell you! It was an awful trip. Why you don't have that oak drive graded and paved, I'll never understand. How's Mama?"

"Middling." Aunt Enid turned to Sophie and held out her hand. "Hello, Sophie. You've certainly changed since I saw you last."

Sophie shook the hand and curtsied politely.

Delia Sherman

"I know I shouldn't be surprised," Aunt Enid said. "Children do grow, after all. How old are you now?"

Before Sophie could answer, Mama said, "Thirteen. Fourteen in July, though you wouldn't think it to look at her."

"I expect she's a late bloomer," Aunt Enid said cheerfully. "Now, you just leave your cases in the car for Ofelia to deal with and come on back to the kitchen. I've got a pitcher of ice tea waiting for you, and biscuits, fresh this morning."

"I don't want you going to any trouble," Mama said.

"Oh, no trouble," Aunt Enid said. "Ofelia made them."

The biscuits were good, but not as good as Lily's. Sophie chewed and chewed, eyes on her plate, thinking of Lily's biscuits, warm and flaky, spread with butter and mayhaw jelly, thinking of Lily, shadow-dark in her white uniform, smelling of laundry and baking and hair oil, sitting at the kitchen table and listening to Sophie tell her about her math teacher and the book she was reading and what Diana said in class.

She missed Diana, but she missed Lily more.

The tea had mint in it, fresh from a little pot on the windowsill, and was delicious. Aunt Enid poured it into cut-crystal glasses from a pitcher she took from the icebox, a rusty metal cabinet with the motor perched on top like a big drum. It looked almost as old as the stove and the long porcelain sink under the window.

Sophie edged off her pumps and doused her biscuit with Karo syrup. Aunt Enid sat back in her chair and picked up her glass. "Well," she said, "now you've taken the edge off, I want to know how you're doing, Sister."

Mama's mouth tightened. "As well as can be expected, under the circumstances."

Sophie winced at the chill in her voice, but Aunt Enid just laughed. "Lord, Sister, you know that tone doesn't work on me. Now, tell me about this job you've gone and taken. A secretary, of all things! Didn't that fancy lawyer of yours get enough from Randall to keep you and Sophie comfortable?"

Clearly, Aunt Enid had her own way of dealing with Mama. Mama sighed. "I can't complain. Randall's taking care of the mortgage and Sophie's tuition. But between paying Lily and Sam and Sophie needing piano lessons and uniforms and new glasses every whipstitch, some months I hardly know how to make ends meet. A secretary's salary just doesn't cover it all. So I've decided to sell the house, rent a little place in town, and take an accounting course at Soule College so I can be a CPA and make some real money."

Sophie noticed that Mama didn't mention that her bridge friends had stopped inviting her over or that she spent nearly all her evenings in the city. She hadn't mentioned those reasons for moving into town to Sophie, either.

Aunt Enid took a sip of tea. "I see. And what about Sophie's schooling?"

"That's a worry," Mama admitted. "Randall's been complaining about how expensive private school is, but I just can't see my way clear to sending her to public school. No daughter of mine is going to sit in the same classroom with little Negro children, no matter what the Supreme Court says. It's not natural."

"Of course not," Aunt Enid said. "The very idea."

Mama buttered a biscuit. "I'm going to send her to St. Mary's."

"St. Mary's!" Aunt Enid set her glass down with a snap. "That's a Catholic school!"

Mama shrugged. "What if it is? There's no danger of enforced desegregation, and the fees are very reasonable. And I've heard that the education's excellent."

Aunt Enid raised her eyebrows. "Have you? Oh, I'm not going to say a word—she's your child, and I'm not one to stick my nose into other folks' business. Just don't you let Mama get wind of it. You know how she feels about Catholics."

There was an uncomfortable silence, during which Sophie saw that Mama and Aunt Enid looked more alike than she'd thought.

The icebox kicked on with a rattle and began to hum loudly. Aunt Enid cleared her throat. "Well. It's a long drive from New Orleans, Sister. Why don't you go lie down on your bed for a spell while Miss Sophie and I get reacquainted?"

Mama nodded crisply. "I believe I will. Sophie, sit up straight. And comb your hair before supper. You look like something the cat dragged in."

When she was gone, Aunt Enid poured the last of the tea into Sophie's glass. "Now, what shall we talk about, Sophie Fairchild Martineau?"

Making conversation, Mama always said, was the art of asking questions. But the only question Sophie could think of was "What's wrong with Catholics?" which would probably start things off on the wrong foot.

Aunt Enid smiled at her kindly. "I expect you're shy. I was shy at your age. Do you like to read?"

Sophie didn't like being told she was shy, even though it was true. "Yes," she said firmly. "As a matter of fact, I like to read very much."

"Good. I have plenty of books here, although I doubt your Mama would consider most of them suitable for a young lady. Have you ever read Dickens?"

"We read *Great Expectations* in school."

"Did you like it?"

"Yes, ma'am."

"Do you play chess, by any chance?"

"No, ma'am."

"Pity. I like a nice game of chess. Maybe I'll teach you. Now. Do you want to see the garden first, or your room?"

She sounded very hopeful about the garden, but Sophie's head was beginning to spin with all the changes of subject. "My room, please, ma'am. If it's not too much trouble."

First she had to get her shoes back on. Since her heels were rubbed raw, this wasn't easy. Aunt Enid got her a couple of Band-Aids, thankfully without comment, then led Sophie outside and up the stairs to the back gallery.

"Oak Cottage was built by Creoles," she said, "back in 17-something—your grandmother will know. French plantation houses don't have inside stairs. Your room's down there"—pointing down the gallery—"overlooking the garden. It was my room when I was a girl. I'm on the other side now, next to your grandmama."

A faint, silvery tinkle sounded inside the house. Aunt Enid looked flustered.

"That's Mama now. Where's Ofelia got to? I told her to get the cases, but she should have been in to make Mama's coffee by now." She hesitated. "Sophie, you go in and tell your grandmama it'll be up directly. Go on. She doesn't bite."

Sophie wasn't at all sure of that. Mama always said that Grandmama was a Great Lady, which Papa said meant Grandmama liked telling folks where to sit and spit. Sophie remembered when Grandmama had made her girl (not Ofelia. A funny name. Asia—that was it.) scrub Sophie's feet with a bristle brush after she'd been running around outside in her bare feet. She remembered the story Grandmama had told her, too, about a little girl who'd gotten ringworm in her big toe and had to have her foot cut off. It was a stupid story, but the way Grandmama had told it gave Sophie nightmares. She could still hear that gentle, sweet voice saying, "And you know what they had to do? They had to cut it off with a saw. And the little girl never danced again."

The last thing on earth Sophie wanted was to see Grandmama alone, but she knew an order when she heard one.

All the bedrooms in Oak Cottage opened off the double parlor that took up the better part of the second floor. During the day, the gallery doors were shut to keep the heat out. Sophie opened a long French door and a pair of wooden shutters, then pushed through two sets of curtains. In the gloom, the sofas and chairs looked like the ghosts of furniture waiting for ghostly guests. The air smelled of roses.

Her eye caught a pale, slender shape in a shadowy corner.

She gasped and reminded herself that there was no such thing as ghosts. The tinkling sounded again, shrill and impatient, from the very corner where the pale shape hovered.

Sophie took a step forward. The shape came into focus, and she let out her breath: it was only a bunch of white roses in a silver vase.

Feeling foolish, Sophie marched straight to her grandmother's room and opened the door onto pitch darkness.

"Grandmama? It's Sophie. Aunt Enid said Ofelia would be along with your coffee directly."

"Sophia Fairchild Martineau." Grandmama's voice was low-pitched and gentle, just as Sophie remembered. "My only grandchild. I'd get up and greet you, dear, but I haven't put my foot to the floor for almost a year now. My great regret is that I can't get to church to hear the Lord's Word. But the Reverend D'Aubert drops by most Sunday afternoons, and that's a great comfort."

Sophie was trying to think of something to say when a colored woman pushed by her with a tray. Ignoring Sophie, she set the tray on the washstand, pulled back the heavy curtains, and jerked the shutters open with a brisk rattle, letting in the late sunlight and a drift of damp air.

Sophie stared. Grandmama's room looked more like those fancy antique shops on Royal Street Mama liked to poke around in than a person's bedroom. In addition to a massive armoire and a lady's dresser, a marble-topped washstand and a full-length pier mirror, the room was cluttered with incidental tables, side chairs, and embroidered footstools. Photographs in silver frames and assorted knickknacks crowded every flat surface, and paintings in gold frames covered every inch of wall space. Between the shuttered windows, a huge tester bed rose above the clutter like a royal barge with Grandmama sitting against a mound of pillows, clutching a silver handbell like she was fixing to throw it.

"I've been ringing for a good twenty minutes, Ofelia," she said, gently reproachful.

"Yes, ma'am." Ofelia poured coffee into a gold-rimmed cup, added hot milk from a pitcher, and put the cup into Grandmama's hand. "Here's your coffee, Miz Fairchild. You just visit with your little granddaughter here, and I'll be back with your supper in two licks."

She stumped out of the room, leaving Sophie alone with her grandmother.

"What are you doing all the way over there?" Grandmama beckoned irritably. "Come closer, so I can see you. Where's your dear mama?"

Sophie negotiated a careful path over a footstool and around two straight-backed chairs and a spindly table covered with bright little boxes. "The snuff boxes!"

"I asked you a question, Sophia."

Sophie touched a blue-enameled lid, smooth and cool under her finger. "Mama's resting. It was a long drive from New Orleans."

"When I was a girl, it took two full days," Grandmama said. "Come here and let me look at you." Reluctantly, Sophie obeyed, standing uncomfortably while her grandmother's watery blue eyes moved over her face and hair like weightless fingers.

"I'm glad to see you favor the Fairchilds," Grandmama said at last. "Not the eyes or the chin, of course. But you have your dear grandfather's hair, and the Fairchild nose." She sighed. "I must say, they looked better on him. It's a pity about the spectacles, but I suppose they can't be helped." She took a sip of coffee. "Do you do fancywork, dear?"

Sophie shook her head. Mama had tried to teach her embroidery once. It had not gone well. "No, ma'am."

"In my day, young ladies had accomplishments. I will teach you to tat, just as I did your dear mama, so you can start laying up some linens for your hope chest." She turned her head toward the window. "I do believe I have had enough company for today. You may go away now, Sophia."

Sophie curtsied and went.

Tatting. What *was* tatting, anyway? Sophie imagined herself sitting among the cups and spindly tables day after long, hot day, tatting under the direction of that gentle, impatient voice. She'd go crazy, she just knew it. She'd start throwing knickknacks, and Grandmama would send her back to New Orleans. Where she would get in the way of Mama's househunting and schoolwork and be a burden.

16

As she crossed the parlor, she heard Mama calling her from her bedroom.

"Yes, Mama?"

"Come in here. I want to have a little talk with you."

Mama had folded back the shutters and was sitting by the open window in a rocker. Her shoes were off, her stockinged feet were propped on a needlepoint footstool, and her eyes were closed. "Come here, darling, and sit by me."

The closest seat was the cushioned bench of a mirrored vanity. Sophie sat down, trying to keep her back straight.

"Your Aunt Enid has a green thumb," Mama said. "She has her church work to keep her busy, and Mama, of course, but that garden is her pride and joy. She always did like making mud pies."

"What about worms?" Sophie hated worms.

"She loves them." Mama hated worms, too. She gave a comic shudder, turned to share the joke, and then the inevitable happened. "Oh, Sophie," she said. "What have you done?"

From long experience, Sophie knew that answering "I took off my stockings because I was hot" would lead to a speech about disobedience and ingratitude, followed by a freezing silence until Mama got over her disappointment. But then, so would any other answer.

"Sophia!" Mama's voice sharpened. "Do you hear me?"

Sudden, furious tears blurred the sunlight into an unbearable glare. "I hear you." Sophie knew she should stop right there, but she couldn't. "I know you work like a slave to buy me stockings and things, and then I don't appreciate them. I slouch and I mumble and my hair is a disgrace and I don't have any manners and you're very, very disappointed in me."

Mama's dark amber eyes opened wide with shock. "I'm surprised at you, Sophia Martineau, speaking to me in that tone of voice. How many times must I tell you that irony is not attractive in a young lady?"

"I guess I'm not a young lady," Sophie said thickly and stumbled out of the room with her mother's voice following her, calling her to come back, right this minute, before she was sorry.

There were three doors at the end of the back gallery. The first one she tried led into a bathroom, the second was locked. Sophie jerked open the third door, slammed it behind her, sat down on the floor, and cried.

It didn't last long. Sophie never cried long—there wasn't any use in it. "Go on, honey, and have a nice cry now," Lily always said when Sophie brought home a disappointing report card. "It'll do you the world of good." But the report card never changed, no matter how many tears she shed over it, and neither would Mama.

Sophie wiped her face and glasses on her skirt. She couldn't see in the gloom, and the air smelled damp and slightly sour, like musty paper. Sophie pulled off the torturous pumps, padded over to a window, folded back the shutters, raised the sash, and turned to see where she'd be sleeping all summer.

It could have been worse. Next to Grandmama's room, the furniture was downright sparse—just a rocker and an armoire and a writing-desk and a bookcase stuffed with old books. The walls were papered with faded cabbage roses, and the bed was white iron, with a mint green chenille spread. Beside it, a rickety nightstand held a painted tin lamp, a book, and an electric alarm clock. One of the windows had a seat built into it, just exactly the right size and shape for reading in.

It was like a room from a book, and very much the kind of room Sophie had always dreamed of having. It was the crowning misery of a miserable day that she was too unhappy to appreciate it. Leaving the seersucker suit in a wrinkled pile on the floor, she put on an old skirt and blouse, opened the suitcase with the books, picked up Edward Eager's *The Time Garden*, carried it to the window seat, and pulled back the curtain, revealing a scene like a watercolor illustration in an old book.

Sophie knelt on the faded chintz cushion and looked out. The watercolor effect came from the glass, she realized, which was old and wavy. She looked down into a neat garden shaded by a big live oak. Under the oak, a flowering vine draped a cabin with scarlet trumpets. In the field beyond, she saw a big, dark bushy blob, too low to be a grove and too big to be a hedge.

What she didn't see was any sign of the famous brick Big House.

Sophie opened *The Time Garden* and read until she heard Aunt Enid shouting up the back stairs that supper was ready.

Chapter 3

Mama was still not speaking to Sophie at supper time. By breakfast, she'd thawed enough to ask for the salt, but it was clear she was still in a state. When Aunt Enid realized nobody was going to eat the fried eggs and grits she'd made, she got up and cleared the table. Sophie watched her stack the dirty dishes in the sink and run hot water over them.

Mama folded her unused napkin neatly. "I know Ofelia doesn't come in on weekends. Would you like me to help you with the dishes?"

"I thought I'd let them soak. No use doing two or three little washings when one big one will do." Aunt Enid turned off the water. "Why don't you go up and see if Mama wants anything?"

Mama went, her opinion of Aunt Enid's housekeeping unspoken but clear as glass.

Aunt Enid hung her apron by the door. "Come see my office, Sophie. I think you'll like it."

She was right. Sophie stood in the open door and stared, enchanted, at the cozy clutter of rose clippers, garden gloves, seed packets, and balls of brightly colored yarn. Books filled the shelves that covered the walls, bristled from two free-standing rotating bookcases, lay in shifting piles on the long table behind the sofa and the giant desk under the windows.

Aunt Enid stepped over and around the clutter to the big square fireplace at the end of the room and took a pipe off the mantel. "That was your great-grandpap's," she said, laying it in Sophie's hands. "I have the whole collection around here somewhere."

Sophie rubbed her thumb over the pipe bowl. The polished wood felt like silk.

There was horrified gasp from the door. Sophie jumped guiltily and thrust the pipe behind her back as Mama found her voice. "This place is a pigsty, Enid! How you can live like this, heaven alone knows. Daddy must be turning over in his grave!"

Sophie's hands tightened nervously, but Aunt Enid just snorted. "I expect he's gotten used to it by now. Did Mama finish her breakfast?"

Mama looked irked. "She did. And now she says she wants her bath, but I don't think I can get her out of bed by myself."

"There's a trick to it," Aunt Enid said. "I'll come up and help you."

"Thank you," said Mama, and the two sisters exchanged tight smiles that made Sophie think having a sister wasn't really much fun as *Little Women* made it seem.

Left alone, Sophie explored the library, finding a complete set of Dickens and several paperback mysteries with titles like *The Saint in Action* and *Hot Ice* that looked a whole lot more exciting than Nancy Drew. Around dinnertime, the morning rain cleared and Aunt Enid took Sophie on a tour of the garden.

It was a lot more businesslike than Mama's garden in Metairie, with vegetables as well as flowers, and more kinds of roses than Sophie had known existed. Aunt Enid hunkered right down by the okra and started picking bugs off its leaves and squishing them between her fingers.

21

Mama glanced at Sophie and wrinkled her nose. Sophie wrinkled back, relieved that things were back to normal again. For now.

Supper that night was actually fun. Sophie picked okra out of Ofelia's chicken fricassee and listened to her aunt and her mother reminisce about being the Fairchild girls of Oak River, with special emphasis on the numerous beaux who had squired Mama to church picnics and danced with her at parties.

"You got the best-looking ones," Aunt Enid said. "But my beaux had spirit. Remember when that William Kenner dared Jeff Woodley to spend a night in the Big House, and he fell through the steps and broke his leg?"

"Served him right," Mama said. "Wasn't it Jeff who tied Cleo's old apron on Apollo?"

Aunt Enid grinned. "No, that was Burney Fitzhugh. You remember how Mama wanted Daddy to get rid of all the statues in the maze? He told her, 'They're not naked, Isabel, they're nude. Naked is wickedness. Nude is art.' I thought she'd pop a vein, she was so mad."

Sophie remembered the dark blob she'd seen from her window. Could that be the maze? And did it still have naked statues in it? Maybe, when Mama was gone back to New Orleans, she'd take a look for herself.

"Probably gone to rack and ruin now," Mama said. "Didn't we have fun, Enid, losing Cousin Nick in it?"

"What a nuisance that boy was!" Aunt Enid said.

"Still is, according to Elizabeth," Mama said. And they plunged into family gossip, much to Sophie's disappointment.

On Sunday afternoon, Mama went back to New Orleans, her job, and Soule College. Before she went, she gave Sophie a light hug. "Good-bye, darling."

Sophie buried her face in her mother's familiar smell of Shalimar perfume and fresh-ironed cotton. Mama patted her back and pushed her gently away. "Be good for your Aunt Enid, now."

She got into the Ford and drove off, leaving a large, hot silence behind her.

"Well," Aunt Enid said. "That's that."

She went back into the house, and Sophie kicked the bottom step so hard she had to sit down and squeeze her toe.

The screen door squeaked and Aunt Enid reappeared. "I brought you some lemonade."

"I'm not thirsty, thank you," Sophie said without looking up.

Aunt Enid set the frosted glass beside her. "In case you change your mind."

Sophie nodded. A moment later, she felt a light touch on her hair. Then the steps squeaked under Aunt Enid's feet and the parlor door opened and closed.

What was wrong with her, Sophie wondered, that everyone left her? Was it her frizzy hair? Her glasses? Was it because she read all the time? Would Papa have taken her to New York with him if she'd been the young lady Mama wanted her to be, who read *Seventeen* magazine and knew all the words to "Teen Angel"?

Because then she was doomed.

Sophie wiped her face and got up. Now Mama was gone, she was free to explore. She'd start with the garden shed, poke her nose into the maze, maybe even mount an expedition to the Big House, assuming there was anything left of it to find.

Close to, the garden shed looked like a woodcutter's cottage from a fairy tale, with two small windows peeping out among the vines and a low wooden bench by the half-open door. She pushed it all the way open and went inside.

Given Aunt Enid's housekeeping habits, Sophie was surprised to see that her gardening tools were clean and polished and laid out neatly on an old wooden table. The rest of the room was a jumble of broken furniture and flowerpots piled higgledy-piggledy between the door and a huge stone fireplace that took up nearly the whole back wall.

Sophie knew perfectly well that young ladies did not crawl into fireplaces, no matter how big, much less stick their heads up the chimney. She did it anyway, right on through a sticky barrier of ancient cobwebs. When she'd finished picking the clinging threads out of her hair, she settled her glasses and looked up into a close and total blackness that smelled sourly of old wood smoke and soot.

Luminescent amber eyes opened above her, narrowed a little, then winked.

Sophie gave a startled yelp. The eyes disappeared. There was a faint scrabbling, a shower of soot, and the chimney was clear.

Sophie ducked out of the fireplace, blundered out the door, and scanned the roof. Yes, something was definitely moving among the leaves, something splotched black and white and reddish-brown like a calico cat. It leaped down from the roof to her feet, grinned at her, and took off across the field at a leisurely lope.

Sophie hesitated a moment, then took off after it, slipping on the wet grass and banging her toes on loose rocks. About a stone's throw from the maze, she ran out of breath and had to stand with her hands on her thighs, panting.

When she stood up again, the strange animal was squatting between the two stone urns, for all the world like it was waiting for her. Sophie could have sworn it waved at her before it turned and disappeared.

She ran through the gap, tripped over something hidden in the tall grass, and fell flat on her face, gulping like a fish.

"You is a *fine* specimen, you is."

Sophie sat up and pushed her glasses up her sweaty nose. A corridor walled with dusty leaves curved gently away from her in both directions.

"Who's there?" she called.

"Come find me and see."

The voice was high and light, like a little child's—a colored child. Sophie got to her feet.

"That animal I saw in the garden shed—is that your pet?"

A giggle. "You might could say that."

"It sure is strange-looking." She peered up and down the leafy corridor. "Where are you, anyway?"

"Here and there! In and out! Come on and find me."

Sophie saw gaps in the leafy wall—two to the right, one to the left. She remembered reading about mazes, how you should always turn right on the way in and left on the way out. Or was it the other way around?

She shrugged and turned right.

"You fixing to stay a spell?" the voice inquired.

Sophie kept walking.

"Stubborn as a mule," the voice remarked. "Don't listen, don't look, don't mind what she's told. You never going find me, you don't mind what you told. What them things over you eyes, girl? Blinders?"

"That's rude!" Sophie said indignantly. "I can't help having to wear glasses! And you haven't told me anything."

"Have." The voice was smug. "Study on it."

"You asked whether I was intending to stay a spell," Sophie pointed out. "That could mean anything."

"It mean you fixing to get right lost."

Sophie rolled her eyes and turned around. At the end of the path, she went left, then left again, which led her into a dead end furnished with a cracked marble bench.

By this time, she was ready to give up. She didn't like being teased, especially by some sassy little colored child who didn't have any business being in her family maze in the first place. She began to retrace her steps.

"That's right," the voice said. "Go back. Save youself a passel of time and trouble. Ain't nothing in the middle anyways."

Which made Sophie bound and determined to find the middle of the maze—and the sassy child—if only to give it a piece of her mind.

Three turns later, she was in another dead end, this one sporting a sad-looking marble dog.

"You should have drunk that there lemonade you auntie made you," the voice said. "No telling when you see lemonade again."

"That doesn't help," Sophie said.

"See if going right instead of left help better."

For the next few minutes, the voice insulted her, teased her, led her, she was sure, around in circles. Finally, she saw a pair of stone urns just like the ones at the entrance and stepped between them into a miniature wilderness of bushes and weeds.

"What I tell you?" the voice crowed. "Nothing here."

"You're here, somewhere."

"Somewheres."

Sophie looked around for a hiding place, spotted a building-shaped mound of leaves across the garden, fought her way to it and peered into a fly-haunted interior. Two wicker chairs, half-rotten and furred with mold. No child. No multicolored animal.

Grimly, Sophie set in to search every inch of the tiny garden. She found a broken stone bench, an empty stand that may have held a sundial, and more roses run wild than you could shake a stick at, and that was all.

By now, she was hungry as well as thirsty, and her feet were bruised. The lengthening shadows told her she'd been in the maze a lot longer than she'd thought. If she didn't hurry back, she'd be late to supper and Aunt Enid would be put out with her.

"You win!" she called out. "Can you lead me out of here? Please?"

Her only answer was the hysterical shrilling of cicadas. Sophie fought down a rising panic and told herself she wasn't really lost. All she had to do was go back the way she'd come. She looked out the entrance and sure enough, a line of trodden grass led to the right, clear as print.

Piece of cake.

And it might have been, if the voice had led her directly to the center. As it was, Sophie was soon as lost as Mama's Cousin Nick. At first, she was too mad to be frightened. But as she got more and more lost, fear overcame anger. The shrilling cicadas started to sound more and more like voices—frightened, unhappy, whispering voices. Sometimes they went silent, and that was worse, because then she could hear rustling in the hedges and in the grass. Then she thought she heard a little girl laughing, and a man's voice—or was it a bullfrog?—and a dog's excited barking. She wasn't sure if they were real, or she was imagining them, but she was too spooked to think. Before long, she was sobbing and plunging through gap after gap, blinded by tears and panic. When she finally ran out of breath, she was standing in a green square furnished with a bench and one of those statues Great-Grandmama had wanted to get rid of.

Sophie sank onto the bench, gasping, took off her glasses, and scrubbed her hands over her wet face. This was not, she reminded herself, how the children in books behaved when they had adventures. She had to pull herself together and think.

"Sophie!" Aunt Enid sounded as if she'd been calling for some time. "Sophie, where on earth are you? It's supper time!"

Sophie jumped up. "Aunt Enid! I'm here, Aunt Enid."

There was a startled silence, then, "My land! Are you in the maze?"

"Yes," Sophie wailed. "And I can't get out!"

"No need to take on, child! I'll have you out in no time. It would be too much to ask, I suppose, for you to be in a dead end?"

"There's a statue," Sophie said.

"Lady or gentleman?"

"Lady. No arms. There's a sheet around her hips."

"Got it." Aunt Enid's voice now came from over to the right. "Dratted grass. I have to get Henry to mow the paths."

Time dragged. Leaves rattled. Aunt Enid's voice came and went, muttering. "I could have sworn there was one here," and "Drat the child." Sophie wondered nervously what Aunt Enid was like when she was seriously put out.

"Ah. There you are."

Aunt Enid's face was red and shiny with heat. To Sophie's relief, she seemed more excited than irked. "My land," she panted. "Haven't done that in fifteen years. No, twenty."

She plumped down on the bench and squinted up at the statue. "Gracious. To think of good old Belle Watling, still here after all these years. Although I guess she's not likely to wander off, is she? Makes me feel a girl again."

"Who's Belle Watling?" Sophie asked.

Aunt Enid's eyes crinkled. "Belle Watling is a character in *Gone With the Wind*."

Sophie wondered if the title referred to Belle Watling's clothes. "I don't understand."

"And I don't propose to explain it to you. You can read the book and work it out for yourself."

After supper, Sophie found a copy of *Gone With the Wind* and started to read it. She could have done without Scarlett O'Hara, who she thought selfish, vain, and mean as a cross-eyed mule. Still, she was more fun to read about than the saintly Miss Melanie, who was what Mama would call a Perfect Lady. Sophie privately considered Miss Melanie a perfect wet blanket and couldn't see what either lady saw in Ashley Wilkes. Rhett Butler alarmed her. She never did figure out why Belle Watling was a good name for an armless statue. But she loved the descriptions of clothes and parties and the funny things the slaves said, and the plot picked up when the war started, so she kept at it until her eyes closed by themselves.

Aunt Enid laughed when Sophie brought the book down to breakfast and propped it up to read over her cornflakes. "I don't suppose it'll do you any harm, even if you can make head or tail of it."

"I'm skipping some," Sophie admitted. "Aunt Enid, was Oak River like Tara?"

Aunt Enid poured herself a cup of chicory coffee. "Well, Tara was a cotton plantation, but I expect you mean the slaves and balls and so on. Yes, I suppose it must have been."

"Did they have balls at Oak Cottage?"

"Not after the Big House was built. Mr. Charles surely loved company. The dining room could seat forty for dinner and there was a ballroom with mirrors and crystal chandeliers, brought all the way from France."

Sophie's eyes rounded. "What happened to them?"

"Sold, along with the best part of the furnishings, round about the time of the First World War. Just as well. They wouldn't have fit into Oak Cottage anyway."

"So is there anything left of the Big House?"

"Some. Used to be, you could see it from your room, right past the maze, until the oak grove grew up around it." Aunt Enid gave Sophie a hard look. "Now look here, Sophie. I don't want you going anywhere near the Big House. You'd likely go inside, just to take a look, and have a wall fall on you or some such. We've got plenty of ghosts in the family as it is—we don't need another."

She was, to Sophie's astonishment, perfectly serious. "Mama says there aren't any such things as ghosts," Sophie said.

"I'm pleased to say that your Mama isn't the sole judge of what is and isn't so. World would be a pretty dull place if she was. I don't suppose she's seen fit to tell you about Old One-Eye or the Girl in Yellow or the Swamp-Weeper?"

Sophie closed *Gone With the Wind*. "No, ma'am."

"They're part of your heritage, child. Way back before he built the Big House, your five-times-great grandpa Fairchild owned a slave called Old One-Eye. He was a conjure man— that's a kind of heathen witch doctor—and he could conjure up spirits and haints and rain during the sugar harvest. He was nothing but trouble, and when he ran away, Grandpa Fairchild wasn't as upset about it as he might have been. Still, property was property, and it didn't do to have it running away. So Grandpa Fairchild sent out the slave hunters to find Old One-Eye and bring him home."

"Did they find him?" Sophie asked.

Aunt Enid looked grim. "They did that, child. It took them nigh on a year, but they found him, back in the swamp among the cypress and the swamp maple. The slave hunters trussed him up and carried him back to Oak River hanging from a branch like a wild hog. By this time, Grandpa Fairchild was mighty irked, and as I said, Old One-Eye was a heap of trouble. So he had him whipped until the skin fell off his back, and then burned him to a crisp and threw his bones into the bayou. Daddy used to swear he'd heard him when he was a boy, hollering and crackling in the old stable-yard."

Sophie shuddered. "That's horrible!"

"Most ghost stories are horrible," said Aunt Enid. "They wouldn't be scary otherwise."

"Are there ghosts in the maze?" asked Sophie, remembering the whispers.

"Well, there is the Girl in Yellow. I disremember the details, but it's said she walks there just before dawn."

"Does she whisper?"

"I never heard anything about whispering. Why?"

Sophie shrugged.

Aunt Enid studied her for a moment. "You just remember, child: ghosts are only shadows. You say your prayers, they can't hurt you."

"Aunt Enid, have you ever seen a ghost?"

"If I haven't, it doesn't mean they don't exist," Aunt Enid said. "After all, I've never seen Jesus. There's no question that there's strange things around Oak River, and if they're not ghosts, then they're something mighty like."

Chapter 4

Later that day, Sophie went back to the maze and stood at the entrance, listening for the voices she'd heard the day before. The cicadas sounded like cicadas. The leaves and grass rustled only when there was a breeze. No strange animals appeared or childish voices teased her.

Maybe Sophie read too much, like Mama said, but she did know what was real and what wasn't. She knew the animal she'd chased into the maze wasn't just a cat or a rabbit or a muskrat. The more she thought about it, the less she believed that the voice she'd heard belonged to a real child. Which meant she must have been talking to a ghost.

Sophie had been wishing for a magic adventure ever since Papa had read her *Peter Pan* when she was little. What she'd had in mind was a trip to the past or a world like Narnia, filled with magic and talking animals, not being led in circles by a ghost with a taste for practical jokes. Probably she'd be better off reading her way through Aunt Enid's office and learning how to garden, maybe even exploring the bayou, like a normal kid on summer vacation. And she'd start right now.

Aunt Enid was in the kitchen, topping and tailing beans while Ofelia stirred a pot of something spicy smelling. According to

Aunt Enid, Ofelia was a great cook in the Creole tradition, but all Sophie could taste was pepper. She preferred Lily's macaroni and cheese.

"Aunt Enid, I can go swimming in the bayou?"

Aunt Enid looked startled. "I thought you were dead set on the maze."

"Too spooky," Sophie said.

Ofelia picked up a spice jar, shook some into the pot. "That maze is haunted, sure enough. All kinds of shadows in there. Best you keep away."

Aunt Enid chuckled. "They'll leave fast enough when Henry mows the paths. No self-respecting ghost could be expected to put up with the stink and noise of that old mower of mine."

Sophie doubted that. So, judging from the way her mouth pursed up, did Ofelia.

"You'll feel better about the place," Aunt Enid went on, "when you can be sure of not getting lost again. Once the paths are clear, all you have to do is follow the white stones, and you'll be either in or out in no time."

"That will be lovely," Sophie said politely. "But I'd still rather go to the bayou, if that's all right with you."

Aunt Enid gave her permission, along with lots of advice about staying away from 'gators and snakes, in case they might be poisonous. Sophie began to wonder if maybe she should just go ahead and take her chances with the ghosts. But she didn't want Aunt Enid to think she couldn't make up her mind, so next morning, armed with a thermos of Ofelia's cold tea and mosquito repellant, she set out to walk along the bayou.

She clambered over roots and around swampy patches until she got tired, then sat with her back to a shaggy cypress trunk and read *The Dutch Shoe Mystery* by Ellery Queen until the mosquitoes came out. By the time she got back to Oak

Cottage, she was muddy, scratched, bitten up, and late for supper for the second time in a week.

Aunt Enid wasn't happy. "You little hoyden! I know you don't dare carry on at home like this, Little Miss Butter-Wouldn't-Melt, and let me tell you, you should be ashamed! Why, I was fixing to call Henry to start dragging the bayou for your dead body!"

On and on she went. Sophie stared at her dirty feet and listened, feeling smaller and guiltier by the minute.

Aunt Enid stopped fussing mid-sentence. "Goodness gracious, child, don't look like that. It's not the end of the world."

Sophie wasn't at all sure of that. Mama would likely never speak to her again if Aunt Enid sent her home now. "I'm so sorry, Aunt Enid. I didn't mean to be late. I won't ever do it again."

"Of course you will." Aunt Enid sounded impatient. "You're a child. I never heard of a child yet had any more notion of time than a chipmunk. Tell you what. The old plantation bell's around here somewhere. Why don't we hang it on the porch, and then I'll ring it when I want you. And you'll come running. Right away, you hear? No lollygagging."

Sophie risked a glance. Aunt Enid was smiling. "No lollygagging. I promise."

"Good. Go wash your hands, now. And your feet. And better change your clothes. I swear, you're wearing half the bayou." And Aunt Enid began to dish up the jambalaya Ofelia had left warming in the oven.

Next day, Sophie helped Aunt Enid as she dug around in the garden shed like a terrier after a bone. She unearthed her favorite hoe, a split willow basket, and finally, under a moldy tarp, a rusty iron bell about the size of a basketball.

"I knew it was here," Aunt Enid said triumphantly. "Daddy always said old man Fairchild had it cast with a handful of silver dollars, to give it a sweet tone. Doesn't look like it'll ring, does it?"

Once they'd rubbed the bell with steel wool and oiled the clapper, Henry hung it by the kitchen door. It rang with a deep clear tone that carried easily as far as Sophie was likely to wander.

And she did wander. During a run of hot, clear days that made going outside more attractive than staying in, Sophie got acquainted with the bayou. She loved the strange, gnarled cypress knees poking out of the still brown pools, the piping and creaking and calling of animals and birds, the rich smell of living water and growing things. If she sat very still, she could spot muskrats swimming, their eyes bright and anxious as they scouted for 'gators, and watch egrets standing on one leg like feathery statues, heads cocked as they hunted crawfish. By the end of the week, she had lost her straw hat in the bayou and her sandals under the bed. Her arms and legs were mosquito-bitten and scratched, her feet were getting callused, and her skin was turning brown.

Sophie was proud of her tan. She'd never had a nice one before, even when Papa and Mama had taken her to the Caribbean for Christmas vacation when she was ten. Mama had turned golden, Papa had turned a rich leathery color, but Sophie had just gone lobster red and peeled. Now she was a kind of tawny brown, just like the girl in the Coppertone ad.

Grandmama, when she noticed, was not pleased. "You look like a little colored child," she said irritably. "You might just as well plat up that frizzy hair of yours and be done with it."

Delia Sherman

Sophie smoothed her hair self-consciously.

"In *my* day," Grandmama went on severely, "a *real* lady had a peaches and cream complexion. We wore hats and gloves and carried parasols when we went out and bathed our faces with lemon water to bleach out the freckles." She sighed. "I do hope you're not taking your Aunt Enid as a model, dear. Her skin's that weathered, she might as well be a farm woman." A crafty look pulled at the soft wrinkles around her eyes. "Why don't we start those tatting lessons tomorrow?"

Tatting, Aunt Enid had told her, was making lace with a tiny metal shuttle, and that was all Sophie intended to learn about it. "Tomorrow is Sunday," she pointed out. "We're going to church in the morning. And the Reverend D'Aubert is coming to see you in the afternoon."

"Monday, then. First thing. But you will remember to wear a hat when you go out, won't you, dear?"

Sophie crossed her fingers behind her back. "Yes'm. Good night, Grandmama."

The next week turned rainy. Sophie spent it mostly on the window seat, working her way through the children's books filling the bookcase. Some of them were very old: a battered copy of *Swiss Family Robinson* had "Charles M. Fairchild, his book, 1845" written in a spidery script on the inside cover. Mama's name was in *The Five Little Peppers and How They Grew*. *The Story of the Amulet* had belonged to Aunt Enid. It was about time travel and magic creatures, and Sophie loved it.

By Friday she was read out and restless. For once, it wasn't raining, but the air was so hot, just breathing was an effort. Sophie walked slowly upstream to a pool she'd found, still as black silk, flecked with green duckweed. She'd cooled her feet in it before, keeping a sharp eye out for arrow trails on the water and logs with eyes. Today, she stripped to her underpants and slipped into the cool wetness. As she floated, she looked up through the feathery cypress leaves to the white-hot sky above, listened to the cackling of the moorhens, and wondered whether her friend Diana had ever been swimming in a bayou. Probably not—Diana liked swimming pools and white sand beaches and thought wild animals belonged in zoos. Diana didn't belong in the same universe as Aunt Enid and Oak Cottage, any more than Papa did. Mama, now, Mama belonged to Oak Cottage. Maybe that was why she and Papa couldn't be happy together.

Sophie thought of the months before Papa left, with Mama locked in stony silence and Papa hiding in his den, when he was home at all. She hadn't been surprised when he went away for good. "Silence is golden," he always said. "But absence is goldener." Sophie just wished he'd taken her with him.

"Wishing again? You the wishingest girl I ever did see."

Sophie floundered upright, splashing and sputtering as the muddy water got in her mouth.

"Easy now. Ain't no call to put youself in no taking."

It was the voice she'd heard in the maze. "I'm not in a taking," she said. "I'm startled. It's not nice just to say things out of thin air like that."

"It ain't nice to *fib*," the voice said. "Why, you shaking like an old dog with palsy."

"I am not. And even if I was, it would be because I was annoyed. Nobody likes stupid invisible ghosts creeping up on them."

"You think I a *haunt*?" The voice was indignant.

"I don't know what you are, and I don't care. Now, go away, so I can put my clothes on."

"Can't." The voice was smug. "I *is* away. And I ain't going nowhere. That there cottonmouth, though, look like he swimming right at you."

In a heartbeat, Sophie was out of the water and on shore, her blouse clutched to her chest. "Cottonmouth? Where?"

The only answer was a chuckle.

Sophie struggled grimly into the shorts and blouse, too mad to be embarrassed.

"Don't you go away!" the voice commanded. "I got something particular to say to you."

Sophie buttoned up her blouse. "Me, too. Good-bye. I feel silly talking to the air. If you have something to say, come out here and say it where I can see you."

"Ain't you the bold one! I warn you, I mighty powerful juju. I sits at the doorway betwixt might be and is, betwixt was and will be, betwixt here and there. I breaks chains and bends laws, and Old One-Eye himself weren't strong enough to master me. You *sure* you want to see me?"

This sounded even scarier than Old One-Eye, if Sophie had believed a word of it. "I'm sure."

A thousand shades of pink and tan and copper and brown swirled in the air like cotton candy at a fair, spinning into a ball that drifted onto a cypress knee, uncurled its arms and legs, and opened wide, bright, amber eyes. Its podgy body was covered in a short, dense pelt blotched chestnut and white and black, and it had a deer's long and mobile ears above a round, mischievous face. It was like nothing she'd seen before—except maybe the multicolored animal she'd followed to the maze.

It was also even funnier looking than the Psammead from *The Story of the Amulet*. Sophie tried to smother a giggle and failed. The creature's ears pricked forward. "You laughin' at me, missy?"

"No. I'm just—"

"Ain't that just like a Fairchild!" the creature interrupted. "Beg to see me, and when I obliges, she laugh! When I gets done, missy, you going to laugh out t'other side your mouth." It swelled up indignantly.

"I'm sorry," Sophie said hurriedly. "I didn't mean anything by it."

The creature humphed and folded its arms across its fat belly. "You better not."

"Can I ask you a question?"

The creature shrugged. "Free country. Freer than it used to be, anyway."

"What's your name?"

"Don't have a name."

"Everybody has a name."

"I ain't everybody," said the creature smugly.

Sophie had an idea. "Are you Rumplestiltskin?"

The creature laughed delightedly. "I ain't heard that one before. Old Man. Br'er Rabbit. Hobgoblin. Compair Lapin. But never Rumpel—. What that name again?"

"Rumplestiltskin. It's in a book. What are those other names? Are those all yours?"

"Ain't you been listening, girl? I told you, I ain't got no name. Them's what peoples *calls* me. Them's people's names, not mine." It paused, ears twitching. "You auntie calling you."

This sounded like typical magic creature double-talk to Sophie. "No, she's not. It's nowhere near supper time yet."

The deep clang of Aunt Enid's bell rang out, startling two herons into flight. "What I tell you?" The creature immediately began to fade—slowly, like the Cheshire cat, feet first.

"Don't go," Sophie pleaded. "You said people. What people?"

Delia Sherman

"Colored peoples. Black peoples. Red peoples. Even some white peoples. Conjure mens. Two-headed womens." The creature was gone from the chest down now, and grinning like a jack-o'-lantern. Sophie noticed that it had no teeth, only bony plates like a baby. "You can have one more question, if you asks quick."

"Will I see you again?"

The bell rang, an insistent iron summons

"Auntie getting resty." The creature was now all mouth and eyes and twitching ears.

"One more question. You promised."

The creature's ears disappeared and its mouth grew transparent. One liquid eye faded from sight. The other one winked and was gone.

Sophie waited a moment, in case it returned, then reluctantly started home. At the edge of the trees, something tickled her ear—a single word:

"Yes."

Chapter 5

Aunt Enid met Sophie at the kitchen door.

"Where were you?" she asked crossly. "Texas? Your Mama's on the phone."

Sophie ran through to the office and picked up the receiver. "Hello, Mama."

"Where on earth were you? Not by the bayou, I hope. There are snakes, you know, and alligators. And the water is filthy."

Sophie made a face. "No, Mama."

"Have you heard from your father recently?"

Over the past year, Sophie had received exactly two letters and six postcards from her father. They contained descriptions of Broadway and Times Square, funny stories about the neighbors in his apartment building, and all his love for ever and ever. She wasn't sure he even knew she was in Oakwood. "No, Mama."

Silence. "Well. I have a surprise for you, darling. I'm coming down tomorrow to see you."

Sophie hung up the phone with a sense of dread. She'd heard that bright, false voice before. Mama saved it for what she called adventures—like moving to a new school or getting divorced. Whatever it was, Sophie knew it was bound to be unpleasant.

That night, Sophie curled up in the window seat and looked at the sky. Moonlight silvered the roses over the garden shed and made a little mirror of the puddle under the water pump. Out in the field, the maze lay coiled like a sleeping snake.

A cloud covered the moon, pulling a black curtain over garden, shed, and maze. When it moved on and she could see again, everything had changed.

Sophie scrambled to her knees, lifted the sash, and leaned out. The garden paths shone blinding white, as if paved with marble. The live oak was smaller, and the leafy blanket over the shed had disappeared. A dirt yard replaced the field, neat wooden cabins clustered around a tall frame tower. Beyond the maze, yellow light glowed in the windows of a shadowy house.

As Sophie watched, a man in a wide-brimmed hat came out of one of the cabins, moseyed over to the tower with a dog at his heels. A moment later, the deep, clear voice of a bell shattered the stillness like the Last Trump. The tower and the buildings and the white paths shimmered and faded, and Sophie was looking at the familiar garden, the vine-covered shed, the oak grove, and the overgrown field, just as they'd been before.

Wide awake, Sophie knelt at the window, hoping for the vision to reappear. But the moon set and the clouds screened the stars, and then she fell asleep on the window seat and woke up stiff and cranky to a hot, sticky morning and the unwelcome news that she had to clean her room before Mama arrived.

"I don't care, Lord knows, but Sister's likely to blame my slovenly ways for all those books and clothes you got lying everywhere. Better make your bed, too. And when you're done tidying, get in the bathtub and scrub yourself. Those knees are a disgrace."

Sophie obeyed to the extent of pulling up the chenille spread, shelving all the books, and stuffing her clothes in the armoire. She drew a bath, scrubbed her hands and knees until they were sore, and washed her hair. She hid her scratched feet in white ankle socks and sandals and put on the pointless bra and her Sunday blue-gingham shirtwaist. She was scraping her hair back with a plastic headband when she heard a familiar honk and ran out to throw her arms around her mother.

"Hello, darling." Mama pushed Sophie to arm's length and examined her critically. "What on earth have you been up to? You look like a wild Indian!"

Aunt Enid came out the door behind the stairs, wiping her hands on her apron. "And you, Sister, look like a French poodle."

Mama laughed self-consciously and patted her short, tight, chestnut curls. "I got a permanent wave. Do you like it?"

In fact, Mama had gotten a whole new outfit. Her dress was black and white, with a narrow skirt that just covered her knees. Her belt and purse were bright red, and matched her high-heeled, pointy shoes. Sophie was enchanted. "Mama, you look just like a movie star!"

Aunt Enid snorted. "That's as may be. And won't Mama just create when she sees that skirt!"

Aunt Enid served supper in the dining room—fried chicken, succotash, and homemade biscuits—and Mama entertained them with stories about Soule College and her new job and all her wonderful new friends.

Round about coffee and dessert, Aunt Enid lost patience. "I'm sure that's all very interesting, Sister. But it doesn't explain why you drove all the way down here three weeks before we expected you."

Mama's fork, full of gingerbread and whipped cream, paused in mid-air. "Randolph has remarried." She popped the gingerbread into her mouth.

Randolph, Sophie thought, is Papa's name. Randolph Perault Martineau.

"Stop staring, Sophie, and close your mouth. You look like an idiot child. Your father has remarried—an artist woman he met in New York, Judith something." Mama sipped her coffee. "Horowitz. Judith Horowitz. He's moved into her apartment in the Village, wherever that may be. Doesn't sound very elegant, does it?"

Sophie jabbed her half-eaten gingerbread with her fork. She felt slightly sick.

"Judith Horowitz," Aunt Enid said. "That's not exactly a Southern name, is it?"

"Well, Enid, what would you expect?" Mama said, bright as a button. "He clearly didn't want a Southern lady. He didn't want a lady at all. He wanted a beatnik, Jewish—"

"Helen Fairchild Martineau!" Aunt Enid sounded shocked. Mama's cheeks flushed pink.

Sophie stood up. "Can I please be excused?"

Mama lifted one perfectly plucked eyebrow. "Don't you want to see your father's letter?"

Sophie shook her head wordlessly, pushed in her chair, and went up to her room. She took *The Story of the Amulet* from the bookcase and sat down with it on the window seat.

Was it worse when someone died, she wondered, or when they ran away and left you behind? What was Papa doing up there in New York, anyway, apart from getting married? Was it more interesting than playing Monopoly and going to see *South Pacific* with his daughter?

Sophie cried a little, blew her nose, picked up the book again, and opened it. Mama came in, dropped an envelope on the bed, and went out again.

The envelope was addressed to Mama, in Papa's writing. The four-cent stamp honored the American Woman with a picture of a mother and daughter reading a book together. They didn't look as if they liked it much.

Sophie pulled out the single, typewritten page.

> *Helen:*
> *This letter is to inform you that I've remarried—an artist named Judith Horowitz I met at a gallery opening. It was as much of a surprise to me as it must be to you. We'll be living in her apartment in the West Village—address and telephone below. Could you tell Sophie? I'll write her when things get settled down a little, maybe have her come out for a visit so she can meet Judith. But I'd appreciate it if you prepared her.*
> *Thanks. Rand.*

Sophie folded the letter up again and put it back in the envelope because Mama would pitch a fit if she tore it into pieces. Then she went into the bathroom and pushed the envelope under the connecting door.

On Sunday morning, Mama accompanied Sophie and Aunt Enid to church. The good ladies of Oakwood Methodist stared at Mama's permanent wave and short skirt, and the Reverend D'Aubert was moved to speak about how women working outside the home led to desegregation and moral degeneration. Sophie wanted to crawl under the pew, but Mama sat and listened with an interested smile, and was extra-bright and charming to everyone during coffee hour. She chatted about apartment-hunting all the way home, and when they got to Oak Cottage went straight upstairs to sit with Grandmama. At loose ends, Sophie trailed Aunt Enid into the kitchen.

Her aunt gave her a harried look. "After that morning, I think I need a little solitude. Why don't you go cut some roses for Mama's room? I noticed some Gloire de Dijons coming on to bloom this morning. They're the yellow ones, over by the cabbage bed."

It was a sign of how rattled Aunt Enid was that she hadn't even noticed it had come on to rain. Shears in hand, Sophie stood under the gallery, watching the water sheet down over the garden, knowing she should wait for it to let up, or at least put on her aunt's gum boots and oilcloth jacket. Instead, she stepped into the downpour and lifted her face, feeling the lukewarm water soaking through her dress and plastering her hair sleek as a muskrat's. She squelched through the grass to the drooping golden roses and cut a big armful, cradling them in the sling of her blue gingham skirt. Then she ran back to the house, straight up the back stairs to the gallery, and through the parlor to Grandmama's room, leaving a puddled trail across the polished floor.

"Sophie!" her mother exclaimed.

Grandmama squinted. "What is it, Helen? Is the child hurt? You should look out after her better."

Mama's mouth snapped into a hard, bright smile. She grabbed Sophie's shoulder and dragged her up to the bed. "Look, Mama. Sophie brought you flowers. Isn't that nice?"

Grandmama's faded eyes fastened on Sophie, then fluttered shut, as if in pain. "When I was young, girls were taught to cut and arrange flowers *properly*. Go to your room, Sophia, and come back when you're dressed like a Christian."

"Now, Mama. She *meant* well. Look at those beautiful roses. You'd better put them in something, darling. You don't want them to wilt."

Sophie looked from mother to grandmother. Grandmama's face was all pursed up like a shelled pecan; Mama's was as bright and blank as a doll's.

"There's water in the pitcher on the washstand," said Mama. "My land, Mama, if you could just see your face! Didn't you always say a lady should cultivate a pleasant expression?"

She smiled at Grandmama; Grandmama smiled back, sharp as a curved sword. Sophie shivered.

"Hand me that towel, darling," Mama said. "You don't want to catch your death of cold."

Sophie unloaded the roses into the pitcher and found a linen towel. Her mother took it from her and commenced scrubbing at her dripping hair. "I was just telling your grandmama all about my accounting course and how much money I'll make when I get to be a real Certified Public Accountant."

Grandmama picked at her sheet and her bed-jacket, her withered cheeks pink. "This is the Lord's day, Helen. You remember what Our Lord said to the money-changers in the Temple?"

Mama's hands stilled on Sophie's head. "I'm not a money changer, Mama. I'm an accountant."

"It's not *becoming*, Helen. A lady does not speak of money and business. She shouldn't even think of them."

"A lady who earns her own keep must think about them."

"A lady does not work for her keep," said Grandmama decidedly.

"Then how does a lady eat? How does a lady keep a roof over her head and a rag to her back?"

"A lady is provided for. But it's plain to be seen you've given up acting like a lady. I begin to have some sympathy for Randolph, if that is how you spoke to him."

"I treated Randolph exactly the way you taught me to."

Grandmama pursed her mouth. "Don't talk ugly. You were the one insisted on marrying him. It's nothing to me if he ran off and left you without a penny to your name."

It was bad enough for Grandmama to light into Mama, but at least Mama was there to defend herself. Papa was not.

"That's not fair, Grandmama!" Sophie burst out. "Papa gives us money. It's just everything is so expensive, and—"

"You hush up, young lady," Mama snapped. "You know nothing about it. I *like* working. I *like* keeping figures straight and showing other people how to keep theirs, and most of all, I like getting paid for doing it."

Grandmama reached a trembling hand toward Sophie. "Come here, you poor child. You love your old grandmama, don't you? You won't break her heart with foolishness."

Mama dropped the towel and marched out of the room.

"Well." Grandmama felt under her pillow, brought out a little glass bottle. "I declare, that girl will be the death of me. I'd never have dared to speak to my poor, sainted mama in that hard, selfish way. Never." She shook the bottle impatiently. "Well, child? Are you going to open my salts or aren't you?"

Sophie took the bottle and tried to unscrew the tiny metal cap. It wouldn't budge.

"I'm very faint, Sophie," warned Grandmama. "Excitement is bad for my heart."

"It's stuck, Grandmama."

"A lady doesn't make excuses, miss. I told Helen no good would come of marrying that man. His mother was from California, I believe."

Sophie struggled grimly with the smelling salts, wishing she was anywhere except in this dim, overcrowded room that smelled of old lady and damp and suddenly, overwhelmingly, of ammonia, as the neck of the bottle broke, spilling its pungent contents over the crocheted counterpane.

"Clumsy girl!"

Sophie rubbed her nose and streaming eyes. "I'm sorry, Grandmama."

"Well, fetch a towel, girl." Grandmama sneezed and edged away from the spill. "Look at you, haven't even got the sense to stay out of the rain. You'll come to no good, you mark my words. Just like your no-account father."

Sophie looked up from mopping at the sheets. "Papa's not no-account! He's funny and he's good and he loves me."

Grandmama bared her false teeth in a pitying smile. "If he loves you so much, where is he, miss? You'd be better off if he simply knew his duty."

Choking with fury, Sophie flung the ammonia-soaked towel down on the bed and ran, pursued by the irritable silver tinkling of Grandmama's bell. In her room, she threw herself on the bed, remembered she was still wet, and got up again.

"Sophie?" Her mother called from her room. "Sophie, go see to your grandmother."

Sophie went through the bathroom into Mama's room. She had closed the shutters and was sitting in the rocker with her hands in her lap. Sophie could hear her breathing, very slow and deliberate, with a hitch in each breath. She'd never heard her cry before, not even when Papa left. It was unnatural, like the sun rising in the West.

She came closer. "She doesn't need seeing to. She's in a temper." She hesitated. "Please don't cry, Mama."

"Be still, Sophie."

She sounded sad and tired. Sophie tried again. "I'm glad you like school and accounting. I think you're—"

"I said, be *still!*"

Sophie bit her lip. "I'm sorry. I just thought—"

"Nonsense," Mama said flatly. "You didn't think at all. You never think. And you're always sorry. You're the sorriest child I've ever laid eyes on. Just look at you, all covered with mud and soaked to the bone. Your hair looks like a hooraw's nest."

Sophie's hands flew to the hair Mama herself had rubbed into a tangled mess. "I brush it every day, just like you told me."

Mama sighed. "That's a fib. I declare, sometimes it's hard to believe you're my daughter at all. The only explanation is a touch of the tar brush in your father's family. Those French planters didn't care who they married, and that's a fact. Go away and comb your hair, if you can. And change your dress. That one is ruined."

Sophie ran into her room and shut the door. She'd probably cry soon. And then Mama would be mad when she came down to dinner with her eyes all red. Maybe she just wouldn't go down. Maybe she'd read instead. Maybe she'd read until Mama left for New Orleans, and not say good-bye.

Kneeling in front of the bookcase, she reached blindly for a book, any book, that might distract her. *The Time Garden*. Perfect. Magic adventures, and not a parent anywhere in sight. She curled damply in the corner of the window seat.

I should change, she thought, and then, *I don't care.*

"Don't care killed the cat," said a voice in her ear.

Sophie's heart skipped a beat. "Where are you?"

"Here and there. Betwixt and between. Takes a heap of doing. What you in a state about?"

"I'm *not* in a *state!*"

"Yes, you is. The State of Louisiana." It laughed out loud.

Sophie glanced fearfully at the door. "Hush. Mama'll hear you."

"And what can you mama do to me? If'n she can even find me, which she can't?"

"Nothing. She can't do anything to *you*."

"Aw," said the Creature sympathetically. "You all upset. She whup you?"

"No," said Sophie. Mama didn't think much of people who resorted to violence to control their children. "She just hates me, that's all. I wish I was dead!"

"Don't you be saying things like that in front of me, child." The Creature sounded alarmed. "Not less'n you means it."

"Well, then, I wish I wasn't me."

"Who you want to be?"

Sophie held out *The Time Garden*. "I want to be like Ann and Roger and Eliza. I want to travel through time and have grand adventures and brothers and sisters and have everybody love me."

The room was very still. "That a wish?" the Creature asked solemnly.

Sophie was in no mood to be cautious. "Yes," she said. "It's a wish."

"Well, now," the Creature said. "Love is something you gots to earn for youself. I might could see about giving you some family, though. And adventures just come along natural with going back in time."

Sophie stood up, leaving *The Time Garden* on the window seat. "Okay, I'm ready. Is there anything I need to do?"

"You done it," said the Creature. "We's here."

Chapter 6

"Where's here?" Sophie asked.

Her only answer was a fading giggle.

And wasn't it just her luck, she thought, to get the kind of magic creature that would transport her somewhere and leave her without explanation? Just like the Natterjack in *The Time Garden*, come to think of it. And the Natterjack had always shown up when the children really needed it. Irritating as the Creature was, she was sure it would, too.

In the meantime, here she was, back in the Good Old Days, in a room that both was and was not hers.

Every piece of furniture seemed to come from somewhere else. The princessy bed with its high headboard was from Mama's room, but what was that gauzy material hanging from the half-tester? The mirrored armoire and dresser belonged in Grandmama's room, and the last time Sophie had seen that desk, it was in the parlor. The familiar faded wallpaper was gone, and so was the ratty rug, replaced by deep rose paint and pale matting. The only clues to the room's occupant were the striped scarf across the bed and the scribbled paper scattered across the desktop.

Sophie padded over to the desk to investigate, picked up an ivory pen, its gold nib crusted with dried ink. Beneath it was a half-written letter. She couldn't make head or tail of the scrawly handwriting, but the date was clear enough: *June 12, 1860*.

Sophie's hand shook a little.

The War Between the States was due to start in—Sophie thought for a moment—less than a year. She wondered whether she should warn her ancestors about it, decided she shouldn't risk changing the course of history by mistake and returning to the present to find out she hadn't been born. She might, however, let the slaves know that they'd be free in a few years—nothing too specific, just a hint, to give them something to look forward to.

But that was for when she'd actually met a slave. She put the letter back where she'd found it.

On the marble-topped nightstand, she found a white leather Bible and a copy of *Hiawatha* by Henry Wadsworth Longfellow, which had been used for pressing flowers. Inside the nightstand were a white porcelain pot and a faint stink that reminded her of a not-very-clean public bathroom. She shut the door quickly. Chamber pots were a part of the past she'd never thought much about.

Neither were corsets, which she found in the big mirrored armoire, hanging on hooks next to mysterious white cotton garments and pastel dresses with long, bulky skirts. She touched a flounce, wondering whether the Fairchild it belonged to was old or young, and if she might let Sophie try on her clothes.

Next, Sophie went to the window. In 1860, there was no window seat, just a square bay with a vanity table set it in to catch the light. A white gauze curtain framed the view she'd glimpsed by moonlight two nights before. Then, it had disappeared like smoke. This time, it wasn't going to go away.

Sophie caught sight of her reflection in the triple mirror on the vanity. She looked like she'd been dragged through a hedge backwards. There wasn't much she could do about the mud on her dress and arms, but she couldn't bear to meet her ancestors with her hair looking, yes, like a hooraw's nest. Sophie searched through the clutter of bottles and jars and ribbons until she found a silver brush. It wasn't polite to use someone else's brush without asking, but this was an emergency.

As she raised the brush to her hair, the door opened. Sophie spun around to see girl staring at her—a real Miss Lolabelle in a poufy white dress and a striped silk sash around her tiny waist. Her dark hair was bundled into a net and her skin was pink and white. With her eyes and mouth all round with surprise, she looked just like a doll a tourist would buy on Decatur Street.

The girl put one hand to her throat and gave a very Miss LolaBelle-like little scream. "Antigua!" she gasped. "Antigua! Come here!"

A Negro girl appeared at her shoulder. "Yes, Miss Liza."

A slave. A real, live slave. She was very pretty, with rosy-brown skin and eyes the same Coca-Cola brown as Miss Lola—Miss Liza's. Sophie noted the bright yellow turban wrapped around the Negro girl's head and the little silver cross strung on a red thread around her throat and was surprised. She'd thought a slave would look more downtrodden.

"You put Miss Liza's brush down!" the slave girl said. "Right now, you hear?"

Sophie dropped the brush with a clatter.

"I do believe she was fixing to steal it!" Miss Liza's voice was a high-pitched whine, not nearly as pretty as her face. "Bring her along to the office, Antigua. Papa will know what to do." She disappeared in a flurry of white ruffles.

Antigua grabbed Sophie's arm and shook it. "You in trouble, girl! What you doing here, anyway?"

This was not how Sophie had imagined her adventure beginning. She licked her lips. "Um. I got here by magic."

Antigua gave her a vicious shake. "Magic? I never heard of no magic that put folks where they don't belong to be. You crazy, girl? Or just foolish?"

"It's the truth," Sophie protested.

"Crazy *and* foolish," Antigua said. "Listen here, now. You don't want more trouble than you already got, you best find some other tale to tell Dr. Charles. Magic! I never!"

The slave girl took a firm grip of Sophie's arm and dragged her out to the gallery and down the back steps. Sophie was too shocked to resist. Were slaves allowed to hustle white people around like that? Wasn't that the reason the old days were good? Because Negroes knew their place?

Antigua entered the house through a door that didn't exist in 1960 and hustled Sophie down the back hall to Aunt Enid's office—or what would be Aunt Enid's office a hundred years in the future. When she'd knocked, she propelled Sophie across the room to the fireplace, where Miss Lolabelle was sitting by a lady on a sofa, carrying on while a tall gentleman patted her shoulder.

Antigua released Sophie and stepped back, leaving her staring at her illustrious ancestors.

The lady on the sofa was blonde and pale and thin as a rail, and dressed in gray silk and a lacy cap with long side-pieces. Wool and knitting needles lay on the sofa beside her. The gentleman, got up in a stiff high collar that made Sophie's neck itch to look at, had a long, sad face and an aquiline nose. A Fairchild nose, in fact.

The gentleman seated himself in what looked exactly like Grandmama's big wing chair. "My daughter says she discovered you in her room with her silver hairbrush in your hand." His voice was firm, but not unfriendly. "I trust you have some reasonable explanation?"

Sophie was so astonished to hear someone talking just like a character in a Dickens novel that it took her a moment to realize he was actually talking to her. It took another moment to realize she was going to have to answer him.

The lady picked up her knitting. She was working on a sock. "Perhaps a whipping will loosen her tongue, Dr. Fairchild."

Sophie went cold all over. It occurred to her that adventures might not be as much fun to live through as to read about.

"I think we can get to the bottom of this without whipping, my dear," Dr. Fairchild said.

"I cannot agree. The wench is a thief. Even your mother believes in whipping thieves."

"Now, Lucy, we don't *know* she's a thief."

The lady raised her almost invisible brows scornfully. She had a good face for scorn, with ice-blue eyes and a thin mouth. She was knitting without looking at what she was doing. Sophie found her terrifying. "She's bold enough for one. You, girl. Didn't anybody ever teach you not to look at your betters?"

Hastily, Sophie dropped her eyes to her feet.

"You've nothing to be frightened of," Dr. Fairchild said. "If you're innocent. Now. What is your name and where you come from?"

"Sophie," she said, her voice shaking slightly. "I'm from New Orleans."

"There! We're making progress. Can you tell me, Sophie, how you got here from New Orleans?"

It was all too obvious neither of the Fairchilds would believe any story involving magical Creatures and time travel. Why didn't any of the books mention that adventures were like taking a test you hadn't studied for?

"You got here somehow," Dr. Fairchild prompted. "Did you come by boat?"

Sophie had had teachers who couldn't wait for an answer. If she just stood there looking dumb and scared, he'd probably just tell her what he wanted her to say.

"Yes, sir," she answered eagerly. "A boat from New Orleans."

Mrs. Fairchild clicked her needles angrily. "That's a bare-faced lie, Dr. Fairchild. There hasn't been a steamboat by in weeks."

"They probably put her off at Doucette," he pointed out. "Saved themselves some time."

Miss Liza gave an impatient little bounce. "What does it matter where she came from? She was stealing my hairbrush, and she ought to be whipped!"

Mrs. Fairchild turned her icy glare on her daughter. "Your father is conducting this interrogation, Elizabeth. It does not become you to interrupt him."

Miss Liza scowled.

"The truth now, Sophie," Dr. Fairchild went on. "Did you get off the steamboat at Doucette?"

This might have been a trick question, coming from someone else. But Dr. Fairchild looked to be what Grandmama would call a Perfect Gentleman, and Perfect Gentlemen didn't lay traps. "Yes, sir."

"Nonsense," Mrs. Fairchild said. "We're a good five miles from Doucette. Did someone drive you here?"

Mrs. Fairchild, on the other hand, was not a Perfect Lady.

"No, ma'am," Sophie improvised. "I walked."

"Walked! Dr. Fairchild, I do believe this wench is a run-away as well as a thief. Just look at the state of her!"

"I disagree, my dear. She's not much more than a child. She couldn't have made the journey from New Orleans alone. It's more likely she lost her way between here and Doucette and fell into a ditch. She seems a little simple."

Mrs. Fairchild gave a laugh. "All slaves are simple when they're in trouble."

Sophie looked up, shocked. "But I'm not"—Mrs. Fairchild laid her knitting aside and pulled something from her waistband: a leather strap, about an inch wide. Sophie looked down hastily—"a runaway," she finished.

"If you want us to believe you," Dr. Fairchild said sternly, "you must tell us exactly who sent you here, and why."

Sophie hardly heard him. How could anybody think she was a slave? Slaves were Negroes. She was white. In 1960, white people were white and colored people were colored and nobody had any trouble telling them apart. It was true she was barefoot and she had a tan. Couldn't they tell the difference between tan and black? Hadn't they noticed her Fairchild nose?

The silence lengthened: Dr. Fairchild wasn't going to help her this time. Sophie was on the edge of panic when Mrs. Fairchild said, "If you look at her carefully, Dr. Fairchild, I think you'll see why she's reluctant to answer. Elizabeth, you may leave us."

"*Mama!*"

"Do as your mother says, puss," Dr. Fairchild said.

"But, Daddy!"

"Now, Liza."

Miss Liza flounced away. Dr. Fairchild took Sophie's chin in his large, warm hand and studied her carefully, just like Grandmama. Sophie felt her face heat uncomfortably.

"Well." Dr. Fairchild let her go. "Your master is Mr. Robert Fairchild, isn't he?"

Sophie nodded numbly.

"Robert always did spoil his servants," Mrs. Fairchild observed.

"My brother," Dr. Fairchild said, "treats his servants as he was taught to treat them."

"Which includes sending them on a long journey upriver without so much as a sack? And what about her traveling pass?"

"Very true, my dear. Do you have a traveling pass, Sophie?"

Sophie tensed. "I lost it?"

"You lost it." Dr. Fairchild made an impatient noise. "Don't you know how dangerous it is for a girl like you to be without a traveling pass? If the patrollers found you, they'd put you in chains and drag you back to your master, and that would be a lot of trouble for everybody."

Mrs. Fairchild said, "This is all very well, Dr. Fairchild, but it doesn't tell us what she was doing in Elizabeth's bedroom."

Dr. Fairchild sighed. "Very well, Lucy. Sophie. Why were you in Miss Liza's room? The truth, now."

Because it's my room, a hundred years from now. "I—got lost."

"A likely story! If you ask me, Dr. Fairchild, there's more to this girl than meets the eye. Have you ever seen anything like those spectacles?"

Sophie touched her glasses. They were just ordinary, blue plastic frames with little metal flowers on the temples. "My father gave them to me."

Mrs. Fairchild sent her a glare that could have stripped paint. "If you refer to Mr. Robert as your father again, I *will* have you whipped."

"Now, Lucy, the girl probably doesn't know any better. It's like Robert to have spoiled her, just as it's like him to send her without writing to warn us. Unless, perhaps, he wrote Mother. Or she might have a letter with her. Do you have a letter from your master, child?"

"I lost that, too." Sophie found it all too easy to sound pathetic. "I lost everything."

Delia Sherman

"Convenient. I don't mind telling you, Dr. Fairchild, I don't believe I've ever heard such a collection of untruths since the day I was born."

Dr. Fairchild sighed. "Well, she's a Fairchild—no question about that. I'll talk it over with Mother tonight and write Robert in the morning. In the meantime, we'll just presume she's a new addition to the family. Antigua?"

The slave girl had been standing by the door so quietly, Sophie had forgotten she was there. She acknowledged her name with a little curtsy. "Yes, Dr. Charles."

"Get this girl something to eat, then take her to Mammy."

Mrs. Fairchild took up her knitting again. "You, girl. How old are you?"

"Thirteen, ma'am."

"I thought you were younger. Thirteen is much too old to be running around with your legs showing. Get her something decent to wear, Antigua. As for you, girl, I can't even begin to imagine what you're used to in Mr. Robert's household. In my household, you will behave with proper humility, or you will be punished."

"Yes, ma'am. Thank you, ma'am."

Dizzy with relief, Sophie curtsied and followed Antigua out of the office. She thought she'd done pretty well, all things considered. A member of the family, Dr. Charles had said. Maybe things were going to work out after all.

Chapter 7

It had been raining in 1860, too. The sky was a patchy gray, and the wet grass clung to Sophie's legs as she followed Antigua around the back of Oak Cottage and along the edge of the garden.

A whiff of something good brought water to her mouth. "What's that?"

Antigua snorted. "You don't know roast chicken when you smells it? I thought you just acting simple so's Dr. Charles feel sorry for you. Maybe it ain't an act, huh?"

Sophie was stung. "I'm not simple."

"Then don't ask fool questions."

Sophie shut her mouth and wondered when the friends she'd wished for were going to show up.

They walked up to Aunt Enid's garden shed, looking bare and businesslike without its blanket of vine. Sophie peered through the open door into a noisy, smoky room full of women in long dresses shelling beans, stirring pots, chopping vegetables, and kneading bread on Aunt Enid's potting table. The mammoth fireplace was all cluttered with pots on hooks and a long spit with chickens strung along it like beads on a string. The air was hot and sticky as boiling molasses and hummed with flies.

Sophie stepped back, hoping Antigua would bring her food outside.

"Well, looky there!" a voice exclaimed. "A stranger!"

Next thing she knew, Sophie was standing at the center of a semicircle of curious black faces asking questions faster than she could answer them.

"Where you from?"

"Ain't you light!"

"What-for them things setting on you nose?"

Sophie hadn't been this close to so many Negroes since she was eight and Mama had stopped her going to church with Lily. She'd liked Lily's church, where the singing was a lot more lively than at St. Martin's Episcopal and the ladies were all got up in fancy hats. These women, in their faded dresses and tightly wrapped headcloths, frightened her.

Sophie pushed her glasses up on her nose and smiled nervously.

"Well, Miss High-and-Mighty!" a short, round woman exclaimed. "Can't you answer a civil question?"

"Don't act more foolish than God made you, China. Can't you see the child's scared half to death?"

The woman who had spoken was tall—as tall as Papa, with reddish-brown skin and a blue headcloth. The other women moved aside to give her room.

Knowing authority when she saw it, Sophie held out her hand. "How do you do?"

"Well, I never," China said, and everybody laughed.

"Hush yourselves, now," the queenly woman said. "Ain't you never seen a body with manners before?" Her hand, hard and scaly with work, folded around Sophie's. "I'm Africa, Old Missy's cook."

Antigua appeared at Africa's elbow. "She belong to Mr. Robert. Or so she say."

A dozen pairs of eyes turned to Sophie with a new and intense interest. She felt her ears burn.

"Oh, she Mr. Robert's, sure enough," said a dark, skinny woman.

Someone else laughed. "And ain't it just like him, sending off his high-yellow girl for his mammy to raise up for him?"

Africa ignored them. "What's your name, child?"

"Sophie."

"Sophie." Africa's smile showed missing teeth. "And what're them things on your nose, Sophie?"

"Glasses."

Africa held Sophie's chin and lifted her glasses off her nose. The world disappeared into a multicolored blur. Sophie squeaked and made a blind grab.

"Don't fret, child. I'm just looking," said Africa.

"But I can't *see*! You don't understand!"

"I sure enough don't." Africa dangled the glasses by the earpiece. "Old Missy, she don't have spectacles like these. Dr. Fairchild, *he* don't have spectacles like these, and he's a medical man. How come you got them?"

"So I can see," Sophie almost wailed. "Give them back to me. Please!"

Africa held the glasses up to her eyes, yanked them away as though they'd bitten her. "Whoo-eee! You blind as sin, child!" She handed them back. "Better take good care of them. Oak River ain't New Orleans. If they get broke, you'll just have to do without."

"Not less you ask Mr. Robert to get you some more," said Antigua nastily. "What work you do at Mr. Robert's house, anyway?"

Sophie settled her glasses back on her nose. "Work?"

"Yes," Antigua sneered. "Work. You know—what black folk do and white folk don't?"

Sophie looked down at her feet, sun-darkened and streaked with dried mud. There was a scratch above one arch and a bug crawling on her big toe. The feet surrounding her were mostly darker, but two or three might have been as pale as hers under the dirt. She tried to imagine what would happen if she raised her head right now and announced that she was not a slave, but a genuine white Fairchild, brought into the past by magic.

They'd think she was crazy, just like Antigua had. And if she insisted, they'd probably tell Dr. Fairchild, who would think she was crazy, too. Maybe if she just went along, and was agreeable and polite, she could keep out of trouble until the Creature showed up to rescue her.

Africa clapped her hands sharply. "Y'all get back inside and get on with dinner. Unless you're hankering to tell Mrs. Charles she ain't going to eat until three?"

"No, ma'am," said China with feeling. "I likes my black skin just fine on my back where it belong."

The other women laughed and went back into the kitchen. Africa looked down at Sophie. "I 'spect you wants a corn cake."

Sophie hesitated. That kitchen was probably as full of germs as it was of flies. And none of those slaves looked very clean. Still, she *was* hungry, and she loved corn cakes. Lily used to make them, light and spongy and a little sweet. Besides, she was the heroine of this adventure, and heroines never got so much as a head cold.

"Please, ma'am. If it's not any trouble."

Africa led her through the flies and heat to a wooden bin full of flat, grayish things that looked like cardboard cookies. The corn cake tasted even more like cardboard than it looked, but Sophie was empty enough to choke it down anyway, and even remembered to thank Africa for it before going outside, where Antigua was sitting on the bench waiting for her. "Come on, if you done stuffing you face. I gots work to do."

She got up and trotted purposefully away, Sophie at her heels.

As they came into the yard, Sophie was hit with a truly eye-watering stink. "What's *that*?"

"Soap boiling." Antigua pointed to where three Negro women with their sleeves rolled up were stirring a big iron pot over an open fire.

Sophie sneezed. "That's not what soap smells like."

"How else pig fat and lye supposed to smell? What you make your soap from in New Orleans? Manna?"

"I don't know. We buy our soap at a store."

Antigua rolled her eyes. "I 'spect everything better in New Orleans."

Sophie didn't bother to respond. It was obvious the slave girl was bound and determined to take everything she said as a slight and an insult. There'd been girls like that at school. The only thing to do was keep her mouth shut and hope Mammy was friendlier.

Antigua picked her way across the yard with her pink skirts held up out of the mud, with Sophie trailing behind, gaping at the busy slaves like a tourist on Bourbon Street. Each cabin was a workshop, and the work done there spilled out into the yard: barrel making, carpentry, leatherwork, forging iron. They fetched up at a cabin where a woman sat in the door, stitching at a cloud of white stuff. A mysterious, rhythmical clacking came from inside.

"Afternoon, Asia," Antigua said. "This here is Sophie. Mr. Robert send her on a boat from New Orleans. Mrs. Charles say give her some decent clothes." Antigua wrinkled her nose. "Better wash her first. And be quick. I taking her to Mammy, and there ain't much time before dinner."

Asia bundled the white cloud into her arms. "She better come on in, then."

Sophie followed Asia into the cabin. The clacking came from a huge wooden loom worked by a shadowy figure, arms flying, flat, bare feet working the treadles like a giant spider.

Asia shook her head. "That Antigua. She so full of herself, she liable to bust like a bullfrog one fine day. This here's Sophie, Hepzibah. She need some decent clothes, right quick."

The clacking died away, and the weaving woman disentangled herself from the loom. When she stood up, Sophie saw she was thin, and would have been tall if her back hadn't been curled like a hoop. "Welcome, Sophie. That a mighty pretty dress you got there." Hepzibah took a fold of the blue gingham shirtwaist and rubbed it between her fingers. "I ain't never seen such fine weaving. Where this fabric come from?"

Sophie pulled away nervously. "New Orleans. My mama bought it for me."

"Then your mama ain't got good sense," Asia said. "That dress ain't seemly for a big girl like you. Make a nice Sunday dress for one of the childrens, though."

"No!" Sophie crossed her arms tightly, panicked. What if changing her clothes meant she couldn't go home? What if she left her dress in the past and Mama was mad? "It's mine. You can't have it."

Hepzibah frowned. "It ain't Christian, keeping something ain't no use to you when there's a plenty other folks could use it."

Her expression told Sophie that Hepzibah wouldn't hesitate to remove the dress by force. Reluctantly, she took it off—and her bra, and her underpants—and, miserably embarrassed, stood in a corner while Asia sponged her briskly with cold water out of a bucket. Hepzibah gave her a pair of coarse cotton drawers and a nightgown-like chemise, a long brown homespun dress and a sacking apron. When Sophie was dressed, Asia raked through her hair with her fingers and braided it in six tight plaits, tied a white cloth she called a "tignon" over them, and knotted the ends into rabbit ears.

"There," she said. "I 'spect you be getting something nicer directly. Light-skinned girl like you bound to end up in the Big House."

Sophie came out into the yard, feeling awkward and itchy and hot. Antigua sauntered away from the young stable hand she'd been teasing and gave Sophie a contemptuous once-over. "Well, you clean," she said. "Ain't nothing ever going to make you decent."

Sophie spared a wistful thought for the Natterjack, whose magic made the time-traveling children fit in whenever they went. What with wondering what was going to happen to her and Antigua hustling her from pillar to post, she was much too worried to pay much attention to the scenery. She passed the maze without even thinking to look at it.

And then she saw Oak River Big House.

It stood on a rise surrounded by gardens and flowering trees, three stories of bright red brick, with a wide gallery, tall white columns, and a double stair that curved graceful arms around a marble fountain in which a stone nymph poured water out of an urn. It was splendid and proud, and any Fairchild who entered it must be proud, too.

Sophie stood up straighter. She'd asked the Creature for an adventure, and adventures had to be full of misunderstandings and hardships, or what was the point? She was a Fairchild, and this was her ancestral home.

She followed Antigua around the fountain to a blue door that opened onto a long, stone-floored corridor. A young black man in a short blue jacket came out of a door carrying a glass on a silver tray. "Careful, Antigua," he said. "Young Missy send her a note, make her cross as two sticks."

Antigua shrugged and herded Sophie into a room furnished with a big desk and shelves full of papers.

"Mammy, this here's Sophie," she announced, curtseying. "She from New Orleans." And then she left.

Sophie, who'd been expecting someone fat and jolly and Aunt Jemima-ish, studied the Negro woman behind the desk with a sinking heart. She was thin as a rake, nunnishly dressed in black and white, and looked about as jolly as Mama in a temper.

The woman glanced up from the note she was reading, adjusted her narrow steel spectacles, and fixed Sophie with a sharp gaze that reminded her uncomfortably of a particularly strict math teacher she'd had in fifth grade.

"Mrs. Charles has told me about you, Sophie. She says you are rude and spoiled and possibly a thief. I won't tolerate a thief, and I won't tolerate uppity behavior, whatever color you are. The law doesn't care who your father is, and neither do I. If your mother was a slave, so are you. Do you hear me?"

Sophie gaped at her. "You can't talk to me like that!"

Mammy got up from her desk and slapped Sophie across the face.

Sophie put her hand to her stinging cheek. "You hit me!"

"If you don't keep your thoughts and your eyes to yourself, I'll do more than that." Mammy took Sophie's arm in a firm grip. "You need to learn your place, girl. You can sit in the linen room for a spell, think things over."

Locked in the linen room, Sophie had plenty of time to plan what she was going to say to the Creature when it showed up, about throwing her into an adventure and then just abandoning her. She tried to think what she might have said to the Fairchilds to persuade them she wasn't a slave, moved on to imagining how Mama would have handled Mammy, and spent some time worrying over whether Mama would think she'd run away and call the police.

If Mama even noticed.

Sophie closed her eyes, clicked her bare heels together, and repeated "There's no place like home" until she started to cry. When she was cried out, she wiped her face on her apron and distracted herself by poking through the sheets (heavy linen) and towels (heavier linen). She stood by the window and watched the shadow of the Big House creep slowly over the geometrical beds of the formal garden. Mid-afternoon, she saw a procession of slaves trotting into the house carrying big tin boxes slung on poles. She wondered what was in the boxes. She wondered if anybody was going to give her anything to eat.

Time passed. The shadows crawled. She wished she had something to read.

The slaves brought the boxes out again and carried them around the corner of the house and out of sight. The light faded, palmetto bugs whirred against the ceiling and shadows of hunting bats flitted silently across the sky. And then it was night, and a slave she hadn't seen before was at the door with a lantern, telling her to come along.

"Mammy, she say you sleep in the Quarters tonight, maybe it teach you to mind you manners."

As the slave girl led her through the fragrant, buggy darkness, Sophie leaned that her name was Sally, that she was a housemaid, and just about the nosiest person Sophie had ever met. Too tired to think of any answers to her questions about New Orleans and Sophie's mother and Mr. Robert, Sophie just shook her head, which brought on a furious speech about folks who thought they were better than other folks that kept Sally busy until they reached the oak grove.

"See this here?" Sally swung the lantern to illuminate the first few feet of a narrow path. "Just follow it on a ways, and you come to the Quarters. Africa say she take you in, the good Lord know why. First cabin to the right."

It's not easy to follow a path you can't see. Sophie groped her way forward step by step, jumping at every noise and stubbing her bare toes on every stick and stone. By the time she reached the end of the trees, she was jumpy as a cat. She also desperately needed a bathroom.

In front of her, a double row of cabins glowed faintly in the moonlight, their doors open to catch whatever breeze should happen to chance along. Behind them, a field of young cane rustled sleepily to itself, and cicadas fiddled wildly.

Sophie climbed to the porch of the first cabin to the right and peeked cautiously through the uncurtained window. Firelight flickered on the face of the slave woman who'd given her the corn cake, stirring an iron pot hung over the fire on a hook. On the floor, a child was playing with a baby, and three men sat around a rough table, their faces grim in the flickering light of a smoky candle.

Sophie's pulse stuttered nervously. The men looked just exactly like the kind of dirty, ragged Negroes Mama had warned her against, except they were all working. One was stuffing a sack with what looked like a tangle of black thread; the second was sewing another sack closed. The third man sat in the only chair in the room whittling with his head bent like he was too tired to hold it up. Around them, the walls were covered with clothes and tools hung on hooks; baskets and bunches of herbs dangled from the ceiling. The air was still and hot and thick with grease and sweat and small, biting insects.

If there'd been anywhere else to go, Sophie would have crept away again. As it was, she hesitated until the child looked up and saw her at the window. "Who that?"

Sophie moved shyly to the door. "Sophie."

The child scrambled to its feet. Sophie couldn't tell whether it was a girl or a boy, its hair trimmed like a lamb's wool close to his head, its bony body covered by a coarse brown shirt. "My name's Canada. You come to supper?" The child took Sophie's hand and pulled her forward. "This here's Sophie. She ain't borned here."

"She sure as shooting ain't," one of the men said. "Dr. Charles a good Christian gentleman. Ain't it just like Mr. Robert, though?"

Africa turned from the fire. "Hush, Flanders. Ain't her fault who her pa is. Come here, sugar."

Sophie edged around the table, clutching her skirt so it wouldn't touch anything.

"This here's my husband, Ned." Africa laid a gentle hand on the skinny man's shoulder. He raised his face, pale brown and deeply lined.

"Pleased to meet you, sir," Sophie said shyly.

Ned showed a graveyard of yellow teeth in a wide smile. "I pleased to meet you, too, child."

"The boys are Poland and Flanders," Africa said. "The baby's Saxony. Tote me some water, Canny girl. I'm making us some spoon bread to welcome Sophie to Oak River."

By this time, Sophie was ready to burst. Not wanting to ask about a bathroom where the men could hear, she followed Canada outside. But she couldn't make her understand.

"I don't know 'bout no bathroom," the little girl said. "The water in the cistern here's for drinking. Sometimes we washes in a barrel, but in summer, mostly we swims."

"I don't have to wash," Sophie said. "I have to tinkle."

"Tinkle?"

Sophie was ready to die of embarrassment. "Pee."

Giggling, Canada led her to a little wooden house out in the field behind the cabins. It smelled foul, it was full of flies, and there wasn't any paper, only a basket of scratchy moss to clean up with. Sophie was past caring.

Supper was greens and a little chicken and the water they'd been boiled in—pot liquor, Africa called it—and a deliciously creamy spoon bread, eaten more or less in silence, which suited Sophie just fine. She was tired and frightened, and hadn't the first idea what slaves liked to talk about.

As soon as the last crumb of spoon bread disappeared, Canada and Africa cleared the table, Poland put the baby to bed in a basket, and all three men went out into the night—to hoe their vegetable-patch, Canada said. Sophie sat in Ned's chair, trying to keep out of the way and wondering where she was going to sleep.

A woman came to the door asking Africa to step round to the Big House, as Korea's baby was on the way. Africa bustled around pulling gourds and dried plants from the rafters and tying them in a sack, then left in a hurry.

Canada yawned. "Time we go to bed. Momi, she sometimes out all night when a baby come."

She took Sophie's hand and led her into a tiny back room. Sophie could just make out two ticking mattresses, covered with pieced quilts, taking up most of the floor space. Canada gestured to the smaller one. "This my bed," she said. "But you can share."

Sophie had never shared a bed in her life and didn't want to start now. But there wasn't anyplace else to sleep. She began to cry helplessly.

"Aww," Canada said. "You homesick for you Momi?" She put her skinny arms around Sophie's waist and her head against her shoulder. "Don't you cry. She send you a message, I 'spect, next boat from New Orleans. You going to like it here. Folks is nice, mostly, and Old Missy and Dr. Charles, they don't believe in whipping 'less you do something real bad. Lie down now and go to sleep. Everything look better in daylight. You wait and see."

Chapter 8

An iron clanging woke Sophie while it was still dark.

"Morning bell," a child's voice informed her. "Momi say I supposed take you to Mammy. Can you watch Saxony while I do my chores?"

The mattress crackled as Canny scrambled away. Sophie sat up and rubbed her face. She felt grubby from sleeping in her clothes, hungry, and even more tired than she'd been when she lay down. The adventures of the day before hadn't been a dream after all. The Creature had really taken her back in time, and her ancestors had really mistaken her for a slave. The magic hadn't ended at midnight or when she went to sleep. It looked like she was stuck in the past until the Creature took her home.

If it even intended to. Maybe, Sophie thought, the Creature was an evil spirit, whose treats were really tricks. Maybe it was laughing itself sick in whatever betwixt and between place it lived. She just hoped leaving her here until the war started wasn't its idea of a good joke.

She would have liked a real bathroom with running water and Cheerios for breakfast. What she got was an outhouse, a bucket to wash in, and a hunk of cold cornbread, just like everybody else.

The sky grew pearly with dawn. Africa and her menfolk left for work. Canada handed Saxony to Sophie, who held the dark little thing gingerly while Canada rolled up the mattresses and swept the floors with a straw broom nearly as big as she was. By the time everything was tidy, the sun had burned away the mist and Saxony was fussing.

Canada heaved the baby onto her hip. "I fetch Saxy here down to old Auntie Europe—she look out for the picanninies. Then I show you the bestest way to the Big House."

It had rained in the night, and the morning smelled clean and damp. Sophie waited for Canada on the front steps, scratching at some new bug bites on her leg and trying not to think about whether Mammy would slap her again or if Dr. Fairchild's mama was as mean as his wife.

There was certainly plenty to distract her. Chickens scratched and squabbled in the dusty road between the cabins, ignoring scrawny dogs, who ignored them back. From the cabin next door, a tethered goat gazed with yellow, slotted eyes through the fence slats at the rows of vegetables in Africa's garden. Birds sang from the oak grove and dipped and soared above the restless cane.

The Good Old Days were sure livelier than the present. Sophie thought she'd like them just fine, if she didn't have to be a slave.

Then Canada ran up, and it was time to go to the Big House.

Thinking it over, Sophie decided that Canada must be her official magical sidekick and guide. She certainly acted like one—pointing out the fastest shortcuts to the Big House and the yard, warning her what parts of the gardens were off-limits, telling her how to deal with Mammy.

"She bark like a mad dog," Canny said, "but she don't hardly ever bite 'less you sass her. You just bend real respectful, say yes'm and no'm and keep you eyes down, and she be happy as a goat in a briar patch."

Like Miss Ely, Sophie thought, remembering the strict math teacher. *It's just playacting. I don't really have to mean it.* She grinned at Canny, knocked on Mammy's door, went in, and bobbed politely.

"There you are," said Mammy. "That headcloth looks like a possum's been nesting in it."

Sophie glanced up, caught a fierce dark glare, and looked down again. "I'm sorry. I didn't have a mirror."

"Sass and excuses!" Mammy whipped off Sophie's tignon and refolded it. "If it were up to me, I'd send you right back to Mr. Robert. But Mrs. Fairchild's a kind, Christian lady and she takes her responsibilities seriously. Just you keep in mind that kind is not the same as weak. Mrs. Fairchild ran this plantation all alone when Master passed and Dr. Charles was off North learning to be a doctor. She still runs it. She's not likely to be impressed by a mongrel slave wench who thinks she's as good as white folks." Mammy yanked the tignon tight. "Follow me."

A few moments later, Sophie was on the gallery of the Big House, curtsying to her five-times-great-grandmother, Mrs. Charles Fairchild of Oak River Plantation, with her eyes fixed on the spreading pool of her wide black skirts. She felt slightly sick.

"So you're Sophie," a sweet, slow voice said. "Look up, child. I want to see your face."

Shyly, Sophie lifted her gaze to a round, rosy face framed by a frilly white cap, a little rosebud mouth, a very unFairchild-like button nose, and clear blue eyes.

"What an adventure you've had!" Mrs. Fairchild said merrily. "And how like Mr. Robert not to tell us he was sending you. I've written to scold him. Now. What shall we do with you? I suppose you do fancy sewing?"

Sophie considered lying, decided it would lead to disaster. "No, ma'am."

"We shall have to teach you, then. Dr. Charles tells me you're well-spoken. What are your accomplishments?"

"Accomplishments, ma'am?"

"Can you dress hair, for instance? Starch and iron?"

What did slaves do, anyway? Sophie wracked her brain for some useful skill. "I like to read. And I won a prize once, for my handwriting."

"I declare!" Mrs. Fairchild produced a fat leather book from the folds of her dress. "Can you read this?"

The spine was stamped in gold: *Little Dorrit*, by Charles Dickens. Sophie opened the book eagerly. If there was one thing she was good at, it was reading aloud. Whenever teachers wanted something read in class, she was always the first to be called on. She found the first chapter and began: "*Thirty years ago, Marseilles lay burning in the sun, one day. A blazing sun upon a fierce August day was no greater rarity in southern France then, than at any other time, before or since.—*"

"You read very well, child." Mrs. Fairchild sounded surprised. "Isn't it just like Robert to have you taught! He never did give a snap of his fingers about the law. What do you think, Mammy?"

"I think she's next door to useless. But she can fetch and carry and help Aunt Winney see after your things."

"You're right. Winney will be glad of the help, and there's no one better to train her up as a lady's maid." Mrs. Fairchild gave Sophie a friendly smile. "It will be nice to have a bright young face around me. Not dressed like a yard hand, though. You ask Winney if she can find something in that armoire full of gowns Miss Charlotte left behind when she married."

Aunt Winney, it turned out, was Mrs. Fairchild's body servant. She was older and even stouter than her mistress, and couldn't go up and down stairs without puffing and groaning from the pain in her legs and back. She'd traveled from Virginia to Oak River with the former Miss Caroline Wilkes Berry when she was a bride, which was why, as she told Sophie, she had a Christian name instead of one of them heathenish Oak River names.

"You be grateful you ain't called New Guinea or Mexico," the old woman said. "Missy Caro say old Massa's grandpappy begun it when he buy the firstest slaves for Oak River. He name them Asia, America, Africa, Europe, Australia, and England."

Aunt Winney reminded Sophie of the old ladies at St. Martin's, chatty and cozy and full of gossip and pats on the cheek. So what if she was leather-colored and had her hair tied up in a jaunty red-checked tignon? She was friendly and more than happy to answer Sophie's questions.

"England? The other names are continents. Why not South America or Antarctica?"

Aunt Winney chuckled. "You so sharp, you going cut youself. Old Massa's grandpappy come from England, that why-for. Now, lets us see what Miss Lotty got you might could wear."

By the time the bell rang at noon, Sophie was the proud possessor of two high-necked calico dresses, two petticoats, white calico stockings that tied at her knees with string, a crisp white apron, and a pair of scuffed brown boots with buttons up the side that were too big and had to be stuffed with rags to keep her feet from sliding.

Aunt Winney smiled. "You pretty as a picture, sugar."

Pretty? Sophie turned and stared in the mirror.

A stranger stared back at her with dark, surprised eyes. With her hair hidden by the white tignon and a shape created by layers of petticoat and a fitted top, she looked almost grown-up. But pretty? Mama certainly wouldn't have thought so.

Aunt Winney's dark, round face appeared over her shoulder. "Now don't you go running away with the notion that yaller skin make you better than other folks. You hear what I say?"

Why did people kept telling her to be humble? The girl in the mirror looked meek enough to Sophie. "Yes, ma'am."

"Good. Now, run on down to the kitchen and fetch me a bowl of mush. You can catch a bite while you down there, but no lollygagging."

The shortcut to Oak Cottage passed behind the maze. Sophie was tempted to run in to look for the Creature, remembered it was off-limits, decided she'd let it go. Being a slave wasn't as bad as she had feared, now she'd been assigned to the Big House. She liked her many-times-great-grandmother, and it seemed like her grandmother liked her, too. Maybe they'd get to be friends, and Sophie could tell her about the present. That would make a good adventure.

When she reached the kitchen, Sophie asked a slave woman shelling lima beans on the bench outside for two bowls of mush. The woman glared at her. "Bowls is in the blue dresser and mush in the iron pot. Wait on your own self."

Sophie took two steps into what felt like a steam bath perfumed with pepper and onion and browning butter, and her stomach turned over. She'd been feeling off all morning—nerves, she'd thought. Maybe it was just hunger. Careful to keep out of everybody's way, she found the blue dresser and the bowls. The iron pot hung at the side of hearth. Sophie looked in and saw yellow mush mixed with unidentifiable lumps that might be potatoes or yams or chunks of fatty meat. There were flies struggling on it—and probably in it, too.

Delia Sherman

Heat washed over Sophie like scalding water, her stomach clenched, and she threw up on the stone hearth.

First she thought she'd die of shame, and then she just thought she'd die. Everything inside her seemed to be trying to get out and her head beat like a thousand drums. Shrill voices pierced her ears, pinching hands pulled at her as she was heaved up like a bundle of laundry and carried out into the air.

After that, Sophie was conscious of very little except how miserable she was. At some point, her fouled clothes were taken off. She felt water cooling her burning skin, then a coarse gown that rasped her like sandpaper. Large, cool hands touched her rigid belly and her forehead. She heard a voice she knew was Dr. Charles's saying that Robert should never have sent a city girl to the swamp in fever season.

She dragged her eyes open, saw her arm stretched over a white basin. Dr. Charles was beside her, holding a knife as bright and painful to look at as a bolt of lightning.

The knife bit into the crook of her elbow, and she felt very weak and sleepy and Papa was squeezing her arm and telling her that he'd come to take her home.

"I miss my Punkin-Pie," he said, and opened his mouth wider and wider, swallowing her arm clear up to the elbow. Sophie was wondering, without real interest, whether he intended to eat her clear up when she noticed the Creature floating in the air beside her, its face all puckered like a baby about to cry. She opened her mouth to give it a piece of her mind, then got distracted by Papa turning into an old man with a tall hat like Abraham Lincoln's. But he couldn't be Abraham Lincoln because Lincoln was white and this old man was black as his hat, black as the crooked stick he carried, wound with red thread and white shells.

He waved the stick toward a door outlined with a thread of blinding light. As Sophie watched, the thread widened to a scarf, then a ribbon. The door was opening.

"Fetch Africa," a woman's voice said. "This girl going fast."

What girl? Sophie wondered. And where was she going?

"Papa Legba." She saw the Creature crouched at the old man's feet. "Can you save this-here white girl? I go to a lot of bother to get her, and there ain't another one will do as well."

The old man gave the Creature a look that could have skinned a mule. "Serve you right, duppy, if she do die. You can't just go dragging folks through time like it was a railway station!"

One amber eye peered up impudently. "Don't serve *her* right, though. Dead, she ain't worth nothing. Live, she might could do some good."

The old man studied the Creature, his face still as a carving. Suddenly he laughed. "That plan of yours, duppy, is like something Compair Lapin and Bouki might hatch when they been drinking corn likker. Going to be fun to watch. But you best remember all doorways belong to me. I choose when they open, where they lead, and who may pass through."

The Creature touched the old man's boot. "I remember."

Sophie was about to ask the old man if he could open a door and send her home when a dark blue void opened over her bed. She saw a light sparkling in the heart of it, crystal blue. The scent of salt water tickled her nose; the taste of molasses filled her mouth. The bed rocked under her, floating on a gently swelling sea. A wave leapt up, caressed her body coolly, withdrew. The void filled with a velvety voice singing a wordless song, and a queenly figure appeared, crowned with gold and veiled with strings of pearls.

"Yemaya," said the old man in the hat.

"Don't you know better than to lead a child through into this time with no preparation? The water and the food are poison to one who is not used to them. You play a dangerous game, Legba." The musical voice was stern.

"I *am* dangerous," said the old man silkily.

"And I am not?"

For a moment, the air around the two entities crackled and buzzed. Then the old man laughed. "You're barking up the wrong tree, Yemaya. This game belongs to the little trickster, who plots but never plans."

The Creature grinned sheepishly.

"You play with forces you do not understand," the woman told it, angry and amused. "Do not do so again."

"No, ma'am," the Creature said. "Not 'less I needs to. Can you fix her?"

"I can," the velvety voice said. "I will."

The door snicked shut, darkness fell, and Sophie was asleep.

After a dreamless, drifting time, Sophie woke to an unfamiliar room, the crimson glow of a fire, and a woman bent over a big-bellied pot like a witch in a fairy tale. She felt like she'd done three thousand sit-ups and run fifty miles in a desert, but she wasn't sick anymore.

The woman turned. Without her glasses, Sophie couldn't see her face, but she was dressed in blue with yellow around her head, like Yemaya, and held herself like a queen.

"'Bout time you woke up," the woman said. "I ain't got no root for sleeping sickness."

It was a beautiful voice, but it was human, and Sophie recognized it. "You're Canada's mother. Africa."

"That's right, and I'm right glad you know it. You been clear off your head since Dr. Charles bled you yesterday." Africa put aside a curtain of gauzy fabric, slid an arm under Sophie's shoulders, and held a steaming cup to her lips.

The mixture was bitter and mossy and thick with bits of leaves. As Sophie choked it down, Africa said, "I don't know what to make of you, and that's the truth. The Master of the Crossroads, he goes his own way. That way sometimes bright and sometimes dark, but it ain't never what I'd call easy."

Sophie frowned. "Do you mean the old man, or the Creature?"

"What creature is that, sugar?"

"The one that brought me here. I have to find it, so I can go back home."

Africa smoothed her hair gently. "This your home now, sugar, less Mr. Robert change his mind. You rest."

Next time Sophie woke, Dr. Charles was taking her pulse.

"Strong and regular," he said. "Mrs. Fairchild will be pleased. A couple of days of rest, and you'll be as good as new."

Dr. Charles gave her hand a pat and moved away. Sophie found her glasses under the pillow and put them on. The room snapped into focus. Sophie looked around at four iron beds draped in gauze, and a cabinet full of jars and bottles beside a table where Dr. Charles sat unrolling a long strip of linen around a slave woman's arm. A second slave, an older woman in a big white apron, stood beside him with a jar.

Dr. Charles snipped off the bandage, tied the ends, and tucked them in neatly. "There, Rhodes. I don't want you back in the fields for another few days yet. I'll tell Mr. Akins to assign you something light."

Delia Sherman

The woman Rhodes thanked him and left. The older woman, whose name was Aunt Cissie, fetched in a skinny man with a hacking cough, followed by a big man complaining of a griping in his guts, an old woman bent over with rheumatism, and three or four more. Sophie watched Dr. Charles examine them, peering into mouths and eyes, sounding chests, instructing Aunt Cissie to give them liniment or spoonsful of foul-smelling liquid, asking after the health of a brother, an aunt, a father, a wife, listening to the soft-voiced, respectful answers. When the last patient had left, he dismissed Aunt Cissie, pulled out a long black book, and started to write in it.

The pen scratched softly, the flies buzzed lazily against the ceiling. Sophie was on the edge of drifting off to sleep again when a clattering on the porch jerked her awake. The door flew open and a man stomped in. He was dirty and roughly dressed. Sophie thought he was another field hand until she saw that he kept his broad-brimmed hat on his greasy curls and looked Dr. Charles straight in the eye.

"Devon Cut needs a new gang-driver," he said.

Dr. Charles kept on writing. "Give it to Old Guam."

"Guam? That pipe-sucker?" His voice was like a street car braking. "He ain't done an honest day's work since the day his mammy weaned him."

"Mrs. Fairchild has chosen Old Guam, and I agree." Dr. Charles laid down his pen. "By the way, Akins, I've had a letter from Chicago. The new evaporators are on their way to New Orleans and should be here, God willing, in a few weeks. Have you read those articles I gave you?"

Akins tipped his hat to the back of his head. "Yessir," he said. "That there evaporator's a fine machine, but I'm thinking it's a mite complicated for them niggers to run."

"Given that a black man invented the apparatus, I have no doubt black men can learn to operate it, given the proper training." Dr. Charles got up and put on a black frock coat. "Come along to the Big House, and we'll discuss it. Why, hello, Canada. Have you come to visit Sophie?"

Sophie saw Canada, looking very small and black and meek, standing in the door with a large covered basket on her arm. "Yessir." Her voice was so low Sophie could hardly hear her. "I brung her some broth."

Dr. Charles patted the little girl's head as he left. Akins ignored her completely. As soon as they were out the door, Canada turned and stuck out her tongue.

"Who's that horrible man?" Sophie asked.

"That old Mist' Akins, the overseer. His mama beat him with an ugly stick so hard, it gone straight on till his soul."

Sophie laughed. "You're funny, Canada."

"White folks calls me Canada." She pulled a canister from the basket. "You call me Canny."

Sophie pulled herself up against the thin pillow. There was so much she didn't know about living in the past. If she was going to be stuck here for a while, she'd better learn—preferably before she saw Mammy again. "Canny, will you tell me about Oak River?"

"Sure. What you want to know?"

"Everything, I guess. I never lived on a plantation before."

Canny giggled. "You surely ain't. Flandy like to bust himself laughing when he hear 'bout you asking for a bath-room!"

Sophie flushed. "I know I've got a lot to learn."

"What you want to know?"

"Well, how soap is made and what a gang-driver does and why there's a curtain over the bed, to start off with."

Canny nodded. "Well, a gang-driver, he watch the field hands so they don't slack off. The mosquito bar keep the mosquitoes from eating you all alive in the night. I don't know nothing 'bout soap-making 'cept it stink to Heaven, but I know lots 'bout doves. I takes care of all the doves in the pigeon house."

"Tell me about the doves, then," Sophie said. "But I also need to know about cooking and washing and ironing and—"

"Ain't nobody know all that," Canny said. "And if'n they did, they too busy to hang round here telling you about it." She thought a moment. "Tell you what. Tomorrow's Saturday. Everybody gots a plenty of chores, but I asks around some, see who can maybe come by for a spell. That suit you?"

"That suits me just fine," Sophie said. "Thank you."

Canny unscrewed the canister and poured a fragrant golden stream into a tin cup. "Momi say if this set well, she see 'bout trying you on boil chicken and white bread. You gots to drink, too—water, milk, sassafras tea."

"Your Mama sure knows a lot about sick people."

"Momi know everything there is about everything," said Canny. "Momi a two-headed woman."

"Huh?"

"A two-headed woman. Sometimes, when she bring the babies and tend to folks and make *gris-gris*, she not just herself, but the other one, too."

"The other one?" Sophie remembered the velvety face in her dream. "You mean Yemaya?"

"Shush—that name a special secret. Maybe Momi tell you about it by and by." She made a face. "Maybe she tell me, too. Now drink up you soup, and I tell you a story. You ever heard how come snakes got poison in they mouth and nothing else ain't got it?"

"No," said Sophie.

"Don't they tell no stories in New Orleans?"

"They tell lots of stories. Just not that one."

Canny settled down cross-legged at the foot of the bed. "When God make the snake, he put him in the bushes to ornament the ground. But things didn't suit the snake, so one day he get on a ladder and go up to see God."

Sophie finished the fragrant chicken broth, took off her glasses, and listened sleepily as the snake complained to God about getting stomped on and God gave him poison to protect himself. Canny described how, when the snake got a little carried away with his gift, the other animals climbed the heavenly ladder to complain in their turn. Sophie's eyes grew heavier and heavier. About the time God was coming up with an answer to their complaints, she fell asleep.

Chapter 9

First thing next morning, along with a basket containing broth and ashcakes and sassafras tea, Canny brought a skinny girl called Tibet and a lively, round-faced boy called Young Guam and Sophie's education on plantation life began.

At first, Sophie was too shy to open her mouth. Tibet and Young Guam were closer to her age than Canny, maybe eleven or twelve. They were dark and dusty and ragged, and their talk was full of words she didn't know, like billets and crushers and black moss, and how lazy white folks were, making other folks do things anybody with gumption would know how to do for themselves. Sophie couldn't help wondering if Lily and Ofelia said the same things about Mama and Aunt Enid—about Sophie herself, come to that.

If the children of Oak River didn't think much of the Fairchilds, they purely hated Mr. Akins. "He ugly as a 'gator," Tibet said, "and twice as mean. He catch you sucking on a tee-niny piece of cane, he whup you bloody."

"Worth it, though," Young Guam said. "I sure do love me some sugar cane. You ever chewed cane, Sophie?"

Sophie, who had never seen sugar that didn't come in a bowl, shook her head.

"'Course she ain't," Tibet scoffed. "City girls don't got no call to chew cane. City girls eats white sugar, double refined."

"I'd chew cane, if I could get it," Sophie said shyly. "I wouldn't want to get whipped, though."

All three children hooted, even Canny, and started in boasting about how many whippings they'd had and how long it had been before they could sit down afterward, with each teller outdoing the last and laughing like a beating was the funniest joke in the world.

Sophie didn't know whether she was supposed to laugh along or feel sorry for them.

Tibet gave her a measuring look. "Hush up you mouth, Young Guam. Sophie here ain't well enough for this kind of talk."

"What kind of talk she well enough for, then?"

Canny poked Young Guam in the shoulder. "I told you! You supposed to tell her 'bout Oak River!"

"Oak River a big place," Young Guam said. "What you want to know?"

"Everything," said Sophie. "I've never lived on a plantation, you see."

"We ain't never even been to New Orleans," Tibet said wistfully. "I hear it a mighty fine place."

Canny brightened. "Why don't we tell Sophie 'bout Oak River and she tell us 'bout New Orleans, turn and turn, like hoeing cane?"

Everyone agreed that this seemed fair and then looked at Sophie, waiting for her first question.

"Um. What's black moss?"

Tibet answered. "You know that old grandfather moss hanging from the trees? Well, you takes that and puts it in a barrel of water for a week or two and . . . Wait—I show you."

She ran outside, returning a moment later with a handful of something black and drippy that smelled strongly of spoiled vegetables. She stripped off the rotten leaves and dumped what was left in Sophie's lap.

"This here's black moss. You lying on it. White folks sits on it. We picks it, and Dr. Charles, he sell it in New Orleans and give us the money."

Sophie touched the springy, wiry black stuff. It felt like soft steel wool.

"Cutting wood for the sugarhouse boilers pay better," Young Guam broke in. "When I gets big, I going to cut me about a million cords, buy my freedom, and go to New Orleans. Now you tell 'bout your master's house. I bet it ain't as big as Oak River."

That day and the next, whenever any Oak River children could get away from their chores, they came to the slave hospital to explain things to Sophie. Some told her about sugar-making, from planting chopped-up sections of cane—billets—in the spring to burning the fields after the harvest was over. Others told her about the French Cajun peddlers who traded printed calico and pins for homemade jam and pickles and whittled wooden toys. In return, Sophie told them anything she could think of about New Orleans that didn't sound too modern: the shops on Royal Street and the old Negro men playing trumpets in the French Quarter and the big houses in the Garden District where her godmother lived, and the balls her mother went to, dressed in silk and pearls. Sometimes she'd forget, though, and mention streetcars and movie theatres.

The children listened to these unlikely wonders openmouthed. Finally Young Guam said, "Sophie, you lie faster than a horse can trot."

The way he said it, Sophie realized he was paying her a compliment.

❧

At dawn Monday morning, Sophie woke up to Africa folding back the mosquito bar, and two white petticoats and a yellow dress lying across her bed.

"Dr. Charles, he say you fit to go to work, so I brought your clothes."

By now, Sophie knew that the only servants on Oak River more important than Africa were Aunt Winney, who looked after Old Missy, Uncle Germany, the Oak River butler, and Mammy. Cooks were special. And Africa was not only a cook, but a two-headed woman. "Thank you," she said. "For being so nice to me."

Africa smiled. "You welcome. My Canny's taken a shine to you. Lie back now and let me take a look at you."

When she'd dug her strong fingers into Sophie's belly and peered into her eyes, she said, "You're mighty spry for a girl nearly dead with fever less than four days ago. The Orishas must be looking out for you. Still, no harm in helping them along some."

She pulled a little leather bag from her apron pocket, tied up with red yarn and smelling pleasantly of mint and lavender, and hung it around Sophie's neck. "That's a *gris-gris*," she said. "For protection. Don't you never take it off, now. And don't let nobody see it."

Sophie touched the bag, the soft leather smooth and warm under her fingers. Another mystery, another thing she ought to know and didn't. "I won't." She looked up into the rosewood face. "Thank you for taking care of me. I thought I was going to die."

Africa laughed. "Not for a long time yet, the Good Lord willing. You put on that frock, now, and get your tail on up to the Big House."

It was a good thing, Sophie thought later, that she'd seen in the hospital how slaves acted around white folks, or she'd never have gotten through her first day with Mrs. Fairchild. It was like living with Mama, only more so: never speak until she was spoken to, never raise her eyes, never sit down, always do what she was told, promptly and without argument.

The children had told Sophie everything they knew, but being yard-children, they had no more idea than she about what a lady's maid was supposed to do. Aunt Winney was despairing. "Can't iron, can't mend, don't know a buttonhook from a corset-stay! My land, Missy Caro, what we going do with her?"

Old Mrs. Fairchild was sitting at her vanity in a vast ruffled wrapper, looking like a big white hen. "Now, now Winney—it's not the child's fault. If she's spoiled, it's her upbringing that's to blame." She patted Sophie's cheek. "She's a bright girl. I just know she'll make us proud."

Sophie, not used to praise, felt a rush of affection for the old lady, who was, after all, her grandmother. "Thank you, ma'am," she said. "I'll surely try."

Mrs. Fairchild smiled. "Now, stand over by the armoire and stay out from underfoot while Winney gets me ready to face the world."

It was quite a production, involving a chemise tucked into long white drawers, a stiff corset, a hoop skirt like a steel bird cage, and an undershirt with long, balloon-like black sleeves that filled out the short, open sleeves of her black silk dress. Finally, Aunt Winney brushed, oiled, braided, and coiled her mistress' long gray hair and covered it with a frilly white cap that looked very much like one of Aunt Enid's toilet roll covers. The final touches were a pair of pearl and gold dangly earrings, a cameo brooch, a gentlemanly gold-handled cane, and a lace handkerchief, which Mrs. Fairchild tucked into her belt.

"Thank you, Winney. I'll be spending the morning with Mammy and the accounts, so you and Sophie can make a start on her training. Be good, now, Sophie, and mind what Aunt Winney tells you."

She was hardly out the door before Aunt Winney had hustled Sophie into the dressing room, sat her down on a three-legged stool, and got down to brass tacks.

"Missy Caro, she don't care a lick if you can read or write or fly to the moon if you can't do nothing useful. You ever thread a needle?"

Sophie said she had, and when Aunt Winney challenged her was proud to knot the thread one-handed, as Lily had taught her. Aunt Winney rewarded her with a ripped petticoat to sew up, then settled down to mending a lace collar and lecturing Sophie on her duties, stopping from time to time to criticize the size and evenness of her stitches.

Sophie hoped the Creature didn't mean her whole adventure to be devoted to learning how to be a lady's maid, because the number of things she'd need to know was as vast as Mrs. Fairchild's wrapper. Besides arranging hair and lacing corsets, there was cleaning hairbrushes and airing dresses, mending, fancy ironing, getting spots out of silk and stains out of linen, and, last but not least, making her mistress's morning coffee on a spirit stove in the dressing room.

By the time Mrs. Fairchild came upstairs to change for dinner, Sophie was rigid with boredom and heat and so hungry that the thought of cornmeal mush was making her mouth water.

Mrs. Fairchild gave her a shrewd look. "Why, you're white as a sheet, child. Run along now and get something to eat."

After what had happened the last time she was in the kitchen, Sophie was nervous of the reception she might get.

Delia Sherman

There was some giggling, but mostly everybody was too busy to bother her. She got her mush without incident and carried it outside. A group of yard slaves was gathered under the oak, eating and talking.

Asia waved her wooden spoon. "If it ain't young Sophie, back from death's door. Come over here and sit down by me. That Miss Lotty's yellow you wearing, ain't it? The trouble them sleeves give me, I like to give up sewing and beg Mammy to send me to the fields. But I ain't done such a bad job of it in the end."

Sophie perched gingerly on a root. "Who's Miss Lotty?"

Before long, she knew everything there was to know about Miss Charlotte Fairchild, Old Missy's youngest and most recently married daughter, who lived in all the way up in Georgia with her husband, Mr. Franklin Preston, and their new baby, Franklin Humbolt Preston III. She also wished that, if she had to learn to mend, she could learn it from Asia. Aunt Winney wasn't very good company.

She wished it even more that afternoon, when she helped Aunt Winney with the ironing. Despite the heat, Sophie had to build up the dressing-room fire, then haul glowing-hot irons to an iron stand to sit until they were cool enough not to scorch the fine linen. Sweating and sore, Sophie wished for an electric iron and an outlet to plug it into. Also a hotdog, or some macaroni and cheese, or an ice-cream cone.

She would have done almost anything for a cold Coca-Cola.

Supper was mush again, with greens and chicken and pot liquor. Exhausted, Sophie nodded over the petticoat until Mrs. Fairchild came up to be unpinned, unbuttoned, peeled out of her layers of silk and cotton, rinsed off with water heated on the dressing-room fire, and bundled into her nightgown. She climbed into bed, Aunt Winney unrolled the mosquito bar so it draped the whole bed from tester to footboard, and then it was time for Sophie to read aloud.

The book was *Little Dorrit*. Mrs. Fairchild was already halfway through it, but Sophie was too tired to care that she didn't know what was going on.

She started out well enough, eager to please, but it wasn't long before she started stumbling over words. Mrs. Fairchild said, "That's enough, Sophie. You've done well today. Winnie has given me a good report of your industry, and I've seen for myself how quick you are. Keep on as you've begun, and I'll have good reason to be proud."

Surprised at the warmth in Mrs. Fairchild's voice, Sophie looked straight at Mrs. Fairchild, who smiled at her. She smiled back, shyly, then turned down the oil lamp as Aunt Winney had taught her, stumbled off to the dressing room, unrolled her pallet, lay down, and fell asleep. Next thing she knew, someone was shaking her and telling her the dawn bell done rung and she best shake a leg if she didn't want a licking.

She didn't want to get up, but she had to anyway. She was a slave, and slaves didn't have choices.

What she did have was mosquito bites all over her face and arms because she'd forgotten to pull up her mosquito bar.

All week, the routine was the same. Up at dawn, into the yellow dress and white tignon, roll up the pallet, make coffee on the spirit stove, open the curtains, roll up the mosquito bar, set the cup where Mrs. Fairchild could reach it. Help Aunt Winney down from her attic bedroom, light the dressing-room fire, put a pan of water to warm for Mrs. Fairchild's morning wash.

Empty the chamber pot.

The first time Aunt Winney pointed to the stinking pot and told her it was her job to clean it, Sophie had looked at her in disbelief. "No! Ew! I'll be sick. Can't Sally do it?"

Aunt Winney gave her a whack with her walking stick. "Sally ain't Missy Caro's body servant. You is. You get used to it by and by. Scoot, before I tells Mammy you being uppity."

Nose wrinkled, Sophie carried the pot downstairs, emptied it in the outhouse pit, rinsed it at the pump, and left it to air while she went down to the kitchen for breakfast. She felt too sick to eat, but she'd learned enough to put a corn cake in her apron pocket for later.

And then the real work of the day began.

Mrs. Fairchild had decided that the best way for Sophie to learn her way around Oak River was to use her as a messenger service. When Mrs. Fairchild wanted Mammy, Sophie ran and got her. When Mrs. Fairchild wanted to talk to Mrs. Charles, Sophie ran down to Oak Cottage to let her know. When Mrs. Fairchild had a question about the roses or the new colt, Sophie ran and got a gardener or a stable boy to answer it. And when dinnertime came at two o'clock, Sophie stood behind Mrs. Fairchild's chair to fill her glass and pick up her napkin when it slid off her lap.

Sophie didn't mind the running around, but she hated waiting at table. Waiting was a good word for it, since it involved standing with her hands folded over her apron and her stomach growling, watching the Fairchilds tuck into their soups and gumbos and roasts and vegetables, and counting the minutes until everyone was done eating. Even then, Sophie had to wait to eat her own dinner until Mrs. Fairchild was settled on her daybed to rest.

When she wasn't running errands, Sophie was keeping the bugs off Mrs. Fairchild with a big palmetto fan, bringing her lemonade, keeping track of her books and her workbasket and the contents of her lap desk. She had no time to herself, no moment of the day when she wasn't working or waiting for orders. Some days, the only time she wasn't on her feet was when she was sewing or reading *Little Dorrit*. The only thing that kept her going was knowing it couldn't last forever. The Creature might be tricksy, but she didn't think it was mean. Soon, when she least expected it, it would appear, floating in the air and grinning, to take her home to the cozy clutter of Oak Cottage. Come Sunday, her adventure would have lasted two weeks. Maybe the Creature would take her home on Sunday.

And if he didn't, at least she'd have a day off.

It was only part of a day off, really—Old Missy couldn't dress herself any better on the Lord's day than any other day of the week. And then Aunt Winney said it was time for church and made Sophie help her down to the yard, where they stood in the heat and the sun while a red-faced minister read out a text from Matthew:

"For unto every one that hath shall be given, and he shall have abundance: but from him that hath not shall be taken away even that which he hath. And cast ye the unprofitable servant into outer darkness: there shall be weeping and gnashing of teeth."

It wasn't a comforting text, or particularly easy to understand, which must have been why it took the minister over an hour to explain it. Sophie shifted from one aching foot to the other, her rose-sprigged calico Sunday best glued to her skin with sweat, wondering if it was actually possible to die of boredom.

When the minister finally closed his book and went away, Aunt Winney groaned and rubbed her back. "Well, we done with that foolishness for another week. Now we go praise the Lord our own way."

Sophie very nearly rebelled at the thought of enduring another sermon. But everybody else was heading toward the bayou, and Aunt Winney had already hooked her firmly by the arm and started walking. And there was the niggling fear that the Creature might punish rebellion by leaving her in the past another week. So she went along.

As the path wandered into a swampy grove, Aunt Winney puffed like a steam engine and weighed on Sophie's arm like lead. Grimly, Sophie helped her along, falling farther and farther behind the others, wondering if they were walking clear back to New Orleans. Just when she thought she'd have to sit down and rest, they were in a clearing, where what looked like every Negro on the plantation was swarming around a big rough-built barn down by the water like bees around a hive.

Aunt Winney waded into the swarm and found a seat on a hay bale next to Mrs. Fairchild's butler, Uncle Germany. There wasn't anywhere for Sophie to sit, so she stood by the wall, wishing she was back home with Mama among the polished pews and bright stained glass of St. Martin's Episcopal, and looking forward to eating shrimp remoulade and strawberry shortcake at the Hotel Ponchartrain.

When everybody had quieted down, a tall man in rusty black climbed up onto a plank table against the back wall.

Sophie leaned forward to whisper in Aunt Winney's ear. "Who's that?"

"That Old Guam, and he fixing to preach. Hush up now, and listen."

While Sophie was wondering if Old Guam was any kin to Young Guam, he raised up his hands to heaven—big hands, with one finger missing—opened his mouth, and began to preach.

Old Guam's preaching was about as far from the red-faced minister's as Alaska is from Louisiana. He told stories Sophie knew from Sunday School, about Moses and Pharaoh and the Children of Israel, about the fiery chariot of Elijah and how the Lord had promised a heavenly home to all those who suffered here below. But even the Reverend Lucas at Lily's church hadn't told them like he'd been there, personally standing behind Moses on the shores of the Red Sea. All around her, heads nodded and straw fans waved and voices shouted "Hallelujah!" and "Amen!"

Sophie leaned against the wall and closed her eyes, half dozing on her feet. Suddenly, everybody was singing and Aunt Winney was poking her. "What you doing, standing there glum as Monday morning? Praise the Lord, girl."

Obediently, Sophie clapped while the slaves around her sang, *"I know when I going home, true believer. I know when I going home."*

Well, that was more than Sophie knew. She couldn't deny that her adventure had been interesting, but she was ready for it to be over now. She'd got what she wished for. Mrs. Fairchild treated her more like family than Grandmama did, and Canny and Africa were definitely friends. She'd learned valuable lessons, too. Mama's ideas about Negroes were flat-out wrong, for instance, and the Good Old Days were a lot more complicated than Grandmama—or her history teacher—had led her to believe. If the Creature didn't appear on its own, she'd just have to go and find it.

The hymn ended with a rolling *"Amen!"* and everybody filed out of the barn, laughing and chattering. A pair of thin, strong arms grabbed Sophie around the waist.

"Sophie!" Canny squealed. "You gots a new dress. I gots one, too. Want to see?" She twirled, showing off a very familiar blue gingham dress, taken in at the waist and shoulders, deeply hemmed, and much too big for her.

Sophie took a deep breath. "You look pretty as a picture, Canny."

Canny grinned. "You want to come fishing with Young Guam and them? We can catch us some wall-eye for supper."

"I'd like to, Canny, but—"

"I knows." Canny sighed. "House folk ain't got all day Sunday free, like we do. Momi, neither. We catches any extra, I asks Momi to fry it up for you, special."

Sophie surprised herself by giving the little girl a hug. "You're a real friend, Canny," she said and barely stopped herself from telling her she'd miss her when she went home.

Oak River slept in the afternoon heat. The kitchen was quiet, the Oak Cottage garden empty, the yard and field between it and the Big House drowsy in the sunlight. The gardeners were busy hoeing and watering their own plots; the Fairchilds were dining with the Robinsons next door at Doucette. There was nobody to see Sophie slip between the white urns into the maze.

The Oak River maze wasn't spooky or mysterious in 1860. The marking stones were white, the hedges young and neatly trimmed. Sophie took the time to check on Belle Watling, who was clean and new and looked even more nude with an unbroken nose and both her arms. The central garden was bright with roses, flowering camellia, and oleander, the summerhouse painted green and white like a shiny toy, with pots of flowers beside the steps. The air was scented with lavender and glittered in the heat like an old movie, with a sound track of cicadas.

Sophie looked around for a place suitable for calling up magical creatures. In the center of the garden was the white marble column—whole and new, surrounded with ferns and lilies, and sure enough, with a sundial on top. Sophie went up to it and laid her hand on the warm bronze, next to the motto engraved on the rim: I Measure None But Sunny Hours.

"Creature," she said softly. "I want to make a wish. I want to go home. Please take me back. Please."

Nothing happened, no shadow over the sun or shiver in the grass. Nothing.

Sophie stayed in the maze as long as she dared, trying everything she could think of to get the Creature's attention. She cried, she stormed, she wished on Africa's *gris-gris*. She thought of asking Papa Legba and Yemaya to help her, but that felt too dangerous. After a while, the plantation bell rang, and she ran up to the Big House just in time to escape a scolding from Aunt Winney.

Thinking about it that night on her pallet in the dressing room, Sophie was sad and madder than a wet hen. But she wasn't really surprised. Sometimes it seemed to her like she was always getting sent somewhere she didn't want to be and left there, like luggage in a railway station. She should be used to it by now.

Besides, there was always the possibility that the Creature would make things worse.

Chapter 10

Sophie began her third week in the past in a fog of misery. Everything that had been difficult when she'd thought she'd be going home soon got ten times harder as she lost hope. The only good thing was that she was too tired to think too much about how she missed hamburgers and TV and all the modern conveniences of 1960. She tried not to think at all about how much she missed Aunt Enid and Lily and Mama and Papa. Sometimes she'd wake up in the dark with her face wet, grasping after a fading dream of Papa and the house in Metairie or giggling with Diana or sitting in the Oak Cottage kitchen with Aunt Enid, eating fried chicken.

She was beginning to wonder whether she was ever going to see any of them again.

Aunt Winney, who knew homesickness when she saw it, prescribed prayer and hard work.

"This a world of sorrow and woe, a vale of tears without number. Just you keep in mind you got a brother in Jesus and a hope of joy in Heaven. Now, here a bundle of Missy Caro's linen for the wash. Tell Asia to take care with them corset covers. Lawn tear if you look at it crossways."

If Mrs. Fairchild noticed Sophie's state, she chose to ignore it.

Over time, Sophie got used to Mammy and Mrs. Charles, though she was always careful to be extra-humble around them.

The other house servants were friendly enough, even Uncle Germany, who reminded Sophie of an English butler out of an old movie, except for being tea-colored. She was still shy of the houseboys—particularly Samson, the tawny young man who had winked at her on her first day in the past. He was twenty and very handsome, and sometimes he told jokes that Sophie didn't understand but made Sally the housemaid screech with laughter.

At first, Sophie was shy of Sally, too, in case she might still be mad that Sophie wouldn't answer her questions her first night at Oak River. But she soon realized that Sally had forgotten the whole thing. She was just sixteen, with honey blonde curls that escaped around the edges of her flowered tignon and a friendly nature. It was Sally who told Sophie about the Saturday night dances.

"Everybody go, picaninnies and all, and there's fiddling and dancing and everybody have a fine old time. You ask Old Missy can you come, too."

A night away from Aunt Winney and the mending basket sounded good; a dance, less so. Mama had sent her to dancing school, where Sophie had learned to box step and a vague idea of a foxtrot, but she doubted that either would be useful at a slave dance.

"I don't know, Sally. Maybe Mrs. Fairchild won't like it."

"How you know 'less you ask? You scared?"

"No." Sophie thought for a moment. "Yes. It's just—what if nobody dances with me? What if somebody does? I don't know much about boys."

Sally laughed. "Ain't going to learn no more hiding in Old Missy's skirts, Soph. She say yes, you put on you Sunday dress and meet me at the back door at sundown."

So Sophie asked for permission to go to the dance, half hoping to be refused. Still, she was more happy than not when

Mrs. Fairchild said yes. "You've earned a treat. But you must be back before midnight. I suspect we're about to find out what Mr. Pancks has discovered about Mr. Dorrit."

Feeling like Cinderella, Sophie put on the rose calico and went to meet Sally at the back door.

Sally looked her over critically. "That dress suit you fine. But that old white tignon dull as dishwater." She pulled something from her sash—a red tignon with black stitching along the hem. "Here," she said. "This'll make the boys sit up and take notice."

Sophie blushed almost as red as the tignon.

On the long walk through the woods to the barn, Sally filled Sophie in on all the comings and goings between Oak River and its next-door neighbor Doucette. There'd be Doucette folks at the dance tonight, just as there were Doucette folks who came to hear Old Guam preach. Ned had been a Doucette slave until he'd married Africa and Mrs. Fairchild had bought him from Mr. Robinson.

"Old Missy think a heap of Africa," Sally said. "Korea done marry a Doucette man, and they never sees each other but Saturday nights."

Sophie slapped at mosquitoes and midges and tried not to jump every time something rustled in the alligator grass. Finally, she saw yellow light twinkling through the trees and the rumor of distant shouts and laughter.

"Come on!" Sally grabbed Sophie's hand and ran down toward the barn, which was even more crowded than it had been on Sunday.

As they reached the door, Samson popped up beside them, all got up in a fancy vest. He winked at Sophie, grabbed Sally by the waist, and swung her up in the air as if she weighed no more than a piglet, while she squealed happily to be put down, this *minute*, you hear? Then they both disappeared, leaving Sophie hugging the door frame and wishing she hadn't come.

The barn was a sea of dark faces bobbing and turning as they danced past, laughing or solemn with concentration, eyes flashing in the smoky light of a handful of lanterns hung from the rafters. At the far end of the room, two men frailed away on fiddle and banjo, their shadows bending and swaying crazily in the lamplight. Sophie had never heard music like it before, lively and sad and full of odd rhythms. She wasn't sure whether she liked it or not.

A lanky shadow separated itself from the crowd and offered her its hand. If it had been anybody but Canny's brother, Poland, Sophie would have bolted. As it was, she smiled shyly and allowed him to pull her into the dance.

The packed earth juddered and shook beneath Sophie's feet; dust flew up in clouds. Poland put both hands on her waist and spun her around until she was hot and dizzy and breathless. It wasn't in the least like Miss Leblanc's Dancing School. For a little while, she forgot about everything but the beating of the music in her blood and bones and the hot wind in her ears and faces whizzing by in a kaleidoscope blur of brown, red, blue, pink, green, and white. Everybody was whooping and yelling— even Sophie, until the rising dust caught in her throat and sent her coughing.

Poland guided her out of the dance and to the rain barrel. He scooped up a tin dipperful of water and watched her drink it.

"You want to go 'round again?"

Sophie handed the dipper back. "Maybe later. You go on, though."

Poland shrugged and plunged back into the dance. Sophie splashed water on her hot face and wished she'd gone with him. A woman sitting on a hay bale called out, "Ain't you Mist'

Robert's girl from New Orleans-way? I hear tell you got conjure spectacles can see clear through walls and know Ma'amzelle Marie LaVeau like she was you own ma."

Sophie had given up trying to explain her glasses. She just shook her head mysteriously when someone pressed her for details as the stranger woman was doing now, gathering a little group of Doucette women.

"I can't tell you," Sophie said. "It's a secret. But I can tell you this—they're no great shakes in New Orleans. Any of you ever been there?"

A woman named Alice allowed as how she'd seen the docks and the slave market when she was sold, and another had heard about the quadroon balls, where mixed-blood mothers took their light-skinned daughters to dance with rich white men.

"Sophie know all 'bout them." It was Antigua, her voice edged with malice. "I think you mama planning to take you there in a year or two, sell you to the highest bidder."

Sophie looked around. Antigua was lounging in the barn door, looking like butter wouldn't melt in her mouth. "You got a tongue like a water-snake, Antigua," Alice said. "The child ain't to blame for her mama's skin or her daddy's sins, only for her own."

"Is that so?" Antigua said. "Well then, lying's a sin, and she's told a passel of lies. My sister Canny told me some of her stories 'bout New Orleans—carts that run by themselves and black men playing horns and suchlike nonsense. She got no call to go lying like that. She just laughing up her sleeve at all the poor dumb plantation niggers, don't know no better than to believe her."

The women turned their eyes to Sophie. She opened her mouth to protest that everything she'd said was true. Except it wasn't—at least, not in 1860.

She stood up. "I didn't mean—" She stopped. "It's not like that. I'm sorry."

Antigua hooted with laughter, and Sophie fled, careening into someone—Poland again. "Don't you mind my sister," he said, his hands warm on her arms. "That girl'd kick over an ant hill just to see them run around. Come back inside and dance with me." He grinned. "You a fine dancer, Sophie."

Sophie shook her head. "I can't. I—have to get back to the Big House. Old Missy likes me to read to her at night, and—"

"You best scoot, then. You wants me to walk you back?"

If his voice was warm or his smile extra-friendly, Sophie was too upset to notice. "No," she said. "You stay and dance. I'll be fine."

The moon was just bright enough for Sophie to pick out a path she thought she recognized. As the noise of the dance faded behind her, clouds crept over the moon. A tree frog piped nearby and a hunting owl hooted dismally.

"Where you think you going, girl?"

Sophie stopped dead. She could have been at the bottom of a well for all she could see, but she recognized that voice. "Creature! Where have you been?"

"I don't know as I likes that name," it said thoughtfully. "Don't seem like a *real* name to me. Kutnahin, that a *real* name. Or Br'er Rabbit."

Sophie recalled she had a bone to pick with the Creature. "Howabout I call you dirty, cheating *liar*?"

"What you talking, girl?" The Creature sounded surprised. "Ain't I give you the wish of your heart, just like you asked? As I recall, you wish you was somebody different."

Delia Sherman

"I didn't mean I wanted to be a *slave!*"

"You didn't say what you meant."

"Yes, I did. I said I wanted to have magic adventures. You just threw me into the past, and then you *disappeared*."

"Moving folks through time be hard work," the Creature said. "I was wore out for days and days—couldn't hardly raise a corn on Mammy's little toe. Not that I'd waste my time on suchlike nonsense, no, ma'am."

Sophie felt they were getting off the subject. "But why did you make me a slave?"

"Me? I ain't got that kind of power. You done sold your own self down the river, missy. Ain't even made a decent profit on it, either," it added thoughtfully.

"I did not! I didn't have a choice. Everybody thought I was a slave from the very beginning. They'd never have believed me if I told them the truth."

"You might could invent a better lie," the Creature pointed out. "Don't make no never mind now, howsomever. Yes, ma'am, no ma'am, tell me where to set and spit, ma'am, like you ain't got no more gumption than a tadpole."

"I do too have gumption! Didn't I go to the maze and call you? Why didn't you come?"

"Didn't want to. 'Sides, I got my own problems," the Creature said. "Papa Legba, he none too pleased with me."

Sophie smiled. "He said you plot but never plan."

"He a big one to talk," the Creature snapped. "Why, I could tell you stories 'bout Papa Legba—"

"Stop trying to change the subject! I'm making a wish, and I really, really, really mean it, so you have to grant it. I wish I was home. Please, Creature, take me home!"

"I can't," the Creature said. "Maybe in books adventures is laid out nice and neat like a length of cloth, just cut it out and

108

sew it up into a dress or a pair of britches. Real adventures ain't like that."

"So you won't send me home?" Panic squeezed Sophie's voice to a squeak.

"Not won't. Can't," the Creature said apologetically. "The story ain't near over yet."

"What story? You didn't say anything about a story!"

"The story of how you done what it is you supposed to do, of course—the thing I brung you here to do."

Tears of anger and frustration prickled Sophie's eyes. "Can't you just tell me what it is, so I can do it and go home?"

"Nuh-uh. That not how stories works. Aww, now, don't you go be crying. I can't bear a crying woman."

"I'm not a woman. I'm only thirteen, and I want to go home!"

The Creature sighed noisily. "I tells you what. You stops crying, and I give you some wisdom, straight out. You listening? There a time to speak and a time to shut you mouth, a time to stand still and a time to run, a time to keep to the truth and a time to make a little detour around it. You already knows more than you think, but it don't do you no good less'n you pay attention. Keep you candle beside you, but remember: sometimes you just gots to take a jump in the dark."

Sophie waited a minute for it to go on, then realized it had gone and left her, just like it always did. She took a step forward, felt the ground squelch wetly under her bare toes, stepped back hastily. Maybe she should just wait. If this was the right path, somebody was bound to come along soon, on their way home from the dance. She groped around until she found a tree to sit against, then tucked her bare feet under her skirts and peered anxiously into the dark until at last she fell asleep.

Next morning, Ned found Sophie by the bayou, curled up among the roots of a willow with her feet almost in the water. When he woke her, she sat up, stared at the bayou, at Ned, at the hot, horrible reality she was stuck in, and started to cry.

Ned hunkered down beside her and put his arm around her shoulders. "River take a whole mess of things down to New Orleans," he said. "Cotton, sugar, molasses, black folks, white folks. But it ain't going to take you, honey, not unless Mast' Robert come up and fetch you." He stood up and pulled her gently to her feet. "Come along now. Mammy in a taking as it is. Don't want to make it any more worse."

Mammy greeted Sophie's return with her mouth pleated up like she'd been eating pickled lemons.

"She weren't running or hiding," Ned said. "She sleeping right out in the open, where anybody can see."

"All I care about is Mrs. Fairchild's mighty put out. Get along, Ned, and tell Mr. Akins to call off the hunt. The lost sheep is found."

Ned bowed and left. Sophie studied her muddy feet and figured this was one of those times to keep her mouth shut.

"Blood will tell," Mammy said, sounding a lot like Mama. "You come along to Mrs. Fairchild now, and I hope you're ashamed of yourself."

"I got lost," Sophie offered humbly.

"A liar as well as a runaway," Mammy said. "What you need is a good whipping." Taking Sophie by the ear, she pulled her painfully upstairs to the parlor, where Mrs. Fairchild was sitting very upright in a wing chair, her plump hands folded on the head of her gold-handled cane, scowling like an angry baby.

"Here she is," Mammy announced. "Full of sass and excuses."

"Why did you run away, Sophie?"

"I didn't run away, ma'am. I got lost coming back from the dance."

Mammy gave her ear a painful shake. "I'm warning you, girl. I can smell a lie like a dog can smell a coon."

"It's not a lie. It was dark and I was alone and I got lost."

There was a long silence. Sophie's heart was beating so hard the calico fluttered over her chest.

"I'm inclined to believe you," Mrs. Fairchild said, and Sophie went limp with relief. "But it's a very serious matter for a house servant to stay out all night without permission."

Sophie bit her lip. "Yes, ma'am. I'm sorry, ma'am."

"Well, we'll just pray you are." Mrs. Fairchild turned to Mammy. "Mammy, you run along. Sophie, I was too worried over you to go to church this morning. You shall make some small reparation by staying here and reading aloud from the Bible while I rest my eyes."

Mammy ran along, her opinion of Sophie plain in the set of her head. Sophie fetched the big Bible and turned, as Mrs. Fairchild directed, to St. Paul's Epistle to the Ephesians. It was pretty heavy going, but she plowed on ahead, not paying much attention to what she was reading until Mrs. Fairchild said, "Now, I want you to read verse six with particular attention, Sophie."

"Yes'm. '*Servants, be obedient to them that are your masters according to the flesh, with fear and trembling, in singleness of your heart, as unto Christ; not with eye service, as menpleasers; but as the servants of Christ, doing the will of God from the heart*'."

"Well?"

"Ma'am?"

"What did you learn from reading that verse, Sophie?"

Sophie thought for a moment. "That I should obey you as if you were Jesus?"

111

There was a startled silence. "I hope," Mrs. Fairchild said coldly, "that you do not take my leniency as permission to say whatever foolishness comes into your head."

Sophie glanced up, met an angry blue glare, looked down hurriedly. "No, ma'am."

"Sophie, you have disappointed me. You've caused us all a lot of worry and fuss looking for you. Mammy said you were selfish and willful, but I didn't believe it until now. I prefer to guide my household with kindness, not rule it by force. But I will not be taken advantage of, and I will not be defied. If you do anything like this again, I will have to discipline you severely. I trust I make myself clear."

Sophie knew this speech. She'd been hearing variations of it, mostly from Mama, ever since she could remember. Mrs. Fairchild was just more direct. The Creature didn't understand. Sophie had gone along with being treated like a slave because she didn't know what else to do. And Mrs. Fairchild, well, she wasn't all that different from Grandmama—sugar until she was crossed, then vinegar straight through.

Mrs. Fairchild's voice cut impatiently through Sophie's thoughts. "I'm waiting for an answer, Sophie."

"I'm sorry, ma'am. I was thinking about St. Paul." The lie came easily. "I didn't mean to be disobedient. You've been very kind to me, kinder than I deserve. I won't stay out late ever again."

"See you don't," Mrs. Fairchild said. "Now, close the shutters and soak a cloth in lavender water—you'll find some in the dressing room. Then help me to the day bed and bathe my temples. I do believe I could sleep."

Chapter 11

After Sophie's Saturday night adventure, Aunt Winney kept her as close as a mule keeps his hide. The only time Sophie was allowed out of the Big House was when she went down to the kitchen for meals. Even that was no relief, because somebody who had been at the dance was bound to tease her about magic horseless carriages. On good days, Sophie teased them right back with tales of machines that could let Old Missy talk to Dr. Charles at Oak Cottage without getting up from her chair. On bad days, she just gritted her teeth and pretended she hadn't heard.

Eventually, something came up a whole lot more interesting to talk about than the new girl's lies. Miss Liza had a beau.

His name was Mr. Beaufort Waters, and he came from Seven Oaks Plantation upriver in Iberville Parish. His family had sent him down for the summer to Doucette, the plantation next to Oak River, so he could learn the sugar trade from Mr. Robinson. According to the gossip under the kitchen oak, Mr. Waters had asked Miss Liza to dance no fewer than three times at the Midsummer Ball in June. He'd followed this up by fetching her fried chicken at the Romero's picnic a week later. Soon he took to riding over to Oak Cottage every few days so he could make himself agreeable to Mrs. Charles over tea and walk with Miss Liza in the garden. On the days he didn't come, he wrote, and Miss Liza wrote him back.

Delia Sherman

"I like to run my feets off between Doucette and Oak River," Antigua complained one heavy afternoon as she ate her mush and clabber.

Asia shook her head. "You a pure fool, Antigua, you don't get two cents out of him for each of them letters. When Master Francis sweet on Miss Lotty, I done made me five dollar before she get bored."

Antigua looked sly. "Ten cents apiece."

Asia gasped. "Whooee! Ten cents! My land! He one open-handed gentleman!"

"Pretty-spoken, too," Antigua said. "Yesterday, he say he hope Miss Liza treat me kind. I say just as kind as she treat him, and he laugh real big and give me five cents more."

The women exchanged glances. "You just take care," Hepzibah said, "that fifteen cents ain't buying something you don't aim to sell."

"Pooh," said Antigua. "He don't mean nothing by it. He a perfect gentleman, Mr. Beau is."

Saturday, Sophie got a chance to see Mr. Beau for herself, sitting by Miss Liza at dinner, discussing vacuum extractors with Dr. Charles and asking Old Missy respectful questions about plantation management. He was a slender young man with sandy hair slicked back with pomade and a small, sandy mustache that he stroked from time to time with his thumb and forefinger, like he was checking it was still there. Sophie thought he was good-looking, though his eyes did bug out a little, like gooseberries.

In mid-July, the steamboat *Pretty Lady* pulled up at the Oak River dock to deliver the long-expected vacuum extractor apparatus. Samson gave Mrs. Fairchild the news, and she insisted

114

on going down to the bayou to chat with the captain, bringing Sophie with her to carry her reticule and her palmetto fan. Mr. Akins and Dr. Charles were already there, overseeing the delicate operation of unloading the heavy crates from the steamboat and onto the flat-bedded cane wagons pulled up to the landing.

For the next two hours, Sophie stood on the steamboat's upper deck while Mrs. Fairchild drank coffee with Captain Shaw and caught up on the news of the world outside of Oak River. She could hear the squeaking of the pulley and the groaning of the ropes and Mr. Akins and Dr. Charles on the dock, shouting to the hands to be careful.

"Don't think much of that Douglas fella," Captain Shaw said. "Next door to an abolitionist, if you ask me."

"Surely he's not so bad as that Black Republican Lincoln."

"You ask me, no Northerner's going to understand the Southern states' rights to control our own slaves as we see fit, without no Yankee meddling."

"Dr. Charles thinks some compromise is possible, but I just don't know. Would the South still be the South under a Republican president?"

Captain Shaw looked grim. "It don't bear thinking about, ma'am. Why, didn't them abolitionists send rifles to John Brown? There's already fighting up the Mississippi over whether settlers can bring their slaves into Missouri. No ma'am. If Lincoln wins this election, we Southerners will have to take care of our own interests." He gave the rifle leaning against the railing behind him a significant pat.

Mrs. Fairchild looked shocked. "I do hope, Captain Shaw, you aren't talking about fighting here in Louisiana!"

"Well, we must hope it don't come to that. But if it does, I'm ready for it. By the way, Miz Fairchild, we got a trunk from Mr. Robert for you."

"Thank you, Captain Shaw. Sophie, tell Peru to step here when he's free and fetch Mr. Robert's trunk up to my room. Sophie?" She shot an annoyed look at Sophie, who'd stopped fanning. "Stop gaping, child, and run along."

Sophie curtsied and ran to find Peru. This was it. This was when Old Missy found out Mr. Robert hadn't sent her to Oak River. Sophie would be exposed as an impostor, a stranger, a liar, and possibly a runaway. Mrs. Fairchild would have her whipped for sure, and probably sell her off first chance she got. Surely the Creature would take her home before that happened.

But she didn't trust the Creature anymore.

By the time she'd found Peru and helped Old Missy off the steamboat and back to the Big House and got her some lemonade and Peru had deposited the trunk by her chair, Sophie was just about beside herself.

"I'm surprised he didn't wait and send it with you," Old Missy said. "Just as well, I suppose, given what happened to your papers and all. Here's the key."

Sophie unlocked the trunk with trembling fingers and lifted the domed lid. Inside, a thick stack of papers tied up in black tape and a small wooden box were packed with a pretty white dress with a scarlet sash, a paisley shawl, and a silk bonnet. On top of it all lay a letter, sealed with red wax.

Old Missy took the papers in her lap, broke the seal and handed the letter to Sophie. "My eyes aren't what they were. I hope you can read writing."

Mr. Robert's writing looked like a bird had stepped in ink and danced across the paper. Sophie stared at the scrawl, wondering if she dared make up a story about how he was sending his daughter to Oak River to be brought up like a lady. Then the words began to come clear.

"*My darling Mama,*" she read slowly. "*As you read this missive, your humble and most disobedient child will be smoking a cheroot on the deck of a steamer bound for France. The papers contain the reason for my somewhat precipitate departure—you may safely guess the rest. Having heard there are no slaves in France, Louisette insists upon accompanying me, and my faithful Russia also. The shawl is for you, the bonnet for my esteemed sister-in-law, and the dress for my little girl. Please tell her from me to be good and mind what you tell her, lest she suffer the fate of*

Your Prodigal Son,
Robert Fairchild."

Mrs. Fairchild squinted at the papers. "Well. That's that, I suppose. Everything sold for debt—horses, house, slaves, furniture. Louisette is your mother, I collect." She glanced at Sophie, who nodded dumbly. "Hand me that letter and fetch Dr. Charles. No, he'll be fussing over those vacuum pans. Fetch Mrs. Charles then—no, fetch Mammy. A frilly dress. Isn't that *just* like Robert?"

Old Missy never mentioned the letter or Mr. Robert again, not in Sophie's hearing, anyway. The white dress was hung up on a hook in the attic room Aunt Winney shared with Sally and Korea, for Sunday best. Sophie wondered about "my girl" until her brain fizzed, but couldn't come up with any reasonable explanation except that Mr. Robert had maybe meant the dress for Miss Liza.

If he had, though, it would have been too small for her. It fit Sophie pretty well.

Mr. Robert's letter put an end to any mystery lingering around Sophie and her place at Oak River. Before long, everybody but

Antigua had stopped teasing her about her glasses and asking for stories about New Orleans.

As the days passed, Sophie herself became less and less clear in her mind about where and when home was. Grandmama and Aunt Enid, even Mama and Papa and Lily, began to feel like characters in a book she'd read when she was little. Diana and Metairie Country Day and math class and her room at home faded from her mind. Real life was waiting on Old Missy, being initiated into the mysteries of hair arrangement by Aunt Winney, reading *Little Dorrit* by yellow lamplight, listening to two sermons on Sundays, avoiding Antigua, keeping on the bright side of Mammy and Mrs. Charles, and listening to the stories and gossip under the kitchen oak, weather permitting.

In July, the talk was all of whether or not Mr. Beaufort Waters was going to marry Miss Liza.

It began when Luxembourg the gardener heard Mr. Beau asking Dr. Fairchild for his daughter's hand in marriage through the office window one morning. Before the evening bell, the whole plantation knew as much about it as if they'd been right there in the flower bed, listening. Dr. Charles had said Miss Liza was too young to think of getting married, and Mr. Beau himself in no position to support a family. Mr. Beau had taken it pretty well, Luxembourg said, but when Miss Liza and Mrs. Charles found out, they were fit to be tied.

"Mrs. Charles, she so stuck on that man, you think she the one walking out with him," Antigua said. "She dead set on Miss Liza marrying him. And she will, too. You just wait and see."

Sophie was not surprised when Mrs. Charles showed up in Old Missy's room next morning with Miss Liza in tow, looking pale and red-eyed. "Well, Mother Fairchild," she said, brushing past Sophie as if she wasn't there. "What are we going to do about Charles?"

"Charles?" Old Missy said blankly. "What's wrong with Charles?"

Miss Liza wailed, "Oh, Grandmama!" and burst into noisy hysterics.

Sophie had to admire her stamina. Not even Miss Liza could possibly scream all morning, but it certainly seemed like she did. Old Missy sent Sophie running for vinaigrettes and hartshorn and glasses of restorative cold tea, but Mrs. Charles didn't do a thing to make her stop. She just patted her hand and told Old Missy how wonderful Mr. Beau was and how rich a plantation Seven Oaks was and how her little girl's heart was broken past repair. She wouldn't be surprised, she said, if Miss Liza stayed an old maid for the rest of her life.

Miss Liza, an old maid! It was all Sophie could do to keep from laughing out loud.

Old Missy was not amused. "Don't talk nonsense, Lucy. Charles is absolutely right. Liza is far too young to commit her future to the first passably handsome young man she meets, especially with the political situation so unsettled. Oh, do stop crying, Liza. You'll make yourself sick."

Miss Liza cried even harder.

Next day, Mrs. Charles came over to inform her mother-in-law that Miss Liza was laid down on her bed, pining away with love. Old Missy went down to Oak Cottage with the intention of shaming her granddaughter out of bed. But Miss Liza could not be shamed. Over the next week, Sophie watched mother and daughter wear Dr. Charles and Old Missy down bit by bit. On Sunday, Mr. Beau Waters was invited to dinner, and by suppertime, he and Miss Elizabeth Fairchild were engaged to be married.

The oak-tree gossips were shocked.

"She ain't nothing but a baby!" said Hepzibah.

"She plenty old enough to make a man's life a misery," said Antigua. "Besides, there ain't going to be no wedding for two years, nearly. Dr. Charles, he put his foot down she can't marry until she turn eighteen."

China said, "Your life ain't going to be worth living, girl."

"It ain't now." Antigua sighed. "Mrs. Charles, she promise Miss Liza to celebrate with the biggest ball this parish ever seen. They already making up the guest list."

The ball was set for the second week in August, to give Old Missy's daughters, their husbands and their children, time to travel to Oak River, stay for a nice visit, and get home again in good time for harvest. That would make at least ten guests sleeping and eating at Oak River for two weeks or more, plus their servants. Forty guests were invited to dinner before the ball, and two hundred more to the ball itself.

This meant that every room in both houses had to be turned out and cleaned. Feather beds had to be beaten and aired, the guest linen pressed, the rugs swept, the spare lamps cleaned and filled, the furniture rubbed with beeswax and linseed oil, the doodads dusted, and all the good china and crystal washed and dried and set out in the pantry.

It was too much for Sally, Korea, Samson, and Peru to accomplish, even working dawn to dark, so Old Missy loaned Sophie to Uncle Germany to help.

"Library needs dusted," he told her. "Take all them books down—every last one—and wipe the shelves clean. And put them back just like they was, or Dr. Charles'll have my hide. Don't you go reading none of them, though."

It was like telling a starving person not to eat.

Fortunately, most of the Fairchild library was made up of books Sophie would never dream of reading, books with titles like *The Seven Lamps of Architecture* and *Cyclopaedia of Useful Arts and Manufactures*. More tempting were the set of Jane Austen and the works of Sir Walter Scott and James Fenimore Cooper. *Leatherstocking* she shut after the first page, but *Ivanhoe* was harder to put down. And when Sophie discovered *Emma*, she was lost. She was standing by an empty bookshelf, feather duster forgotten, immersed in *Emma*, when the library door opened. She started guiltily, then relaxed when she saw it was only Antigua.

"My land, Antigua, I thought you were Uncle Germany!"

Antigua stepped over the stacks of books and snatched *Emma* away.

"That's not yours," Sophie said indignantly.

"Ain't yours, neither." Antigua laid the book on a pile. "What you doing here, anyway?"

Sophie flourished her duster. "Dusting!"

"That ain't what I mean." Antigua grabbed Sophie and dragged her to the mantelpiece mirror. "Look at you," she said. "You near as white as Miss Liza. Your hair ain't nappy, your nose ain't wide, and you ain't got no more lips than a chicken. You could run away North easy as Elijah going to Heaven."

Sophie studied their doubled reflection, Antigua's pale brown beside her own fading tan. They didn't look all that different to her, with their rabbit-eared tignons and their hand-me-down dresses and their faces flushed and troubled.

"I don't understand," she said.

Antigua released her with a disgusted shake. "You don't *understand*? Sophie, you duller than a broken knife. Your master give you a traveling pass and a purse of money. And what do you do? You loses them!"

Delia Sherman

"They were stolen." Sophie remembered it clearly—the panic she'd felt when she searched for her bag on the steamboat and found it gone.

Antigua was shaking with fury. "Don't make no never mind. You was free. Nobody watching you, nobody looking for you, nobody to know if you light out North or West or wherever you likes. And what do you do? You crawls here to Oak River and holds out you hands for the chains like they was bracelets."

Up to now, Sophie had kept her temper with Antigua. She'd ignored the teasing and the insults, even gotten in a few herself, when she could think fast enough. But this was too much. She flew at Antigua, both hands raised. Antigua grabbed her wrists. They reeled, staggered, tripped over a pile of books, and fell on top of the embroidered fire screen, which collapsed under them with a sickening crack.

"Lord God Almighty," whispered Antigua. "Get up."

"Yes," said a chilly voice. "By all means. Get up."

Mrs. Charles stood in the doorway, her hands folded at the waist of her lavender afternoon dress, calm as a cat at a mouse hole. "Who is responsible for this mess?"

Sophie scrambled to her feet and hung her head, too frightened to speak.

"Fighting? I'm shocked." Mrs. Charles took her rawhide strip from her sash and slapped it lightly across her hand. "Antigua, step forward."

Antigua threw Sophie a sulfurous glance, stepped forward over the ruins of the fire screen, and knelt in front of Mrs. Charles. Sophie's ears buzzed. Was this a time to speak or a time to keep silent? She didn't want to be whipped, but she didn't want to see Antigua whipped either.

Mrs. Charles raised the strap high.

"Wait!"

Mrs. Charles lowered her arm and lifted her eyebrows.

Sophie licked her lips. "It wasn't Antigua. I got mad and pushed her. I'm sorry."

Antigua couldn't have looked more startled if Sophie had suddenly grown another head.

Mrs. Charles shrugged. "Get up, Antigua. Sophie, kneel." Sophie took a reluctant step forward. "Hurry up, girl!" Sharp fingers seized Sophie's shoulder and thrust her to her knees. Sophie tensed and the rawhide whistled down and cut across her back.

The first blow was a sharp sting, painful, but not unbearable. Sophie gasped, more from shock than pain. The second and third blows, laid over the first, hurt much worse. Sophie cried out and tried to crawl away, but Mrs. Charles held her tight. Again and again the rawhide slashed down across her shoulders and back. Sophie huddled in on herself, screaming and sobbing, sure the beating would never end. And then it did.

Mrs. Charles nudged Sophie with her foot. "Stop that screeching, girl! I never heard such a fuss over a little whipping. As for you, Antigua, don't think you've got off scot-free."

Through her fog of pain, Sophie heard the whistle and slap of rawhide and Antigua's grunt. Mrs. Charles said, "Send someone in here to clear up this mess and take the fire screen to the carpenter. Then get yourself back down to Oak Cottage. Mr. Waters is coming to take Miss Liza riding." And she swept out of the room.

Sophie tried to sit up. The movement rubbed the sore skin of her back against her dress, which hurt almost as much as the beating. She gave a yelp.

"Hush," Antigua said urgently. "You doesn't want Young Missy coming back, does you?"

Sophie clenched her jaw and tried to stop crying. "I'm sorry."

"For what? For telling the truth? I ain't surprised. I ain't never heard of such foolishness since Compair Lapin met Tar Baby. Come on, now." She helped Sophie up and held her steady when she swayed dizzily. "Aunt Winney'll fix you up. You just lean on me."

Up in Old Missy's dressing room, Aunt Winney clucked and shook her head. "Sounds like quite a licking. Not that she ain't got it coming."

Sophie, who'd just about pulled herself together, fell apart again.

Aunt Winney reached for her stick and hauled herself painfully to her feet. "T'aint no good carrying on that-a-way. What's done is done. I reckon you best come up yonder so's I can take a look at you. Don't want Missy Caro coming in and getting all exercised. Antigua, you can help me up them stairs. I swan, they gets steeper ever day."

The three of them crept up the attic stairs, Antigua dragging ruthlessly on the old woman's arm.

"You jumpy as a bird on a cat's head," Aunt Winney said.

"Miss Liza waiting for me, and I still gots to find Peru. One licking's enough for one day. There." She heaved Aunt Winney up the last step. "Sophie, you take care, hear?" And she was gone.

Aunt Winney sat Sophie down and helped her ease the yellow dress from her shoulders.

"Could be worse," she said, poking painfully at Sophie's back. "You ain't cut more'n a lick. In Old Massa's day, I sees mens cain't hardly stand, they's cut so bad, hoeing cane while the overseer watch to make sure they keeps working." She shook her head. "Them was bad days, but they over now, and so's your whupping. I gots some ointment Africa give me will take the fire out of it."

The ointment smelled of herbs and stung like fire ants. Sophie hissed at the pain, but she managed not to cry out. Aunt Winney wrapped her ribs with a torn-up apron, helped her dress, and sent her down to finish her task.

When she got to the library, the fire screen was gone, the books stacked neatly. Sophie painfully replaced them on the shelves in alphabetical order. She wasn't tempted to open a single one.

That night, she dreamed about Mrs. Charles, fanged like a great, pale snake, biting at her back as she fled up endless steps. Whoever she ran to—Aunt Enid, Papa, Old Missy, Mama—slapped a rawhide strip against a giant hand and grinned at her. She woke to the airless dressing room, the throbbing of her back, and an overpowering sense of helplessness. When she finally went back to sleep, she dreamed she was with the Creature in the summerhouse, dressed up in her blue gingham shirtwaist and eating candy from one of Grandmama's gold-rimmed plates.

The Creature said, "You ain't got good sense. But it ain't nowhere writ down that good sense always the best guide to follow. You make a good choice, young Sophie."

"Is that the end of the story?" Sophie asked eagerly. "Can I go home now?"

"Bless you, child, that just an incident. The real story just starting."

Chapter 12

Thanks to Africa's ointment, the welts on Sophie's back faded quickly.
The welts on her mind faded, too, though not entirely. Sophie
had had lessons before in keeping her head down and her
expression pleasant. This one was just harder than most.

Still, there were times when acting like she didn't have a
thought in her head was just not possible.

About a week after the whipping, with the family expected in
a few days and everybody's nerves in rags, Old Missy sent Sophie
down to Oak Cottage with a message for Miss Liza. She wasn't
in the garden and she wasn't in the parlor, so Sophie went to look
her bedroom. The door was shut. Sophie knocked and went in.

And there was Miss Liza, parading her white gauze ball-
gown in front of the long lookingglass. She'd cut out the neck
of her gown so low she was in danger of falling right out of it.
Her eyes met Sophie's in the mirror, and her face blazed furious
scarlet.

"Don't you know to knock?" she snapped.

Sophie curtsied. "I did knock, Miss."

"You did not." Miss Liza tugged at her neckline. "You're
a nasty, sneaking girl who doesn't know her place. Mama says
you've been spoiled rotten."

Sophie didn't laugh, but the effort must have showed. Miss
Liza turned redder still, grabbed a pair of heavy metal shears off
the nightstand, and heaved them at Sophie's head.

Luckily, Miss Liza's aim was terrible. The shears hit the washstand pitcher and smashed it into smithereens, along with the bowl it was standing in. Sophie gasped, Miss Liza gave a furious little scream, and then, like a bolt out of heaven, Dr. Fairchild appeared in the door, demanding to know what in tarnation was going on.

Sophie folded her shaking hands on her apron and did her best to look simple.

Miss Liza hastily snatched up a wrapper and threw it around her bare shoulders. "It's not my fault, Daddy—it's that girl. She sassed me something *terrible*."

Dr. Charles picked the shears out of a heap of blue-flowered shards. "That's not a sufficient reason to throw dangerous things, Elizabeth. Had you hit her, you might have cut her, gouged out her eye, even killed her."

Miss Liza pouted. "She's not hurt. And it would serve her right if she was. After I'm married, how will my slaves respect me if I let them sass me?"

"It is to be hoped," Dr. Charles said, "that by the time you're married, you will have learned to command your temper. Whatever she may have said to you, Sophie is not your servant to punish. And you've destroyed a very expensive bowl and pitcher, sent all the way from England. I'm ashamed of you, daughter. Deeply ashamed."

Miss Liza collapsed on the daybed in a fit of whooping hysterics. Sophie noticed that she was not too hysterical to keep a tight grip on her wrapper.

Dr. Charles sent Sophie for smelling salts and applied them to his daughter's nose. She sneezed and stopped whooping, although tears cascaded from under her dark lashes.

Dr. Charles took her hand. "Listen to me, puss. When you correct a servant, you must do it firmly but gently. Would you throw a knife at a horse that threw you or a dog that growled at you?"

Miss Liza shook her ringlets meekly, but the set of her mouth told Sophie that she very well might, if she had a mind.

"Of course you wouldn't," Dr. Charles said indulgently. "Your mama is an excellent woman, but in the matter of managing the servants, I would prefer you to take your Grandmama as your model. Do you understand?"

Miss Liza sat up on the daybed and lifted large, wet eyes to her father's face. "Of course, Papa."

"That's my good puss." He gave her hand a pat, apparently satisfied with the effect of his lecture.

Which proved, Sophie thought as she went in search of a chambermaid to sweep up the mess, that Dr. Charles was a lot stupider about people than he was about broken bones and fever and vacuum-effect evaporators. Only a blind man wouldn't see that Miss Liza was mean as the devil and twice as tricky. She just hoped Mr. Beau was good and blind.

A few days later, the Big House was ready for company. Everything that could be polished had been polished, the storeroom was full, the beds were made up, and there were fresh flowers in every room.

The day the Fairchild daughters were due to arrive, Old Missy set up camp bright and early in a wicker chair down by the floating dock so she'd be sure to be on hand to greet them. Standing behind her with a sunshade, Sophie watched the steam launches pull up the bayou one by one, whistles shrilling, with wide-hatted ladies leaning over the rails and waving their parasols. Samson and Peru helped the crew tie up to the floating dock. Then a Fairchild daughter would herd her children down the gangway to kiss their grandmother and pester her for a boiled sweet while her husband oversaw the unloading of all the trunks and valises and dressing cases necessary for a two-week visit.

By late afternoon, everyone had arrived and Oak River overflowed with Fairchild women and their ruddy planter husbands, talking and laughing and needing to be waited on.

Miss Lotty and Mr. Preston had brought their new baby and his nurse with them, but Miss Sukey and Mr. Kennedy had left their two younger children at home, bringing only Miss May Frances Kennedy, a prissy-faced ten-year-old with chestnut hair cut to her shoulders. Miss Kate's twins, Augustus and Marcus Becker, were, as Aunt Winney said, as alike as blackstrap and molasses and mischievous as monkeys. Not an hour after they arrived, their father was tanning their backsides for sliding down the banister.

They made a great deal of noise over the whipping, then ran off immediately afterward to climb a tree. Sophie couldn't believe it was just because they were used to it. Maybe people didn't hit their children as hard as they hit their slaves.

Sunday night supper was a more than usually formal affair. The Fairchilds and Kennedys and Prestons and Beckers alone made twelve at table, plus Mr. and Mrs. Robinson from Doucette and Mr. Beaufort Waters.

Sophie stood in her usual place behind Old Missy's chair and watched Uncle Germany and Peru ladle out soup and pour wine for the gentlemen and Korea supply the ladies with lemonade and barley water. Samson pulled steadily at a big, square silk-covered fan suspended over the table, cooling the company and keeping the flies off.

The soup was followed by a side of smoked pork, a treat Mr. Becker had imported from Virginia. As everyone tucked in hungrily, Sophie distracted herself from her own growling stomach by studying the Fairchild daughters.

Miss Sukey, plump and fair and kind-faced, favored Old Missy. Miss Lotty and Miss Kate's narrow lips, dark eyes, and eagle noses were slightly softer reflections of the portrait of old Mr. Fairchild that hung over the sideboard. All three grand-children favored their fathers. While the adults made polite conversation, Marcus and Augustus Becker, all dressed up in blue velvet suits, made faces at Miss May, who fiddled with the string of coral beads around her neck and pretended to ignore them.

From the place of honor at her father's left, Miss Liza gazed possessively at her fiancé, who was enduring Miss Kate's very thorough, very polite investigation of his family, his prospects, and his politics. Sophie found herself feeling almost sorry for him.

When the smoked pork was down to scraps and bones, Mrs. Fairchild rang her silver bell. Sophie leaned around Mr. Beau to take up his plate and felt a sly hand squeeze her leg through her petticoats.

Startled, she jerked back, tipping dirty silverware and a greasy bone onto the rug.

There followed a small flurry. Mr. Beau laughed, Miss Liza glared blue murder, Old Missy tutted in distress. Ears burning, Sophie bent down to clear up the mess.

"Who's that girl?" Miss May Kennedy's voice cut through the buzz of conversation. "The one who looks like Cousin Liza?"

Time stuttered, then started up again as Miss Sukey and Old Missy struck up a lively conversation about the finer points of Georgia and Louisiana society. Uncle Germany snatched the plate out of Sophie's hand and shooed her into the pantry, where Korea was standing with her apron thrown over her face, shaking with suppressed laughter.

"Lordy, Lordy," she gasped. "Bless me if I ever heard the like! 'The one who look like Cousin Liza!' That's some plain speaking, yes, indeed."

"You shut your mouth, Korea, and get your self on out there and clear."

Sophie was almost in tears. "I'm sorry, Uncle Germany. I didn't do it on purpose. It was an accident."

"I ain't blaming you," Uncle Germany said wearily. "Now, you run on down to Africa and tell her we's ready for them pies. And don't go showing that Fairchild nose where anybody but Old Missy can see it."

Next morning, Mrs. Fairchild told Sophie she wouldn't be waiting on her at meals any more.

"Not when there's company," she said. "At least until you're older and more experienced."

"Yes, ma'am," said Sophie, much relieved.

Old Missy gazed into the vanity mirror and adjusted the white ruffle at her neck. "I'll be devoting all my time to my family while they're here. You won't have much to do, bar making my coffee—and reading to me at night, of course. I've decided send you—temporarily—to the yard." She glanced up at Sophie's reflection. "Mammy will tell you where you'll be most useful. Don't look so stricken, child. I'm not angry with you."

Fuming, Sophie presented herself in the office, where Mammy greeted her with grim satisfaction. "It's more than time you did some real work. Go tell Africa she's got a new girl to scrub the pots and sweep the floors. And see you're back in good time for the reading."

Sophie set off for the yard in a fine, sullen temper. Old Missy wasn't angry with her? Well, Sophie was plenty angry with Old Missy. She was mistress of Oak River, after all. If she wanted to keep her granddaughter beside her, what business was it of anybody's? Did the Fairchild daughters think Sophie would stop existing because they didn't have to look at her?

At the entrance to the maze, Sophie stopped. She'd gone in before without getting caught. No reason she couldn't do it again. It was a Fairchild maze, after all, and she was a Fairchild. With a hasty glance around to see if anybody was looking, she ran to the central garden, where she sat on the stone bench under the rose arbor and spread her skirts as if she had as much right to be there as any other member of the family.

Somewhere in the maze, a man spoke, low and teasing. A girl—Miss Liza—giggled in response.

Sophie sprang up and looked around frantically for a hiding place. Not the summerhouse—they might go inside. Maybe behind it.

She wiggled carefully between a big camellia bush and the summerhouse wall. There wasn't space for a snake between it and the hedge, but there was a hole in the latticework foundation plenty big enough to crawl through.

Thinking of snakes, Sophie hesitated, thought of Miss Liza's probable reaction to finding her, decided she'd take her chances with the snakes. She bundled her skirts up as best she could, scrambled through the hole, and tumbled straight down a steep incline to land, unhurt but winded, on something that smelled powerfully of mold. Afraid to move, she listened to the crunching of two sets of feet walking toward the summerhouse and struggled not to cough.

The steps halted and Mr. Beau Waters said, "What a pretty garden, darling. Not nearly as pretty as you, though."

Sophie heard a brief scuffle. Then Miss Liza said, "Not here, Beau. Anybody could come."

"Where then, darling? Because I vow and declare, if I don't have a kiss right this minute, I'm going to wither into dust. And then what would you do for a husband, eh?"

Another giggle. "Why, Beaufort Waters, how you do talk! Come into the summerhouse, then, and we'll see what we see."

Footsteps shook the boards above Sophie, sending a fine rain of dirt down on her head. "Oh, Beau," said Miss Liza, and silence followed, punctuated by murmurs and rustling.

Sophie's eyes adjusted to the dimness. Someone, a long time ago by the look of it, had hidden in this hole before. The thing she'd landed on was a moldy mattress on a board. Beside it, she saw a shuttered tin lantern and a wooden bucket with a lid. A rough wooden ladder led up to the lattice.

Above her, Miss Liza giggled and the floorboards creaked. Sophie wondered whether kissing someone with a mustache tickled.

"I need to see you alone, away from your parents and all those aunts and cousins, not to mention your grandmother," Mr. Beau said. "Will you meet me here tomorrow, after dinner?"

"Oh, yes." Miss Liza's voice was soft. "Yes. This is *our* place, yours and mine, and I'll *always* meet you here if you send word. Oh, Beau. I *do* love you so!"

Another embarrassing silence, then Mr. Beau's boots and Miss Liza's shoes left the summerhouse and crunched out of earshot.

To give them time to get out of the maze, Sophie counted slowly to two hundred, then scrambled up the ladder and out the hole, slapped the dirt from her skirts, and started out of the maze.

She was almost to the entrance when she came face-to-face with Miss May Kennedy.

The two girls stared at each other with startled curiosity.

"You got me into a peck of trouble last night," Miss May whined. "Mama sent me to bed directly we got up from supper."

Sophie was used to being ordered around, threatened, and generally treated like a domestic animal by adults. But she didn't see why she had to put up with being scolded by a girl half her age. "You brought that trouble down on yourself," she said.

Miss May gasped. "You can't talk to me like that!" she said, and actually stamped her foot. "You're nothing but a dirty yard child. I'll tell my mama you sassed me. I'll have you sent away. I'll have you whipped."

If a yard child was what Little Missy wanted, then that's what she'd get. Sophie cocked her hands on her hips. "I *been* sent away already, on account of *you* can't hush."

Miss May started to cry.

"Quit that bawling!" Sophie said recklessly. "I ain't hurt you none. Prissy little crybaby."

"I'm not. Take it back. I'm a Kennedy of Ash Grove, and you're a nigger slave wench."

Now it was Sophie's turn to gasp.

Seeing the impression she'd made, Miss May stopped crying. "Nigger!" she crowed triumphantly. "Nigger, nigger, nigger!"

"Now, now."

Sophie whirled around. Mr. Beau was standing in one of the unmarked gaps, holding a newly lit cheroot and grinning under his mustache. "I can't believe your mama would approve of you using that word, Miss May."

Sophie watched with satisfaction as the little girl went from furious red to pasty white and clamped her hands over her mouth. She couldn't resist adding, "You shouldn't ought to call names, miss."

"From what I just heard, she had good reason," Mr. Beau said.

Sophie hastily dropped her gaze to her feet.

"Do you know what happens to uppity slaves?" he went on pleasantly. "They get sent to work in the cane fields, where nobody will see whether they're whupped or not. So I'd mind my manners, if I was you. And stay out of places you don't have no business being."

"Yessir," Sophie muttered.

"Scoot then," said Mr. Beau, "and we'll say no more about it. Will we, Miss May?" He smiled down at the little girl's tear-splotched face. She sniffed and slipped her hand into his.

"Whatever you say, Mr. Waters."

"Good." He turned to Sophie. "One good turn deserves another. You understand me, wench?"

Sophie shot him a glance, standing free and easy beside Miss May, his long brown cheroot poised for a puff. "Well," she said doubtfully. "I ain't too acute, being a nigger and all. But I tries." And before she could get herself into any more trouble, she turned around and ran out of the maze to the yard, where she belonged.

Chapter 13

When Sophie showed up in the kitchen, Africa laughed.

"No need to tell me what you doing here—I can guess. Korea told me 'bout dinner last night. 'Just like Miss Liza!' I like to die laughing." The sauce she was stirring blurped thickly, and she swung the pot off the fire. "Nobody here got time to tell you what to do, Sophie. You just help Canny with her chores until after dinner, and then we see what needs doing."

Sophie had never thought about what Canny did all day. She remembered, from her time in the hospital, that Canny was responsible for feeding and watering the pigeons that lived in the round wooden dovecote at the edge of the yard. But Canny had never told her about her other chores. Along with Tibet and a boy named H.C., Sophie traipsed back and forth across the yard, carrying bucket after heavy, sloshing bucket from the big cistern to the kitchen water barrel and trundling a two-wheeled cart full of kindling from the woodshed by the stable to the kitchen wood box. The bucket's rope handles blistered her hands and the wood gave her splinters, but the fear of Tibet's teasing kept her from complaining.

Canny always left the dovecote for last, as a treat. The doves were pretty birds, white and plump and as vain of their ruffled feathers as the proudest Southern belle. But all Sophie could think of, hungry as she always was, was how delicious

136

they'd be when cooked up into the golden pies Africa sent up to the Big House.

That night, Old Missy asked Sophie how she was getting on down in the yard. "It should be a rest for you, really," she said comfortably. "Not running up and down those big old stairs all the livelong day."

Sophie clenched her blistered hands and bowed her head to hide her face. "Yes ma'am. You want to go on with *Little Dorrit*?"

Old Missy leaned back against her soft white cotton pillows. "Dickens seems too much like real life just now. I think I've a mind to try something more romantic. Run down to the library and fetch up *Ivanhoe*."

And the subject was closed.

Working in the plantation kitchen was much harder than running errands. Between the scrubbing and the toting, her arms and back ached and her hands were red and rough as sandpaper. The kitchen was like a bake oven, and she always felt a little dizzy and stupid with the heat. But there were compensations. No Aunt Winney to scold and harry her. No Mammy to look at her like a palmetto bug on a tablecloth. No Mrs. Charles to threaten her with the strap. No Fairchild daughters and granddaughters to turn up their Fairchild noses at her.

Once they saw Sophie did her share of work, the kitchen women got downright friendly. Jane taught her how to shuck beans. Bali, who'd been doing all the pot-scrubbing before Sophie showed up, was glad to show her the finer points of getting scorched food off an iron pot with wet ashes. And round about three o'clock, when the white folks were at dinner and the pots soaking in the trough, Sophie could take her mush and potliquor under the kitchen oak and listen to the servants of four plantations trying to top each other's gossip.

The day before Miss Liza's ball, Sophie sat with her shoulder companionably against Hepzibah's knee while a Bywater woman bragged on her aunt's husband.

"Old Henry, he just light out to the swamp, build hisself a little camp, and fish. When he sick of he own company, he come back and take the fifty lashes Mist' Kennedy got waiting for him and go back to work, cheerful as a jaybird. He done it before, and he fixing to do it again, right 'bout the middle of harvest-time. He a right caution, that Henry."

Uncle Angus, Mr. Preston's bodyservant, took the corncob pipe from his mouth. "We got a wench up to Rich Meadow run twenty mile to Kelderly every month God send. She hang 'round and hang 'round till the overseer catch her and haul her back to Rich Meadow. Last time, Mr. Preston put a big old iron collar on her, with bells on it. But she run anyways, jingling and jangling like an old cow. Miz Charlotte, she say she going sell her."

"What's at Kelderly?" Sally asked curiously. "Her man?"

"Her baby boy," said Uncle Angus. "Sold for a houseboy when he weren't much more than six year old."

Everybody murmured and a Rich Meadow woman said, "They the life and the death of us both. You own flesh and blood—it break you heart right in two when they's sold away."

There was a chorus of amens, just like at church, and then Asia said, "I don't know what things like in Georgia, but we got a law in Louisiana, you can't never sell a child away from his ma till he grown. There's some do it anyway, but not Old Missy."

Uncle Angus said, "World be a better place for niggers if they was more white folks in it like Mrs. Fairchild."

"World a better place for niggers there don't be no white folks in it at all," said the Bywater woman sourly.

"You hush youself, Evaline," said a woman sitting at her feet. "You fixing to talk yourself straight into a whipping."

"Ain't no whupping at Oak River. Ain't you heard? That sorry crick out yonder, that the River Jordan. We done come out of Georgia into the land of Canaan. *Praise* the Lord."

There was an uncomfortable silence. Sophie expected Antigua to set her straight, but it was Hepzibah who said, "You're a fool, girl. Oak River folks working for Pharaoh, same as y'all. Old Missy just the Pharaoh that love Joseph."

"The Pharaoh that love Mammy, more like," Antigua added, and everybody laughed.

"Hush up, Antigua," said Uncle Germany. "Old Missy a kind, Christian woman. She do her best by us."

Siberia, the Oak Cottage housemaid, shrugged. "Ain't all roses. Young Missy sooner whup a nigger than eat her dinner."

"Oh, you safe enough, Siberia," Antigua said, "as long as Dr. Charles recollect who wear the britches in the family."

Evaline wasn't done arguing. "India, she say there more rawhide at Oak River than cornmeal."

"India is a fool." Mammy stepped out from behind the oak and glared at the suddenly silent group. "She brought that rawhide on herself, taking up with that no-good old conjure man."

"Ole One-Eye," Zeb the carpenter said. "I remember. She try and warn him when the patrollers was looking for him. Old Massa, he give her the licking of her life."

"There," said Evaline.

Mammy eyed Zeb over her steel spectacles. "There's no denying Mr. Patrick was a hard man. But Mrs. Fairchild's been a good mistress to me, and I won't hear a word against her."

Delia Sherman

Uncle Angus cleared his throat uncomfortably. "Don't take no mind of Evaline, Mammy. She ain't had no sense from the day she was borned."

Africa spoke up from the kitchen door. "You both wrong. Evaline got plenty sense. There ain't no such thing as a good mistress, on account of a mistress ain't a good thing to be. Think on it, Mammy. Old Missy maybe taught you to read and write and speak as white as her own children. But she ain't set you free."

Sophie waited with the rest of the slaves for Mammy's reaction. She was famous for her tongue-lashings, and it was plain to see that she was plenty put-out enough to deliver one. But she didn't even say a word, just turned around and marched off across the yard, scattering chickens every which way with her stiff, black skirts.

The day of Miss Liza's engagement ball came and went. Sophie helped Aunt Winney bathe and dress Mrs. Fairchild in purple silk and lace, then spent the rest of the day down in the kitchen, far from the festivities, turning spits and scrubbing pots. She didn't get back up to the Big House until well after midnight.

Old Missy was already in bed. "No reading tonight, child. I'm too tired to listen. I do believe I'll spend tomorrow in bed, after all that fuss. And please tell Winney I don't want to see a living soul before suppertime."

This suited Sophie just fine. Because she wasn't exactly a house servant just now, and nobody had told her not to, she decided to give herself the afternoon off.

The weather was soft and gray and hot—perfect for fishing. After Old Guam's sermon, Sophie and Canny headed to the

Quarters to pick up some hooks and lines and whoever didn't have anything better to do, and head out to the bayou to try for some bluegill. Everybody was busy, hoeing their gardens, washing clothes and bedding, mending fences, talking, tending to their lives. Sophie and Canny found their friends gathered in Old Guam's hen yard, with his chickens scratching and clucking around them.

Mindful of her Sunday finery, Sophie hung back while Canny squirmed through to where Young Guam sat cross-legged in the dust, dolefully cradling a large speckled hen in his lap.

She squatted down and gave the hen a poke. "She passed, all right. You going to eat her?"

Young Guam clutched the limp, feathery corpse close. "This here ain't no ordinary hen. This here's Old Betsy, been laying a dozen eggs a week since I was a picaninny. I ain't letting no body make no gumbo out of Old Betsy."

A grubby hand sticking out of an even grubbier white sleeve reached out and smoothed Old Betsy's black and white wing. "We should bury her, then."

The voice wasn't a yard child's. Sophie looked again. Under the grubbiness, she recognized one of the Becker twins, looking perfectly at home squatting in the dirt. Sophie wondered if his mama knew where he was, and what she'd say when she saw the state of his Sunday suit.

Young Guam looked at him eagerly. "You mean in a real grave, like she was folks?"

"Of course in a real grave," the twin assured him. "With a bier and a hearse and horses and all."

"Horses?" the second twin asked doubtfully. "You're crazy, Marcus. How we going to get horses to pull a cart with a dead chicken on it?"

Marcus gave his brother (Augustus, Sophie remembered) a friendly thump. "Pretend horses, stupid. Paris and Rome are about the same size—same color, too, like match bays."

Two reddish-brown boys, brothers by the look of them, exchanged glances. Sophie couldn't tell whether or not they were offended by Marcus's suggestion. She certainly was. She thought Marcus and Augustus had taken charge of something that wasn't any of their business and turned it into a game for their amusement, and she wasn't having any part of it. If Canny and the rest wanted to be ordered around by a pair of filthy-faced white brats, fine. She was going to change out of her Sunday dress and just go fishing by herself.

Marcus stood and brushed the dust off the seat of his britches. "What you all waiting for? Time's a-wasting."

Gently, Augustus took Old Betsy from Young Guam and everybody scattered, looking for the things they'd need to give the chicken a proper funeral: a wood cart, some rope, a shovel.

Tibet ran up to Sophie, her arms full of leafy branches. "Is you is or is you ain't going help me lay out Old Betsy right and proper?"

"Come fishing with me instead," Sophie said. "Master Marcus Becker doesn't own you, or me either. We don't have to do what he says."

Tibet gave her an exasperated look. "Not even if he got a good idea? What kind of foolishness is that?"

"Any more foolish than having a funeral for a hen?"

"Young Guam, he set a heap of store by that there hen," Tibet said. "Mast' Marcus, he recognizing that. Why ain't you?"

She seemed serious. "You really think this funeral will make Young Guam feel better?"

"Sure as I'm standing here," Tibet said. "'Sides, might be some fun."

"All right," Sophie said. "I'll do it. Because I like Young Guam, not because Marcus Becker says to."

Tibet dumped the branches in her arms. "Good. Now, make Old Betsy one of them things Mast' Marcus was talking about."

By the time Sophie had made a kind of nest out of the branches and tied it to the wood cart so it wouldn't slide off, the grave diggers had done their work, and the procession set out to carry Old Betsy to her final resting place.

Eager though she was to find fault, Sophie found the ceremony oddly impressive. Augustus took the lead with his mama's prayer book, then Paris and Rome pulling Old Betsy's hearse, with Marcus driving them by ropes tied to their waists. Canny had tied a black bow around Old Betsy's scraggly neck, and everybody agreed she looked fine. Young Guam, as chief mourner, came next, followed by every Oak River child old enough to walk, singing "Swing Low, Sweet Chariot" at the tops of their lungs.

When the procession reached the bayou, everybody gathered round the grave and laid Old Betsy to rest with psalms and prayers and a white handkerchief between her and the black bayou soil. Marcus donated the handkerchief. Augustus, who was bookish, preached a sermon on the text "We all must die" that was almost as rousing—and much shorter—than anything Sophie had heard from Old Guam. To her surprise, he didn't so much as crack a smile the whole time, and when the service was over, shook Young Guam's hand and said he was sorry for his loss as if he really meant it. Then Marcus thumped Young Guam on the shoulder and the three boys grinned at each other and took off screaming like hawks to climb the nearest tree.

"Men," said Tibet with deep disgust.

"Can we go fishing now?" Canny asked.

Sophie caught two bluegill, which she gave to Africa before she went back to the Big House.

Sophie worked in the kitchen for just about a week. Every night, after the last pot was scrubbed clean, she washed her face and hands and changed out of homespun into yellow calico and ran up to the Big House to read Old Missy to sleep. In this way, she managed to avoid seeing any Fairchilds at all, except, of course, Old Missy.

"I declare, Sophie," Old Missy said one night, "you're getting dark as a yard child. And look at your hands! What on earth have you been doing?"

"I've been working in the kitchen, ma'am. Just like you said."

"I didn't—" Old Missy stopped. "Clearly, there's been some misunderstanding. Go fetch Mammy."

Sophie obeyed, then stood at Old Missy's shoulder as she lit into Mammy.

"I don't know what you were thinking, Mammy, sending her to the kitchen. You know I promised Mr. Robert that we'd train her up as a lady's maid. It shouldn't need saying that I wanted her sent to the sewing house. I'm surprised at you, Mammy. I purely am."

It was peculiar to see Mammy standing in front of Old Missy with her hands folded and her head bent, taking her scolding just like she wasn't any more account than Sophie herself. It was obvious that she hated it.

Sophie just hoped that Mammy wouldn't think of any better ways of getting even.

After the kitchen, the sewing house seemed mighty cool and quiet. Like Old Missy, Asia and Hepzibah clucked over the state of Sophie's hands and made her rub them with goose grease so they wouldn't catch on the fabric. Asia taught her how to darn linen and knitted stockings. Much to her surprise, Sophie liked darning, which was like weaving a tiny piece of new cloth with a needle. She was getting pretty good at it by the time the Beckers left at the end of August. Shortly after, the Kennedys followed, and the Prestons and all their servants, and Old Missy called Sophie back to the Big House.

It was hard settling down to being Old Missy's shadow again. Sophie found herself thinking things that would earn her a scolding and maybe worse if she'd said them out loud. Sometimes she felt like she'd bit her tongue so often, she was like to bite it clear in two.

It didn't make it easier that early September was close and hot as a felt blanket. One day Sophie woke with an aching head and what felt like a belly full of rats. First chance she got, she went up to use the pot and saw her drawers were streaked with blood.

Mama, ever practical, had warned her that this would happen sooner or later. Sophie could almost hear her cool voice saying how messy it was, and that refined folks didn't mention it under any circumstances. But Sophie if didn't mention it, her clothes would be ruined.

Sophie went down to the dressing room and stood in front of Aunt Winney, chewing her lip nervously.

Aunt Winney laid her mending in her lap. "Let me guess. You done ripped Missy Caro's nightdress and you scared to 'fess up. Well, you just bring it here, we see how bad it look."

"It's not that. I haven't done anything. It's just—"

The old woman eyed her sharply. "It gots to be something. You white as a grub."

"I . . . I've got . . . I'm bleeding, Aunt Winney. You know. Down there. I don't know what to do."

"Bleeding?" Aunt Winney chuckled. "Bless you, child, that ain't nothing but your woman's nature coming on you." She held out her hand. "You help me up out this chair, and I ask Missy Caro if she can spare us for a minute or two."

To Sophie's surprise, Mrs. Fairchild laughed and told them to take their time. Then Aunt Winney took Sophie down to the sewing house. What came next was one of the most embarrassing hours of Sophie's life so far. Between jokes about dying her petticoats red, Asia and Hepzibah showed her how to make pads of moss and rags and tie them between her legs. They told her to change the rags at least twice a day and wash herself so she wouldn't smell.

And then everybody went back to work.

Chapter 14

As the youngest engaged woman in the parish, Miss Liza had been looking forward to queening it over every unattached girl within a day's ride of Oak River for the rest of the summer. So when her mother and grandmother informed her she'd be spending every waking hour from now until she married learning how to manage a household, she was very much less than pleased.

"Why can't I go to the Pettigrew's dance?" she pouted. "And why do I have to make mint jelly in this horrible heat? That's why we have slaves, isn't it?"

Sophie had been wondering the same thing ever since she'd gone down to the kitchen with Old Missy right after breakfast. Mrs. Charles was there, enveloped in a bibbed apron, and Miss Liza, looking put-upon and insisting that Antigua fan her while she picked over mint leaves. Antigua's cheek, Sophie noticed, was shadowed with an old bruise. She turned away when she caught Sophie staring.

Mrs. Charles glanced up from the pot of bubbling green liquid she was stirring over the fire. "How many times must I tell you? Servants are only as good as their mistress. If you know how it should be done, then you can be sure it's being done right."

Miss Liza pushed a drooping curl from her forehead. "Why can't I learn it some other time? It's two long years before I get married."

Delia Sherman

"I'd be happier," Old Missy said dryly, "if it were three. You have never attended as diligently as you should to your domestic accomplishments."

"When I was your age," Mrs. Charles put in, "I helped my dear mother make clothes, not only for the family, but for the slaves as well. And I helped nurse them when they were injured or fell ill. Which reminds me," she said, returning to the pot. "You will accompany your father to the slave hospital, beginning tomorrow morning."

Sophie and Antigua exchanged looks behind Old Missy's back. It wasn't hard to imagine how Miss Liza would take to nursing slaves. Antigua rolled her eyes, and Sophie had to bite her tongue (again) to keep from laughing.

After a moment of mute amazement, Miss Liza started in to carry on, but Old Missy thumped her gold-headed cane on the floor. "Be still, Liza! You wanted to marry a young man with his way to make in the world. Such a marriage means economy, self-discipline, and good, old-fashioned hard work. You can count yourself fortunate in having a notable housekeeper like your mother to teach you how to go on."

Mrs. Charles looked pleased. "Why, thank you, Mother Fairchild." She pulled the spoon, dripping green glop, from the pot. "Test this, Liza, and tell me if it's ready to set."

Sophie was not surprised when the lesson ended with the jelly spoiled and Miss Liza in tears. Most of the housekeeping lessons did.

September brought hot, wet days, cooler nights, and the first preparations for the long, hard seasons of harvest and winter. Sophie spent hours with Old Missy, Mrs. Charles, and Mammy, counting candles and bolts of cloth, bandages and ointments, lamp oil and tanned hide for shoes. At meals, Dr. Charles was absent as often as not, and when he was present, could talk of nothing but how long the warm weather would last and whether the new vacuum apparatus would be set up in time.

Antigua kept the kitchen oak gossips entertained with stories of Miss Liza's temper tantrums. There was the time she stamped her foot and knocked over the chamber pot and the time she was ugly to her mama and got locked into her room without supper and the time she cracked her ivory comb over Antigua's head. Antigua's account of that was so funny, everybody like to died laughing.

Sally wiped her eyes. "Miss Liza's a caution, sure enough. She best take care, though. Mens don't like womens to be creating and carrying on all the time."

"Oh, she don't carry on where Mr. Beau can see her," Antigua said. "She all sugar-sweet when he come around."

"I hear he ain't coming round so much," said Sally. "I bet you near rich as Solomon, carrying all them letters to Doucette."

Antigua shrugged. "Rich enough, I guess. Price gone down some now they's promised."

Hepzibah said, "You be careful, girl. That man a big old hungry fox, and you a mighty plump pullet."

Antigua's expression hardened. "I ain't no pullet. I keeps my eyes down and my back round so's he hardly know I got a face."

The women exchanged glances and might have said more, but the plantation bell sent them back to work.

The second week in October, Old Missy announced that Dr. Charles had decided to fire up the sugarhouse and start the harvest.

149

"Mr. Akins swears the new apparatus is ready, and the weather's turning cold. So it's grinding hours from now on, Winney. Sophie, I won't be wanting *Ivanhoe* tonight. Go get a volume of sermons from the library. Mr. Scott is just too exciting for this time of year."

Oak River Plantation at harvest time was an altogether different place from Oak River Plantation in high summer. There were no dances and holidays on Saturday or Sunday, not even an hour for church. The plantation bell rang not only at dawn, noon, and dusk, but after sunrise and in mid-afternoon too, calling up the afternoon and night shifts to cut cane to feed the hungry grinders and boil down the clear juice into sweet, white sugar.

From early morning to dark, Sophie followed Old Missy as she stumped from attic to cellar to yard on her gold-topped cane, supervising, encouraging, scolding, organizing. During meals, she stood behind Old Missy's chair, listening while she and Dr. Charles discussed the weather and sugar prices, whether renting in a dozen more field hands would be worth the extra expense and how much building a light railroad from the sugarhouse to the landing dock would cost. One afternoon, Old Missy took a dizzy spell and Sophie had to run for Dr. Charles, who let blood from his mother's arm and gave her a tonic and told her she had to rest more.

Old Missy took the tonic, but not the advice. There were slaves to be clothed and stores to be put up and decisions to be made about almost everything, and nobody Old Missy trusted to do it as it should be done. Because she couldn't seem to keep track of anything smaller than a hundredweight of candles, Sophie was kept hopping after whatever little thing she'd forgotten—scissors, reticule, pins, handkerchief.

One day, it was her favorite parasol.

"I expect I left it down at Oak Cottage. Run down, Sophie, and fetch it here so we can pack it away for the winter."

It was a beautiful fall day, crisp and dry and fragrant with late-blooming maypop. In the yard, two dogs squabbled in the dust and America the blacksmith honed cane knives on a stone wheel. Sophie sang as she walked, something about *high apple pie in the sky hopes*. She wondered where she'd learned it.

The back gallery at Oak Cottage was deserted. Before she went bothering Mrs. Charles about the parasol, Sophie decided to check the storeroom where all the extra boots and riding crops and suchlike were kept. She had her hand on the latch when she heard Antigua saying, "Now, Mr. Beau, you don't want to do nothing Miss Liza wouldn't like."

Sophie froze.

"Miss Liza ain't going to know." Mr. Beau's voice was thick and unpleasant, like he was talking through a lump of lard. "If you breathe a word, I'll say you made it all up. You'll be whupped for lying, or even sold in New Orleans. It'd be easier all round if you was nice to me."

There was a clatter of things falling, then a strangled sob. Sophie pushed the door open. Mr. Beau was pressing Antigua up against the shelves, holding her by the wrists as she struggled. Her tignon had come off, the front of her dress was ripped open, and the floor was littered with boots and hats and candles.

"Mr. Beau?" Sophie croaked, then cleared her throat. "Mr. Beau, you stop that."

Antigua went still. Ignoring Sophie entirely, Mr. Beau bent his sandy head and planted a kiss on her throat. Sophie snatched up a riding crop and whacked him with it as hard as she could.

That got his attention. He spun around, his face all red and mottled behind his mustache.

"Damn little spoilsport nigger!" he spat. "Give me that crop! Now!"

Sophie brandished the little whip recklessly. "No," she said. "And if you try and take it away, I'll shout."

"Nobody will hear you," Mr. Beau said, but the color faded from his cheeks, and Sophie knew he was afraid.

"I knows they will," she said in her best yard-child voice. "Maybe Antigua catch a whupping, but you likely lose Miss Liza. Dr. Charles, he mighty straightlaced."

Mr. Beau chewed on his mustache. "He won't believe you. You're likely to catch a whupping your own self, you go telling Dr. Fairchild lies on me. Besides, I ain't done nothing." He released Antigua, who stumbled to Sophie's side, clutching the front of her dress closed.

Sophie frowned. "Look to me like it be plenty enough to make Dr. Charles think twice 'bout letting you marry his little girl."

Mr. Beau's hands clenched, and his jaw jutted dangerously. Then he took a deep breath, straightened his waistcoat, and slicked back his rumpled hair. He bowed to Antigua. "Some other time, my dear," he said, then turned to Sophie. "And you, yellow wench, you'll be sorry you interfered."

When he'd left, Antigua collapsed on the floor, weeping quietly. Sophie, knees shaking, sank down beside her.

"Don't cry. He won't bother you again. I think he's frightened Dr. Charles might believe us."

Antigua raised her face, swollen and wet with tears. "And that make him dangerous as a lame bear. What for you use that whip on him?"

Sophie bit her lip. "I don't know. It was there, and he wouldn't stop, and . . ."

Antigua scrubbed the tears from her cheeks and got to her feet. "It done now. And you likely going to pay for it." She did up the buttons on the front of her dress. Some of them were missing. "It ain't your fault. Just please don't say a word to a soul. Not a living soul, you hear me, Sophie? Not Momi, not Sally, not nobody."

Sophie nodded unhappily.

Antigua hugged her very quick and hard. "I mighty happy to see you and that little whip, yes, ma'am. As long as you was hitting, I wish you'd of hit him harder."

Sophie gave a weak giggle. "I wish I had, too. I don't think he could have been any madder. What do you think he'll do, Antigua?"

"I don't know, Sophie, I surely don't. I don't 'spect we need wait long to find out, though."

Chapter 15

Mr. Beau waited three full days to act, which gave Sophie plenty of time to imagine what he might do. None of her imaginings were pleasant. By Tuesday morning, she was dropping things and forgetting things and generally making Old Missy nervous as a cat.

"I declare, Sophie, I don't know what's gotten into you this morning. You'd think you were possessed of a devil. Why don't you go down to the sewing house?"

"I'd rather stay here, ma'am, if you don't mind."

"I do mind. Aunt Winney wants to turn out my dressing room, and she doesn't need to be worrying that you're going to break something the moment she turns her back."

"Poor Aunt Winney's knees hurt so bad in the cold, I should be here to help her. I'm all better now, see?" Sophie picked up Old Missy's nightcap and shook it smartly to smooth the ruffles. One of the ribbons caught a silver buttonhook on the nightstand and sent it tinkling to the floor.

Old Missy sighed. "Go, Sophie. I'll send when I want you."

Down in the sewing house, Asia gave Sophie a pile of field-hand's britches and a handful of wooden buttons. Sophie did her best, but the needle kept coming unthreaded, and she pricked her fingers bloody. Finally, she threw the britches on the floor.

Asia eyed her knowingly. "Ain't nothing more useless than a girl with her nature coming on. Go sweep the floor. You ain't fit for nothing else."

Sophie sniffed furiously, fetched the broom, and was raising dust with it when Sally burst in like mad dogs were after her.

"Old Missy want you," she panted. "Right this very minute, she say. She mad as fire. What you done, girl?"

Sophie felt the blood drain out of her face.

"That bad, huh?" Sally shook her head. "I sure happy I ain't you, Sophie. She got Mrs. Charles and Miss Liza with her, and they's mighty put out."

I'm a Fairchild, Sophie thought. *Old Missy's too proud to sell her own granddaughter.*

Sally led her to the parlor. Aunt Winney opened the door, her face as grim as Judgment Day. Behind her, Sophie saw the Fairchild women all lined up in front of the fireplace. Mrs. Charles had her rawhide strap laid ready across her knees. Old Missy held a red bundle in her lap.

Miss Liza sat between them, looking like a cat with cream on its whiskers.

"Mrs. Fairchild has some questions she wants to put to you," Mrs. Charles said. "Mind you answer truthfully, now, or it'll be the worse for you."

Sophie clasped her hands tight to hide their trembling.

Old Missy touched the red bundle. "Do you recognize this?"

Sophie pushed at her glasses nervously, saw the red was stitched with black. "Is that my Sunday tignon?"

Miss Liza made a small, triumphant sound. "Didn't I tell you, Grandmama?"

"Hush, Elizabeth." Old Missy's voice was stern. "When did you last see this headrag, Sophie?"

The question was a trap. What else could it be, with those clear blue eyes fixed so intensely on her face? But without knowing what she was meant to have done, Sophie couldn't think of a single thing she could safely say.

Mrs. Charles tapped her rawhide. "Come now, girl. The truth shouldn't need thinking over."

Sophie took a steadying breath. "I'm sorry, ma'am. It's just I can't remember exactly the last time I wore it. Not since harvest started, I think, or maybe a bit before."

"But when did you last see it?" Mrs. Charles insisted.

"Hush, Lucy," said Old Missy. "Sophie, where do you keep the headrag when you're not wearing it?"

"Under my pallet, in the dressing room."

"And where do you think we found it?" Mrs. Charles asked.

"Under my pallet?"

Mrs. Charles's hands gripped her rawhide. "Don't be insolent."

"Do you recognize this, Sophie?" Old Missy unfolded the tignon, revealing a silver-backed brush etched with a pattern of roses and lilies intertwined.

"No, ma'am."

Mrs. Charles made an impatient noise. "Why do you persist in this charade, Mother Fairchild? You have only to look at her face to know she's guilty."

Old Missy ignored her. "Look again, Sophie."

Leaning in to examine it, Sophie saw a little flat space in the middle of the design with a monogram engraved: EFc. F for Fairchild. E for Elizabeth. She didn't know what the C was for.

Her heart gave a big, choking thump. "It's Miss Liza's brush," she said. "But I didn't take it, I swear. I haven't been near Oak Cottage."

"You were there on Saturday," Mrs. Charles pointed out. "Mrs. Fairchild sent you. Furthermore, I wonder why you're so quick to deny a crime of which no one has yet accused you."

"Let's not get ahead of ourselves, Lucy. Yes, Sophie, it's Miss Elizabeth's brush. Aunt Winney found it in the bottom of my armoire. The question is, how did it get there?"

Sophie knew Miss Liza had put that brush in Old Missy's armoire herself, just as sure as if she'd watched her do it. "I don't know, ma'am," she said miserably. "When did it go missing?"

"Why do you ask?" Mrs. Charles snapped.

Old Missy quieted her with a gnarled hand. "It's a reasonable question. When did you notice the brush gone, Elizabeth?"

"Yesterday evening," Miss Liza said. "I even had Antigua pick through all the washing piece by piece, in case it might have been gathered up with the dirty linens."

Sophie didn't doubt it. "I wasn't at Oak Cottage yesterday," she said. "I was with Old Missy."

Old Missy shook her head. "Not every minute. There was an hour at least between noon and one when you were nowhere to be found."

"I was eating my dinner," Sophie said, trying to keep her voice steady. "You can ask Africa. Or Sally—she went down to the kitchen with me."

"And both Africa and Sally will say they saw you, whether they did or not. You know perfectly well, Mother Fairchild, that servants can be counted on to lie to protect each other." Mrs. Charles leaned forward. "And what if I said Mr. Beau saw you loitering in the back gallery yesterday afternoon?"

"I wasn't at Oak Cottage, ma'am," Sophie said. "Not yesterday."

Miss Liza widened her eyes. "Are you saying Mr. Waters told a lie?"

Delia Sherman

Sophie's mouth was so dry she could hardly speak. "Oh, no, Miss Liza. He must have been mistaken, is all."

"Mistaken!" Miss Liza gave an angry titter. "And I suppose you don't stick out among the other servants like a grub an anthill."

"That's enough, Elizabeth," said her grandmother. "Nobody doubts that Mr. Waters saw a light-skinned slave near Oak Cottage yesterday. It needn't have been Sophie. I myself am more distressed by what I observed this morning. You can't deny, Sophie, that you were very nervous and most reluctant to leave the house when you were ordered."

"Yes, ma'am. But . . ." Sophie stopped. But what? She couldn't say that she was nervous because she was afraid of Mr. Beaufort Waters.

"No buts, Sophie: that's what happened. And you knew Aunt Winney would be turning out the armoire, because I told you."

Sophie clasped her hands together tightly. "Please, ma'am, I don't know anything about the brush. Please believe me."

Old Missy's wrinkles deepened with distress. "You do admit this is your tignon?"

"Yes, ma'am."

"And you keep it in my dressing room."

"Yes, ma'am."

"And who has business in my dressing room, other than you and Aunt Winney?"

"Nobody, ma'am. But anybody can go in. It's not locked."

"Why would anyone want to go into my dressing room? I hope," Old Missy said coldly, "you don't expect me to believe that Aunt Winney would steal Miss Liza's silver hairbrush and try to make it look like you took it?"

Not Aunt Winney, Sophie thought, but all she said aloud was, "No, ma'am."

Old Missy's expression hardened. "I'll give you one more chance, Sophie. Did you take Miss Liza's hairbrush and hide it in the armoire?"

"No, ma'am. I didn't take the hairbrush. I swear."

"I told you, Mother Fairchild," said Mrs. Charles with satisfaction. "A thief *and* a liar."

"So you did, Lucy," said Old Missy, but she didn't sound at all happy about it.

"Naturally," Mrs. Charles went on, "you can't let this go unpunished."

"I was thinking about sending her to the sewing house."

Mrs. Charles brushed the notion aside. "That's a rest cure, not a punishment. Dr. Charles always says there's nothing like a stint in the fields to give a difficult house servant a new perspective."

Sophie stared at her clasped hands while the debate over her future went on, wondering what she'd do in the fields. She didn't think she could bear to cut cane.

"A good whipping is what she needs," Mrs. Charles said.

A real whipping with knotted thongs, she meant, tied over a barrel. Sophie swallowed nervously, and the room got darker and narrower.

"I promised Robert I'd take care of her," Old Missy said.

"It seems to me, Mother Fairchild, that Robert would thank you for breaking the girl of a pernicious habit."

Old Missy shook her lacy cap. "Whipping does nothing but make servants hard and sly. My mind's made up. Sophie must work in the fields until she's learned the consequences of her actions, but I won't have her whipped. Winney, ring the bell."

Sally answered so fast and looked so goggle-eyed that Sophie knew she'd been listening at the door.

"Bring Mr. Akins," said Old Missy, and Sally scurried away.

Sophie tried to think of something, anything she could say that wouldn't make things worse.

"Look at her," said Mrs. Charles. "Smug as you please, trusting in her face to get her off lightly. I declare, Mother Fairchild, I don't know how you can bear to have the creature near you."

"Her face isn't her fault, Lucy," said Old Missy sadly. "It's Robert's fault, if it's anyone's. And if it saves her a whipping, that's the most it will ever do for her."

Old Missy spent the time waiting for Mr. Akins lecturing Miss Liza on kitchen gardens. She sounded perfectly calm, but Sophie hadn't spent all those weeks waiting on her without learning to read her moods. Old Missy believed Sophie had stolen the brush and lied about it, and she was deeply disappointed with Sophie for being like her no-account father, with herself for having trusted her. She wasn't going to get over it anytime soon.

After a long, uncomfortable time, Sally showed Mr. Akins into the parlor. He looked and smelled as though he hadn't washed since harvest started, but at least his broad-brimmed hat was in his hand rather than on his head.

He grinned, his teeth yellow in the briar patch of his unshaven jaw. "Afternoon, Miz Fairchild. I hear you got a new field hand for me."

Old Missy did not return the smile. "Sophie has been very foolish, Mr. Akins. I'm hoping that honest hard labor will teach her more wisdom."

"Sure to, ma'am." He turned to Sophie. "Come along, wench. You hear Miz Fairchild. Time you do some honest work."

Sophie stared from one white face to another. Mrs. Charles looked satisfied, Miss Liza maliciously gleeful. Old Missy just looked old.

Sophie turned and bolted for the door.

A strong hand closed around her arm and jerked her to a halt. Sophie clawed at it, sobbing that she hadn't done anything, that it wasn't fair. Mr. Akins spun her around and pinned her neatly, with her elbows nearly touching behind her back.

"Now, if you ladies will excuse me, I better take care of this directly and get back to the sugarhouse."

"Of course," said Mrs. Charles. "Thank you."

Mr. Akins hauled her down the back stairs and out through the cool, green garden, muttering under his breath about the time he was wasting on women's foolishness.

"Scrawny thing, ain't you?" he remarked. "Smart thing would be to sell you off in New Orleans." He spat in the dirt. "Women!"

As they reached the cane brake, a panting field hand emerged from the wall of green. "Mist' Akins, sir! Old Guam say come quick to Devon Cut! Henry done sliced his leg near clean off!"

"If that don't just beat the devil! Here—" Mr. Akins shoved Sophie into the man's arms. "Take this wench and shut her up somewheres."

"Where?"

"Don't matter. Somewheres with a lock. And tell Ajax to send a horse for Dr. Charles." And Mr. Akins ran off down the road like the devil was snapping at his heels.

The field hand set out for the yard at a fast clip, jerking Sophie along by one arm, dragging her up when she stumbled, ignoring her tears, and generally making it clear that he had more important things to tend to than a high-yellow house servant who probably deserved just what was coming to her and maybe more.

By the time they reached the stable, the only things keeping Sophie going were the field hand's strong grip and her own stubbornness. She stood stiffly while he talked to Ajax, then staggered after him as he went to the woodshed behind the blacksmith's shop, opened the door, and shoved her inside. The door closed, the bar fell, and she was alone.

The dark inside the woodshed was streaked with sunlight leaking through the gaps in the walls and heavy with the smell of cut wood and dirt. Sophie groped around until she found a pile of wood to sit on, took off her glasses, and dried them on her petticoat.

The last time she'd been shut up was her first day at Oak River, when Mammy had locked her into the linen room for being sassy. Then, she'd more or less deserved it—by Mammy's lights, anyway. She'd been lost and confused, fresh from the steamboat and all the rush and worry of Mr. Robert's sudden departure for France.

It was odd, that she could hardly remember what her father looked like. She did remember he loved to sing, though. She'd even sung with him, sometimes. Her father hadn't thought she was a liar and a thief. He used to take her driving down the River Road by the big white-columned plantation houses and the brick refineries, and he'd sent her a pretty dress to remember him by.

Then he'd gone to his new life and left her behind, just like he'd left his dogs.

Sophie picked up a stick, threw it as hard as she could into the darkness.

That's what she was to all her family—a pet dog. As long as she was quiet, tidy, above all obedient, they'd pat her head and give her treats. Any sign of disobedience brought immediate punishment. She was nothing but a disappointment to Old Missy now, a puppy who had turned out to be a chicken-killer but was too valuable to shoot. She wondered if Old Missy would write Mr. Robert in France to tell him what Sophie had done, what he'd answer if she did. Would he defend her? Would he wash his hands of her? Would he even care?

Would he care if she cut off her leg like poor Henry in the cane fields? Would Old Missy?

Sophie cried then, long and hard. And when she was cried out, she curled up on the dirt floor and went to sleep.

Chapter 16

Sophie was awakened by a creak and a crash and a male voice demanding to know what she was doing in the woodshed.

She sat up stiffly and squinted at the dark shape silhouetted against the door. "Mr. Akins shut me in."

The man came into the woodshed. It was America, the blacksmith. "You Sophie from up to the house, ain't you? The one who stole Miss Liza's earbobs."

"It was her brush. And I didn't steal it."

America laughed. "'Course you didn't. And I ain't seen you lying behind that there woodpile, so there ain't no reason to bar the door."

As soon as America left with his armful of wood, Sophie slipped out to the outhouse, then dipped a bucket of water from the cistern and washed her face and hands. Brushing the woodchips from the yellow calico dress, she hoped she wouldn't have to give it back now she was banished to the fields. It wasn't as nice as Mr. Robert's parting present, but she'd hate to go to church in homespun.

Canny's face popped up beside the cistern. "I hear you in deep trouble, Soph. I hear you steal Miss Liza's pearl necklace and Mr. Akins whup you bloody, but I don't believe a word."

Sophie had to laugh. "It was her hairbrush. And I didn't get whipped, only locked up in the woodshed. But I didn't steal anything. Miss Liza hid it in Old Missy's armoire."

Canny frowned. "Why she go do a thing like that?"

Sophie had been thinking about that. "Dr. Charles scolded her for throwing her shears at me, right in front of me, too. She's always hated me, especially after what Miss May said about us looking alike."

"That sure sound like Miss Liza," Canny said. "What you going to do now?"

Sophie retied her headwrap around her unraveling braids. "Old Missy sent me out to the fields."

"You can help us bring the food to the field kitchen," Canny said. "That in the fields. Come on. We doing that now."

So Sophie joined Paris and Rome and the other yard children, who were ferrying sacks of cornmeal and vegetables from the storehouse to the stable and packing them on flatbed carts with barrels of salt pork. When all was stowed, she clambered up a wheel to the high seat where Canny was sitting by a man with a face like a shelled pecan and a beard that would have put Methuselah to shame.

"This here's Uncle Italy," Canny said. "He the only man alive can make Old Thunder here mind him." She pointed at the mule, which looked almost as old as Uncle Italy, in a mulish way.

Uncle Italy laughed toothlessly. "Old Thunder don't mind me, child, not 'xactly. We been knowing each other nigh on twenty years now, and we got an understanding."

"This here's Sophie," Canny went on. "The Big House folk done took against her, so she working with me for a while."

Uncle Italy turned a rheumy eye on Sophie. "You done anything you ashamed to tell me, girl?"

"No, sir. But I'd rather not talk about it, if you don't mind."

Uncle Italy nodded and slapped the reins against Old Thunder's neck. The mule twitched its droopy ears, sighed windily, and heaved the cart out of the yard.

The sky was clear and the air warm and still between the tall, leafy stockades of ripe sugarcane. Sophie gripped the seat edge to avoid being shaken off her perch as Old Thunder heaved the cart over the rutted track. As they passed Devon Cut, a cluster of cane rats scuttled across the road. Behind them, the cane began to pitch and heave. Sophie saw a dark head appear, a dusty arm grab a stalk, a flat-bladed knife flash once, twice, three times, cutting away the long leaves, and then once again to sever the cane. A moment later, the row was open and Sophie could see clear to where two men were gathering the cut canes and piling them on a cart.

Sumpter Cut, a little farther along, was half-bare, with long leaves carpeting the earth between clusters of sharp cane stumps and groups of three and four hands moving down the unharvested rows like rats nibbling down a row of beans.

There were three field kitchens at Oak River, carefully placed with easy access to shade and fresh water. Old Italy drove to Sumpter Cut, where an old woman with a corncob pipe clamped between her teeth supervised the unloading and stowing of half the sacks in a makeshift wooden shed. Under a tree, Becky and Jane, who Sophie knew from the kitchen, stirred an iron kettle of salt pork and mush and chopped greens on a trestle table. Sophie's mouth watered at the smell. She hadn't eaten since breakfast yesterday, and she felt very empty.

Across the fields, the noon bell rang and a commotion like an ocean wave swept through the fields. Men came out of the rows, sticking their cane knives through their rope belts and wiping their faces with sweaty bandanas, to collect bowls and cups and stand in line for dinner.

The old woman set Sophie to dipping water into each hand's tin cup. One man had a gash on his arm bleeding sluggishly through the coating of sticky cane sap and dirt. Sophie soaked his headrag so he could clean it and asked him if he'd been whipped.

"Not today, sister. Sugar-cane leaf mighty sharp, cut clear to the bone if you ain't careful." He smiled at her. "Cain't say but what I'd sooner catch a whupping."

"I'd sooner catch a crawdad," said a girl behind him. "Hey, Soph. What-for you ain't drinking lemonade up to the Big House? You and Old Missy have a falling-out?"

It took a minute for Sophie to recognize Tibet. She had an inflamed cut on one cheek, and looked much older than the girl who'd talked Sophie into joining Old Betsy's funeral.

Sophie tipped water in her cup. "No, ma'am. I just thought I'd like to have me some of them good times out in the fields you're always going on about."

Tibet laughed—not hard, but enough so Sophie felt she'd said the right thing. Then she stepped aside to make room for the next thirsty field hand.

There were very few women among the cutters, but the looks they gave Sophie told her what they thought of pale-skinned house slaves playing at field work. In their place, she knew she'd feel the same.

After everyone was settled in the shade, three old men came up to the table. They were as ragged and dirty as everyone else, but their sugar-loaf hats and whips of knotted cords marked them as gang drivers. Among them, Sophie was shocked to recognize the preacher, Old Guam.

He smiled at her startled face. "I sure surprised to see you here, too, young Sophie," he said and took his dinner to where the other drivers sat, away from everybody else.

Before they started again, Canny charmed bowls of mush out of Jane for herself and Sophie and Uncle Italy. To Sophie's surprise, it was thick with pork and vegetables and clabber and filled her fuller than she'd been in weeks. Canny licked her bowl. Sophie did, too.

The remaining provisions had to be delivered to the sugarhouse. Blinded by the high walls of cane, Sophie smelled it long before she saw it: a combination of bitter wood smoke and a burned sweetness like caramel. Two plumes of gray smoke smudged the blue sky, the chimneys rose above the sugarcane, bit by bit, and then Old Thunder pulled them out of the cane and up to the door of the real heart of Oak River Plantation.

It looked like a cross between a factory and a town hall, Sophie thought, bigger than the Big House, with brick colonnades all around the first floor. At one end, women spread stalks of cane on a jointed wooden belt that ran up to the shiny metal jaws of the rollers, set high in the wall above.

Even outside, the noise of the sugarhouse was deafening. The workers eating their dinners by the kitchen tent looked even more wrung out than the cane cutters. The men were stripped to the waist and gleaming with sweat; the women's dresses clung wetly to their bodies. There wasn't much talking.

While the provisions were being unloaded, Canny grabbed Sophie's hand.

"You want to come see inside?"

Nervous of the noise and meeting Mr. Akins, Sophie hesitated.

"We got the bestest sugarhouse in the parish," Canny coaxed. "Popi the sugar boss and Poland, he tend the boiler. Ain't nobody in the parish know more about sugar than Popi and Poland."

Sophie laughed. "Well, if your pa's running the sugarhouse, of course I have to see it." And she followed Canny through the nearest arch.

A wall of heat and noise and burned-caramel smell hit her like a giant hand.

Before harvest started, Old Guam had preached about the pains of Hell. Sophie had listened, wide-eyed, as he described the scorching heat, the sullen, red-black glow of hellfire, the screeching of the devils, the moaning of the shadowy damned, and wondered how he knew so much more about hell than she'd read in the Bible. Now she knew.

The sound of her name caught her attention. "Hey, Miz Sophie! How you liking the Biggest House?"

It was Ned, waving from a platform crowded with a forest of metal pipes and tubes and huge iron cylinders.

Mr. Akins appeared, looking thunderous, and pulled Ned back among the machinery. Canny dashed through a maze of rattling wooden belts and troughs toward the platform and up the stairs. Sophie scrambled after her, catching her just in time to keep her from barging into Akins's conference with Ned and making things worse.

Judging from his voice, Mr. Akins was not happy. "You're a damn-fool," Sophie heard him say, "if you think I'm going to take your word. I read a book 'bout this here apparatus, which is more than you can do."

Somewhere out of sight, Ned spoke urgently, too soft to hear over the hissing and clanking of the vacuum evaporator. Sophie caught the words "gauge," "pressure," "Dr. Charles."

"Well, Dr. Charles ain't here. Just you remember, boy, I'm still the white man around here, or I might just forget, temporarily like, how Miz Fairchild feel 'bout the whip."

Canny stiffened. "Mist' Akins the damn-fool," she said. "Popi know that machine like he know his children."

"Is that so?" Mr. Akins face appeared, his hat pushed back to show the white crescent of his untanned forehead. "He doing better than me, if he can keep track of y'all. Which one are you? Timbuktu, maybe?"

Canny stared up at him, her mouth an "O" of terror.

"What you doing here anyways, Timbuktu?" Mr. Akins's hand was on the little whip of knotted cords tucked into his belt. Ned peered around his shoulder, white-eyed with fear. Sophie dearly wanted to run. But Ned would be whipped bloody if he interfered, sugar boss or not. And Sophie was grown-up now—fourteen years old, with her women's courses started. She licked her dry lips and said, "We just leaving, sir. Come on, Canny."

"And who in tarnation are *you*?" Mr. Akins grinned like a 'gator. "Well, if it ain't the little New Orleans octoroon that likes silver hairbrushes. What you doing, minding the picanninies?" Reaching past Canny, he grabbed Sophie's upper arm and squeezed it painfully. "Soft as cotton. Well, don't you fret none. I got a nice easy job all ready for you."

Mr. Akins hustled Sophie off the platform and back toward the front of the sugarhouse, where a wooden trough funneled the raw cane juice down from the grinders into a waist-high iron vat. He yanked a long-handled rake from a woman's startled hands and thrust it at Sophie.

"That there," he said, pointing to a mat of fiber and chewed cane leaves, "is debris. Debris clogs the strainer there." He pointed to a screen of wire mesh tacked across the mouth of a second trough. "Your job is to rake the debris out of the vat and dump it in this basket here. You got that?"

As sugarhouse jobs went, it wasn't as hard as most. But the rake was heavy, the vat too high, and the debris awkward to shift. After a while, Sophie's head was reeling with heat and noise. But when she sat down, a woman with a big stick and a gang-driver's hat appeared and whacked her shins. "Get up, girl! That juice spill over, I take it out your yeller hide."

Painfully, Sophie stood and raked a wad of debris from the strainer.

If it hadn't been for Canny, she'd never have made it through the shift. Canny brought her water and a box to stand on and emptied the basket of debris and entertained her with tidbits of gossip and news.

"George say Flanders sweet on Betsy McCormick. Momi sure going to be happy to hear *that*. Doucette maybe get them vaporators, too, if Oak River harvest be good."

By the time the bell rang at four for the end of the shift, they were both exhausted. Sophie could hardly lift the rake, and her legs were so stiff, Poland had to steady her until she could walk. He swung Canny, protesting halfheartedly, up on his shoulders, and the three of them joined the other slaves heading back to the quarters.

It was a long walk. Everybody was mostly too tired to talk, but when somebody up front began to sing, Poland, who had a nice voice and liked to exercise it, joined in.

I hold my brother with a trembling hand.
The Lord will bless my soul.

All around, voices took up the melody, high and low, rich and cracked, a little bubble of music moving through the cane brakes.

Wrestle on, Jacob, day is a-breaking.
Wrestle on, Jacob, oh, he would not let him go!

The singing kept everybody going until they reached the Quarters, then faded out as they scattered to their cabins. Sophie stumbled up the porch steps behind Poland and Canny, so weary she didn't even think about whether she was welcome.

Delia Sherman

To her joy, Africa was there, ladling something hot and fragrant into wooden bowls.

"You the talk of the Quarters, Sophie," Africa said. "I can't even call to mind all the stories I hear about you today. When Uncle Italy tell me you with Canny, though, I pretty sure you show up here sooner or later." She filled a bowl, shoved it toward Sophie. "Eat up. Then get out of that there fancy calico and wash yourself. Until all this foolishness blow over, you can sleep with Canny. I got a dress you can wear, too."

Before Sophie could thank her, she'd put on her shawl and left to cook Old Missy's supper.

Sitting between Poland and Canny, Sophie fell on the steaming gumbo as if she hadn't eaten in a week, then rinsed her face and hands in a bucket on the porch and stumbled off to bed.

When the plantation bell rang at dawn for the morning shift, Sophie ached in every inch of her body, and she'd started to bleed again. She thought she'd die. But she didn't.

She didn't die the next day, either. Or the day after that.

Since Old Missy prided herself on being enlightened and humane, children under fifteen only had to work one eight-hour shift instead of two. Sophie was on the day shift, eight in the morning until four in the afternoon, after which she helped Canny tend the garden and the cabin and get supper for the menfolks when Africa couldn't get away.

After a couple of weeks raking debris, Mr. Akins put Sophie with the women who skimmed the scum off the clarifying vat. It was hard work, and the smell of the quicklime used to bring the impurities to the surface of the cane juice stung her eyes. But Phronsie and Betty were friendly, and sang as they worked, which made the time go faster.

172

Sometimes Sophie thought of begging Old Missy to whip her if she wanted to, as long as she'd let Sophie back into the Big House world of nice clothes and sleeping warm and dry. But that's not the way things worked. Sophie had been sent to the fields, and in the fields she'd stay until somebody remembered to bring her back out again.

Chapter 17

October passed slowly. Sometimes it rained, sometimes it didn't. In the Quarters, the folks too old to work in the fields watched the caterpillars and the birds for hints of winter, even though not even the oldest could remember a killing frost before mid-November. Sophie washed the yellow calico and hung it on a peg in the back room under Canny's blue gingham. It was hard to believe she'd ever worn that dress, with its skimpy skirt and short sleeves. Whatever could Mama have been thinking of, sending her off to Oak River dressed like a little girl?

Poland and Flanders stopped complaining about her gumbo, which might have meant that her cooking was getting better, or just that they were getting used to it. She learned the words to "Wrestle on, Jacob" from Betty, who'd grown up in Virginia, and some lively French songs from Phronsie. Her life in the Big House was starting to feel almost as much of a dream as New Orleans.

One morning, she was leaning on her paddle waiting for the scum to rise, singing softly to herself, when she heard a pop like a giant cork coming out of a bottle, followed by a deafening metallic clanging and screams like hogs being slaughtered.

"Jesus have mercy!" cried Phronsie. "The boiler's bust!" Dropping her paddle, she ran out of the sugarhouse at the same time that Betty, screaming "George!," was running for the platform. A grim-faced Young Guam flew past Sophie like the devil was after him and out into the yard, where she heard him yelling for a mule.

Something terrible had happened.

A man limped past, leaning on the shoulder of the women's gang-driver. "Please Lord he find Dr. Charles right quick."

"What for?" The gang-driver shifted her corncob pipe from one side of her mouth to the other. "Burns like that, you lives or you dies according to the Lord's will."

Sophie's knees felt rubbery and her stomach hollow and cold. The screaming made her want to run away like Phronsie, but she followed Betty instead, because one of those screams might be Ned or Poland or Flanders. If it was, she didn't know what she could do. But she had to know.

It was the near boiler that had blown. As she reached the platform, Sophie could see shiny brown sludge bubbling slowly out of a big hole in the side. She pushed and wriggled into the shouting, shifting crowd of workers, broke through into a little clear space. Six bodies lay in a row, more or less covered with hot cane juice. The air was sickly with the stench of scorched sugar.

One of them was clearly dead. Feeling sick, Sophie looked away from his raw, ruined body as soon as she made sure he wasn't anybody she knew.

And then she saw that the sixth victim of the explosion was Canny.

Sophie knelt down beside her. The blouse over her shoulder and chest glistened with syrup; her throat and neck were blistered and raw.

Sophie touched her hand gently. "Canny? Can you hear me?"

"Hurts," Canny sobbed without opening her eyes. "Momi! I wants Momi. Hurts *so* bad!"

Sophie swallowed hard. "Hold on, Canny. Dr. Charles is coming."

Behind her, one of the men was moaning "Lord Jesus have mercy on my soul, have mercy on my soul" in a soft, hoarse whisper. Canny clutched Sophie's hand as folk came and went around them, covering the dead with sacking, bringing cold water for the living, cleaning up, getting on with it.

Someone leaned over Sophie's shoulder. Looking up from Canny, she saw Ned, his face grim under a coating of soot and dirt.

He gave her shoulder a reassuring squeeze. "Poland and me, we the lucky ones today. You stay by my Canny, hear?"

Sophie nodded, and he was gone.

Time passed. Canny drowsed, waking to moan for water. Sophie wetted her lips with a cloth and tried to distract her with a rather incoherent story about a girl and her grandmother and a wolf. Finally, she heard Dr. Charles's voice asking how many had been hurt and what was being done and where was the overseer?

Ned answered. "We gots everything shut down, sir. I don't know where Mist' Akins be. Two men is dead and three hurt bad. And my little girl. Canada."

Dr. Charles knelt by the last man, touched his throat, frowned. "Get a board." He glanced down the row of wounded. "Four boards. We have to get them to the hospital quick as we can. There's an empty cane wagon out there. Hitch up the mules and load these men, and the child." He noticed Sophie. "What are you doing here, Sophie?"

"Looking out for Canny, sir."

Dr. Charles grimaced. "You'd better stay with her, then. Last thing I need's a child crying for her mammy."

Loading the wounded into the cane wagon was a nightmare. The men screamed as they were lifted onto the boards.

Canny, thankfully, fainted, or Sophie didn't think she could have borne it. And it had started to rain, a chill, penetrating rain that dripped off the brim of Dr. Charles's black hat and soaked through Sophie's skirts. As the wagon lurched through the mud, Sophie did what she could to keep the rain off Canny's face and herself from panicking. Canny needed her, and that was what was important. Dr. Charles said she was a brave, sensible girl and he'd tell Mrs. Fairchild so. Sophie hardly heard him. Only Canny's hand was real, and her burned chest faintly rising and falling.

By the time they reached the Quarters, the praying man had died. Sophie wondered distantly why she wasn't having hysterics, decided not to look a gift horse in the mouth. The wagon reached the Quarters, and Dr. Charles shouted out for someone to come help, bringing off-shift hands out of their cabins, dragging on their clothes. When the wagon stopped at the hospital, they lifted the wounded with anxious tenderness and carried them inside.

Sophie rubbed her hand, which had gone all pins and needles, and followed them.

Inside, Dr. Charles threw off his coat and rolled up his sleeves, barking orders. In next to no time, the burned men were on the beds and everyone had cleared out except for Dr. Charles's assistant Aunt Cissie, two field hands called Greece and Tom—and Sophie.

Canny moaned. Her eyelids fluttered, then went still again.

"Dr. Charles." Sophie could hardly hear herself, her voice was so pinched. She swallowed and tried again. "Dr. Charles?"

Dr. Charles, examining one of the burned men, grunted absently.

"Dr. Charles, I think Canny's dying."

Dr. Charles took Canny's wrist between his fingers, then lifted her eyelids with his thumb and tilted her chin a little to look at the burns on her throat. The movement burst some of the blisters; a thin, clear fluid ran down and stained the sheet.

"Pulse tumultuous but strong," he said. "Burns not particularly extensive. Nothing to worry about. She'll do until I've seen to the men."

"But, Dr. Charles. . ."

"If you won't hush, you'll have to leave."

Sophie watched impatiently while the two men were laid in long tin baths full of cold water and the burned clothes cut from their bodies. After a while, Greece and Tom lifted them out onto wet cotton sheets, which they folded around them while Aunt Cissie spread ointment on long strips of linen.

Sophie said, "What about Canny, sir?"

Dr. Charles had clearly forgotten she was there. "What? Oh, yes. The little girl. I'll get to her."

Anger rose hot in Sophie's chest, but she kept silent while Dr. Charles and his assistants cocooned the men in linen strips. Little girls just weren't worth as much as grown field hands. And it was true that Canny wasn't as badly burned as the others. But it was hard to bear.

"Momi," Canny muttered. "I wants Momi."

Sophie gave her hand a squeeze and got up. "Dr. Charles, sir, I'm going to go get Africa now. She needs to know Canny's hurt."

Without waiting for permission, Sophie left the hospital and ran for the yard, stumbling over chickens and stones she couldn't see for the rain on her glasses. The kitchen seemed farther away than she remembered, or maybe that was just her wet skirts tangling around her legs and the mud all slippery underfoot and the panic that Canny might die before Africa could get to her.

When she reached the kitchen, she threw open the door. "Africa!" she panted. "Come quick! Canny's hurt!"

Africa didn't waste any time on questions, just handed her spoon to China, snatched her shawl from its hook, and marched Sophie straight back across the yard without even taking off her apron.

As they walked, Sophie explained about the explosion as best she could. "Canny's neck and chest are burned, and I think her stomach, too. Little places on her face and legs." Despite her best efforts, Sophie's voice broke. "She hurts real bad."

"Huh," said Africa and walked faster. "Anybody else hurt?"

"Two men died. But Ned's fine."

"And Poland?"

"I didn't see him."

"Huh."

At the Quarters, Africa ran up to the cabin next to hers and banged on the door. "Rhodes! Rhodes! Sorry to wake you, but I need your menfolk's help. My baby's been hurt."

The door opened, and Rhodes appeared, followed by two young men. Blinking and yawning, they followed Africa to the hospital and waited on the porch while she and Sophie went inside.

"Afternoon, Dr. Charles," Africa said brightly. "I hear you got a 'mergency on your hands. May be I can help you out. Pete, Ireland"—she called over her shoulder—"pick up that sheet and tote my Canny home." She turned to Dr. Charles. "It was a Christian thing you did, sending for me, Dr. Charles. A hurt child is best with her own ma, and you got enough on your hands with them men to tend. With your permission, China can see to the cooking for a spell. China's a real good cook. I trained her myself."

179

By the look of him, Dr. Charles was thinking fast. "As long as you keep an eye on these men as well. They're going to take a lot of nursing, and Aunt Cissie can't do it all herself."

"Of course, sir." Africa bobbed a grateful curtsey and hurried off.

Sophie was slipping out the door when Dr. Charles's eye fell on her. "Sophie," he called sternly. "Africa's leave of absence doesn't extend to you. We need every hand at the sugarhouse. You hear me, girl?"

"Yes, sir," said Sophie, and ran out of the hospital straight to Africa's cabin.

There wasn't any doubt in her mind that Africa needed her help more than Mr. Akins did. Mr. Akins had more important things to think about than Sophie. Still, she'd probably blown her chance of going back to the Big House as sky-high as the vacuum evaporator. And she didn't care one bit.

Canny's burns might not have been extensive, but they were deep.

As soon as she got her home, Africa dosed her with a spoonful of dark liquid from an earthenware bottle, wrapped her in a sheet soaked with water into which she'd rubbed basil and wild watercress, then sat singing over her softly. Sophie fetched jars and rags and chopped ham and okra to add to the gumbo and watched out for Saxony, who was just beginning to stagger around and get into things.

At the end of the afternoon shift, Flanders returned from the fields with the news that Ned and Poland wouldn't be coming home until tomorrow, if then. When he'd sluiced off his crust of cane sap and dust, he knelt beside his sister's pallet and stroked her hand.

Africa touched his shoulder. "Don't go weeping before there's a call for tears," she said. "Come eat your supper and don't lose hope." She gave her son's shoulder a shake. "Yemaya ain't fixing to let our Canny die."

Next morning, the sugarhouse was still like a kicked anthill, with everyone running every which-way, doing whatever came to hand to clean up the mess. Sophie took a twig broom and set to work sweeping little bits of metal and rubber, cane dust and leaves out into the yard. With the crushers still and the steam boilers cold, the hum of voices was like cicadas in July.

"Machine ruint anyways," said a man scraping hardened syrup from the floor. "All burnt to hell and gone."

The man working beside him flashed a nervous glance over his shoulder. "Hush you mouth. Devil always listening when you talk 'bout sin."

"I ain't saying whose fault it was."

"Guilty man think everybody know where the pig hid."

The first man shrugged and scraped harder. Sophie coaxed a pile of dark amber chips into the yard, came back in for more. Somebody had lit a row of lanterns up on the platform. By their light, she saw Dr. Charles, Ned, and Mr. Akins standing in a row in front of the leaking cylinder. With their legs apart, their arms folded, and their heads to one side, they looked so much alike Sophie would have laughed, if she'd had the heart.

She moved a little closer to listen.

Dr. Charles unfolded his arms. "How long do you reckon it'll take to fix, Ned?"

"Two-three day to patch it, sir, another day to check them pipes and all—I ain't so sure 'bout the valve. It *look* fine—"

Delia Sherman

"It *is* fine," Mr. Akins interrupted. "There warn't nothing wrong with it in the first place. Just a little clog, and I already done cleaned that out."

"Ned, you're the sugar boss. What do you think?"

"Might do if we lowers the pressure some. But a mended axle ain't never so strong as a new one."

"There's nothing wrong with this one, I tell you." Mr. Akins locked eyes with Dr. Charles, then looked away. "Anyway, a new one will take weeks to come from Chicago, if it comes at all. We can't afford to shut down for weeks."

Dr. Charles rubbed his hand over his hair. "We can't afford to lose more men, either. I'll have to talk it over with Mrs. Fairchild, but I suspect we'll decide to use the old one—at a lower pressure—until a new one arrives. And resign ourselves to a smaller yield. In the meantime, we'd better check the other pans and the steam coils and all the pipes and valves. I don't want any more clogged pressure valves."

Mr. Akins assured him that the whole apparatus had been taken apart and checked under his own eye overnight.

"When did you last sleep?" asked Dr. Charles. "Never mind answering, I can see you haven't been off your feet all night. Go to bed, man. Ned and I will see to what needs to be done." And he turned his back on Mr. Akins.

Sophie, along with everyone else within reasonable earshot, had been listening to this conversation in a state of semi-suspended animation. As Dr. Charles was dismissing Mr. Akins, they edged quietly away. They exchanged glances, though, glances that said as clear as words, Mr. Akins in big trouble, Dr. Charles mad as a hornet, Oak River Plantation coming on hard times, maybe we get sold off to a worse master, what we going to do?

Chapter 18

Two weeks after the explosion, things were back as close to normal as they were going to get. Dr. Charles had fired the boilers up again, and the grinding was limping along, after a fashion. One of the men in the hospital had died, but the other, a man called Cuffee, looked like he was going to get better.

Under Africa's care, Canny was starting to heal. The cabin always smelled faintly of the basil and rosemary she put into the cool baths she gave her, and of the rum and tobacco she poured into bowls set under the designs she'd drawn by the door and the hearth.

As soon as she washed off the sugarhouse stink, Sophie went to sit with Canny while Africa went to tend Cuffee. On her pillow lay a doll Africa had sewn out of burlap stuffed with black moss. It was dressed in blue calico and had a string of cowries hung around its neck. Canny called it Yemaya, and said the design by the hearth, the one with the stars and the little crosses, was Yemaya's vévé. When Sophie told Canny stories about New Orleans—stories she didn't even believe anymore—sometimes she thought the doll was looking at her.

Along about nightfall, Ned and Poland finally came home. Since Africa was bathing Canny, Sophie dished up bowls of the everlasting gumbo while Poland, tired as he was, bounced Saxony on his foot and sang.

Howdy my brethren, How d'ye do
Since I been in the land
I do mighty poor, but I thank the Lord sure
Since I been in the land
Oh, yes! Oh, yes! Since I been in the Land!

When he stopped, Saxony crowed and bounced on his foot to let him know she'd like him to do it again. Poland groaned. Sophie grabbed the baby under the arms and swooped her through the air, making buzzing noises. Saxony squealed happily and squeezed the air with her plump hands. Ned laughed and told her to stop her foolishness. Even Africa smiled.

"I sure be glad you-all having such a fine time," said Antigua, "with my little sister knocking on death's door."

Sophie swung Saxony down onto her hip. Saxony, balked of her game, yelled angrily. Antigua crossed the cabin, snatched the baby from Sophie's arms, rested her cheek on her wooly head, and sobbed.

Africa took Saxony and handed her, still yelling, to her father. "Ned, see if you can quiet this one before she frets Canny. I declare, there's nothing like girl children for giving a mother gray hairs." And she gathered her oldest daughter into her arms.

By the time Antigua's sobs had trailed off, the baby was gnawing peacefully on a piece of sugarcane and Sophie was standing as far out of the light as she could, hoping she wouldn't get sent away.

"Now you got that out of your system," said Africa, "you want to say what's wrong?"

Antigua shrugged her mother's arm away. "Ain't nothing talking can fix. I better go now."

"Go?" Ned asked. "You just got here. Stay, eat supper with us."

"Miss Liza be wanting me," muttered Antigua. "I don't get back right smart, she pitch a fit for sure."

"Then what you come all the way down here for? You needing a tonic?"

"No."

Africa took her daughter's face in her hand and looked at her steadily. Antigua jerked her head away. Africa said, "You're in some kind of big trouble."

"No, no trouble." Antigua avoided her mother's eyes. "Not if I gets back right smart. Just fretting over Canny getting hurt. And Miss Liza's sore as a 'gator in a trap these days."

Sophie knew she was lying. They all knew. When Miss Liza was being fractious, Antigua was more likely to make a funny story out of it than cry. Sophie hadn't seen Antigua cry since she'd found her in the Oak Cottage storeroom with . . .

"Beau Waters!" Sophie exclaimed.

Antigua went still as a hunted rabbit.

Ned turned to Sophie. "What about Mr. Beau?"

"Nothing, Pa," Antigua said. "Sophie just working her mouth. I ain't had no truck with Mr. Beau Waters."

Sophie watched Antigua twisting up her apron, heard the hopeless, flat tone of her voice, and decided the time for secrets was past. "But he had truck with you. I saw him, remember? In the storeroom at Oak Cottage?" She turned to Africa. "He was trying to kiss her."

Antigua turned on her furiously. "You just hush you mouth, Sophie, or on my Bible oath, you be sorry you's ever borned!"

"You hush your own mouth, girl." Sophie had never heard Ned sound so stern. "I wants to hear what Soph got to say."

"Nothing! She don't know nothing, telling tales to look important, Miss High-and-Mighty yellow bastard!"

"Antigua!" Africa shot her daughter an old-fashioned look. "Shame on you. What you thinking of, talking ugly like that!"

"Maybe it ugly, but it true," Antigua protested. "She a white man's bastard, and her mother nothing more than a whore, like Jezebel in the Bible that the dogs ate. I go drown myself in the bayou before I birth a white man's child." And she broke down into sobs again.

Africa turned to Sophie. "Well, Sophie. Maybe it time to hear the whole story."

Sophie told them everything she could remember about what had happened in the Oak Cottage storeroom, riding-crop and all. "He got back at me by saying he'd seen me at Oak Cottage that Monday." She turned to Antigua, who was glowering at her. "I'm so sorry. I guess I just made everything worse by hitting him. I'm sorry about breaking my promise, too. But I had to tell."

Africa and Ned exchanged a long look. "You did right, sugar," Africa said. "You did right to whup that Beaufort Waters, and you did right to tell us about it. There's some things shouldn't be kept secret." She hugged her daughter. "You come out back with me, baby, away from all the menfolks. We going to have a little talk." And she led her out into the night.

In the silence that followed, Ned and Flanders sat at the table and tucked into their gumbo. Sophie, who wasn't feeling hungry, ladled out a bowl and took it into the back room in case the noise had wakened Canny.

It had. "What Anti creating about?" she wanted to know. "And where Momi? I wants Momi. She ain't sung over me yet."

"Your Momi's seeing after Anti now, but she'll be in directly. Now, you eat your gumbo, and I'll tell you a story."

"'Bout Bouki and Compair Fox?"

"You know those stories better than I do. This is a brand-new one, just for you. Once upon a time, there were three bears who lived in the swamp . . ."

The story flowed out of her just like she was remembering it. By the time Miss Goldy had jumped out the window of Massa Bear's Big House, Sophie had spooned most of the gumbo into Canny's mouth. She brought her some water and sang to her until she slept, then slipped into the front room to find Flanders darning socks and Ned sitting by the fire with his corncob pipe, his face ashen with weariness.

Ned looked up. "She's asleep," said Sophie. "Will Antigua be all right?"

"I surely don't know, honey," Ned said heavily. "It in the Lord's hands now."

Sophie thought that the Lord might have taken an interest sooner, maybe before Beau Waters had a chance to be born. But all she said was "Amen" and went to rake ashes over the fire to bank it down for the night.

"Leave it, Sophie," said Africa from the front door. "Time to sleep. You, too, Flanders. Ned, we got us some talking to do before the shift bell ring."

Antigua was with her, miserable and red-eyed. Sophie looked from her to Africa and Ned's carved-wood expressions.

"I ain't going to sleep," Flanders said.

"Me, neither," said Sophie. "I want to help."

Africa frowned. "You-all can help by not being a nuisance."

"If Antigua's going to run away," said Sophie, "she's going to need help."

"I ain't heard nobody saying nothing 'bout running away," Africa said.

"It's the only thing she can do," said Flanders.

Delia Sherman

"Besides," Sophie added, "she's always wanted to."

"Ain't you the wise woman?" said Antigua, but she no longer sounded furious, just tired half to death. "Let them stay, Momi. It ain't no use nohow. If I dies in the bayou or I dies running North, at least I be shut of Mr. Beaufort Waters."

"Don't talk like that," said Ned. "Ain't nobody going to die. You gots to run, I sees that. But you ain't going to get far if'n you don't have a plan. Sit down, now, and we talk about it."

He sat in his chair by the fire. Everybody else took up their usual stools around the table, except Antigua, who paced like she couldn't bear to be still.

"I ain't got time to talk," she said. "If'n he even look at me again, I kill him dead."

She meant it, and Sophie didn't blame her.

Africa fetched tin cups from the mantel and the coffee pot from hearth. "Here, baby," she said, handing Antigua a fragrant cup. "Drink this. We'll think of something."

"The trick to running away," said Ned thoughtfully, "is you don't run right off. You hides somewheres on the plantation until they tired of looking for you close to home, turned they eyes North—maybe a month, maybe more."

"She don't leave the plantation, how you going to keep the dogs sniffing her out in time for a whupping before sunset?" Flanders asked.

"I gots a plan for that," said Ned. "Somebody take a pair of the runaway's britches or some such and drag it towards the swamp, keeping to the trees like a runaway would. When he come to the water, he wade upstream a ways and drop the britches. Meantime, runaway climb on somebody back and ride to the hiding place so he don't leave no scent. Dogs follows the britches to the swamp, maybe they finds them and maybe not. But they sure as shooting don't find the runaway."

Africa's face was a study. "You got it all figured out, sure enough, and I'd never of thought of it, not if I lived to be old as Methuselah. Flandy can use Anti's petticoat to set the trail, and you can carry her to this hiding place of yours. Where *was* you figuring to hide, Ned, when you up and run off from us?"

Ned shook his head. "Well, that the fly in the ointment, sure enough. There ain't nowhere on this whole plantation one man could hide for more than a day or two, let alone all six of us."

As Africa and Ned smiled at each other, Sophie remembered last summer, when Old Missy had sent her down to the yard. "I know one," she said.

Four sets of worried eyes turned to her. Antigua jumped up and grabbed her arm. "What you talking 'bout, girl?"

"A hidey-hole, under the summerhouse in the maze. There's a way in behind the camellia." Sophie looked from one face to the other. "You really don't know about it?"

Antigua laughed. "We surely don't. Black folks ain't allowed in that maze, except the gardeners—and one nosey, high-yellow house slave, seemingly."

"Who got her wits about her," Flanders said.

Ned scratched his chin doubtfully. "This hidey-hole—you sure nobody know about it 'cept you?"

Sophie considered. "Well, the mattress is rotted out and the lantern's all rusted, so I guess it's been a while since anybody used it. And the hole is real well hidden."

Africa shook her head. "Too risky. The gardeners probably know, and Old Hurley, he's real tight with Old Missy. Old Hurley hears Antigua's disappeared, he tell everything he knows, sure as Sunday morning."

"Old Hurley can't hardly remember his own name no more," Ned said. "We safe enough." He touched Africa's hand.

"The summerhouse Antigua's best chance, Africa. I say we take it."

Africa closed her eyes a moment, then nodded briskly. "Then we better get going. First bell going to ring soon, and if you ain't in the sugarhouse by second bell, the fat be in the fire for sure."

Once the decision was made, things started to move very quickly. Antigua took off her petticoat and gave it to Flanders, who disappeared with it. Africa bundled food and water into a blanket, thrust it into Sophie's arms, and hugged Antigua hard. And then they were out in the chill, clear night.

The moon was up, but somewhere less than half-full. Ned wouldn't risk a lantern, so they stumbled along in the half light, with Antigua riding pick-a-back on Ned and Sophie following close behind, hugging her bundle and trying not to make a noise.

The Big House was dark and massively asleep, the gardens full of tricky shadows. As the trio crossed the field, the plantation bell tolled mournfully to wake the midnight shift. Ned had thirty minutes, at the most, to get to the sugarhouse. They covered the last few feet at a stumbling run.

Even knowing the maze as well as she did, Sophie had trouble finding her way. She was nervous, and the maze looked strange in the half dark, the white stones hard to see in the shadows of the hedges. Antigua began to mutter: "We's lost. I knowed it. The only place you leading us be grief and woe," until Ned told her to hush up.

Three turns later, they reached the garden.

"The opening's in the foundation of the summerhouse," Sophie whispered as she led them across the shell paths. "Watch out you don't fall, Antigua—the hole's pretty near the edge.

There's a bucket in the corner. And be careful crawling in—you don't want to break any branches."

Antigua's only answer was a disgusted "Huh." But her cheeks glistened wet in the moonlight.

Ned took off for the sugarhouse at a dead run, but Sophie plodded back to the Quarters, keeping to the shadows in case anybody might be looking. When she got to the cabin, Flanders was shoveling down a second bowl of gumbo and Africa was hanging a pair of britches, very wet from the knees down, in front of the fire to dry.

"Well?"

Sophie pulled up her skirt to warm her frozen legs. "I'm pretty sure nobody saw us. She's safe for the time being. But we cut it mighty close."

"Ned can move fast when he have to." Africa sighed. "Flandy, Sophie, you best go to sleep now. Morning shift come mighty early."

Curled on her pallet, Sophie tried to follow Africa's advice without success. All she could think about was Antigua under the summerhouse, shivering in the dark on the rotted mattress, listening for dogs. How long would she have to stay there before she could slip away safely? Two weeks? Four? If it rained, would she get flooded out? Catch her death in the cold? And when she did leave, where would she go? Sophie couldn't see Antigua, somehow, making her way through the swamps alone, steering north by the stars.

These thoughts slid into a dream of Antigua sitting in Miss Tucker's eighth-grade American History class, bright as a parrot in her sprigged dress and her bright tignon. She was telling Miss Tucker that the Underground Railway had the most comfortable seats she'd ever sat in, and all the free hot chocolate you could drink. And then the bell rang for the end of class and

Delia Sherman

the dream vanished as Sophie woke to the plantation bell telling the morning shift that it was dawn and time to get up and make sugar.

"You don't know nothing about Antigua," Africa told Sophie. "Anyone ask, she came and ate supper with us and went back to Miss Liza. She came to see how Canny was keeping, and that's all, you hear?"

Chapter 19

The next day was endless. Filtered through the fog of her exhaustion, nothing seemed quite real to Sophie—not the long walk through the half-harvested cane brakes, not the chill, damp wind that cut through her dress, or the sudden furnace heat of the sugarhouse. Not even Mr. Akins, who grabbed her shoulder while she was doggedly skimming the blanket and shouted, "Where's Antigua at, wench?"

Sophie jumped. "Don't know, Mist' Akins, sir," she said in her best field-hand voice. "Ain't she over to Oak Cottage?"

"No, she ain't, as you know just fine. She's run away."

Sophie gaped at him. "She has? Antigua? Whoo-ee. Africa going to create when she hear that. You sure, Mist' Akins?"

He thrust her from him with a snort of disgust and strode back toward the platform, shouting to Ned that Dr. Charles wanted to talk to him. A little while later, she saw Mr. Akins hustling Ned out of the sugarhouse and scowling like a mad bull. Despite the heat, Sophie shivered. What was going to happen to Ned? To Africa? To Flanders and Poland? What was going to happen to Antigua, waiting alone under the summerhouse with nothing to do but think about getting caught?

Betty's wide dark face appeared beside her. "Drink this, child." She pressed a dipper into Sophie's hands. Sweet, cool water trickled into her mouth, and the buzzing in her ears faded a little.

"There be grief and trouble over to Africa's," Betty said sympathetically. "Ain't nobody run away from Oak River since Old Massa day. Bad times is coming. I can smell it."

When Sophie got back from her shift that afternoon, the door was shut, and the homespun curtains drawn tight over the windows. Something was wrong.

Sophie slipped through the gate and around the cabin to the cistern, turned the wooden bucket bottom side up, and stood on it to listen at the window. She heard Africa, speaking softer than usual and slower—her white-folks voice. And then Mr. Akins, harsh as a steam engine.

"Won't do them no harm to set in the smokehouse for a day or three," he said. "Might even do some good, if they tell me where that blamed girl of yours has got to."

"They can't tell what they don't know, Mr. Akins."

"They know. And so do you. Listen here, wench. Miz Fairchild wants that girl found. She leave it to me, I'd whip all you lying niggers till you tell me where she's at. But Miz Fairchild, she won't hear of it, and Dr. Charles seem to think nobody can't run that 'vaporator well as Ned. So I've locked your menfolks in with the bacon to smoke it out of 'em. Now I'm telling you what I told them. It'll be easier on your girl if she give herself up than if the dogs find her."

Heavy boots clomped toward the door. Sophie jumped off the bucket and crouched behind the cistern until Mr. Akins was gone, then ran into the cabin where Africa was in Ned's chair with her apron up to her face.

Sophie knelt down and put her arms around her. "Mr. Akins is hateful. I'm surprised Old Missy puts up with him."

Africa wiped her eyes. "Mr. Akins ain't nothing but Old Missy's mean dog. He bite folks so she can keep her name as a kind mistress." She shook her head. "Don't mind what I say, sugar. I'm just thinking on my poor baby all alone in the cold and the dark. And my man and my boys in the smokehouse. I don't know where to turn, and that's the truth." She sucked her lips against her teeth to still them.

"Why don't I go see Antigua tonight?" Sophie said eagerly. "I can take her candles and some food."

Africa put an arm around Sophie's shoulders. "You're sure enough the best one to go when the time comes. But Mr. Akins is likely to keep a watch on us tonight." She gave her a quick squeeze. "Don't look so sad. Antigua knows it got to get worse before it get better. It won't help her if we lose heart. Go and see if Canny's awake."

Canny was not only awake, but feverish. Africa gave her a dose of willow bark and prepared her herbal bath. As she sponged Canny's burns, the cabin was quiet except for her soft chanting. Sophie sat on the floor by the fire with the baby asleep on her lap, watching the light dance on the stars in Yemaya's vévé and feeling oddly peaceful.

After a while, Africa came out of the back room and took the lid off the iron pot. "Put the baby down, sugar, and go pull me some okra and a handful of peas. This gumbo's thinner than Uncle Germany's hair."

Dark was closing in earlier every night, and the air was frosty. It was the near the end of November—almost Thanksgiving, Sophie thought. Though that didn't mean they'd get a feast, or even a day of rest. Grinding season didn't stop for anything.

Delia Sherman

As Sophie moved between the plants, searching for what Africa wanted by feel, her skirts brushed against the herbs planted everywhere, releasing their sharp or dusty or green scents into the damp air. Sophie touched the *gris-gris* bag around her neck. For some time, she'd been wanting to ask Africa about the vévés, the doll, the chanting, to find out more about the old man and the queen she'd dreamed of while she was sick. But Africa had been busy or she had been too tired, and somehow the questions had never been asked.

Cradling her harvest in her apron, Sophie ran back inside. "Africa, I need to ask you something. Can you tell me about Papa Legba and Yemaya?"

Africa looked up from chopping onions, eyes wide with surprise. "Tell you what, sugar? Seeing as how they take such a particular interest in you, I thought for sure your mama must be a *voodooienne*, teach you the mysteries of the Orishas before you could walk."

Sophie had to laugh. "Mama thinks voodoo is superstitious nonsense."

"You mama's a mighty foolish woman, then. What do you think?"

"I don't know," Sophie said. "I thought I saw somebody when I was sick, but it I guess it could have been a dream. Who is Yemaya, Africa?"

Africa studied Sophie's face intently. "Yes," she said. "It's right that you know. Yemaya is the mother of waters, whose children are as many as the fish in the sea."

"And the old man in the hat?"

"Papa Legba stand at the crossroads. He the master of doorways and choices and time. My mawmaw told me once, 'Papa Legba throw the rock tomorrow that kill the chicken yesterday.'"

196

A memory niggled at Sophie's mind: something about time and railway stations and a strange creature that looked like a possum. Africa moved to the fire, and the memory slipped away.

"This house under Yemaya's protection," Africa said, nodding at the pattern on the wall. "And that vévé the sign of her blessing."

"So why do you have *her*?" Sophie pointed to the colored print of the Virgin Mary that was nailed up over the mantel.

"Think about it like this," Africa said. "White folks call my daughter Canada, you call her Canny. Yemaya whispered me a name for her when she was born. You tell me. Which one is her right name?"

This made sense to Sophie, as much sense as the Father, the Son, and the Holy Ghost did, anyway. "What about the doll, the one you made for Canny? Is that Yemaya, too?"

"A little bit of her," Africa said. "Enough to bring her eye on Canny, give her strength to heal."

Sophie thought for a moment. "Back home in New Orleans, they have dolls like her. They're supposed to bring your enemies bad luck. Is there a doll you can make for Mr. Akins so he'll break his leg or something and can't go hunting for Antigua?"

Africa whirled on her with a look of fury. "Shame on you," she said sternly. "I don't have no truck with that kind of left-handed curse working, and I ain't studying to begin now. My hands are clean."

"I'm sorry," Sophie said humbly. "I just thought—"

"Well, you stop thinking, you hear?" Africa shook her head and went back to her cooking. "Hoodoo don't hardly work on white folks anyhow. The old gods are far from home, with lots of folks calling on them for help. My great-great-granny Omi Saide, she was a priestess in Yorubaland. She had the power to know the future, to kill with a thought, to heal, to bring the rains. Even so, the slavers chained her and brought her in a ship to New Orleans, where Old Massa's granpa buy her and change her own name to Africa. My mawmaw, she say Yemaya told Omi Saide it was so she could take care of her people who went before her."

When the peas were soft and the okra and onions dissolved, Africa and Sophie took their bowls into the back room to keep Canny company. Then Africa put Saxony to bed and tended Canny while Sophie washed up. By the time she was finished, the first bell was ringing for the night shift.

Africa came out of the back room with a bundle of stained bandages. "Time to sleep now, sugar. I'm going to set up for a spell, see if there's something the Orishas can do to get my menfolk out of that smokehouse."

As Sophie lay the back room, she heard Africa chanting softly. And then she slept and her dreams were laced with the smell of tobacco and herbs and rum and the rush and beat of the sea.

Next morning, it was raining hard. It drenched her on her walk to the sugarhouse and again going home, a chilly, soaking rain that washed great ruts in the dirt roads and half blinded the hands cutting cane. Between the explosion and the weather, Dr. Charles decided this was no time to lose the work of three strong hands. So Mr. Akins had to let Ned and his sons out of the smokehouse, and the dogs couldn't pick up Antigua's scent, even if anybody could be spared to look for her.

The news wasn't all good. Ned, Poland, and Flanders had to sleep in the sugarhouse, under guard. Africa was disappointed, but all she said was, "Better than the smokehouse."

After they'd eaten, Africa wrapped up a pile of hard-baked corn cakes, a slab of fat bacon, and a can of fresh water in a

blanket and stuffed them, along with a shuttered lantern, a tin-
derbox, and three candles, into a burlap sack.

"Better take a little sleep now," she told Sophie. "I'll wake
you at midnight."

The rain had let up a little when Sophie crept out of the cabin.
Her skirt tucked into her apron and her head and shoulders
wrapped in a blanket, she slipped through the dark like a
shadow. She was afraid, but no more than she'd been all day. At
least now she was doing something really useful.

In the maze garden, Sophie knelt in the sticky mud by
the hole in the summerhouse foundation. "Antigua? It's me,
Sophie. Are you there?"

"I ain't up North."

Sophie let out her breath gratefully. "Well, you will be. In
the meantime, I've got food, and a lantern and some candles.
And fresh water."

Sophie crawled under the summerhouse, pushing the
bundle in front of her. "Here's another blanket, though I'm
afraid it got wet. We can light the lantern and talk a little, if
you want."

Antigua made a sound between a laugh and a sob. "I don't
mind."

Soon the two girls were sitting side by side on the rotted
pallet with both blankets over their shoulders and the shuttered
lantern making a small pool of light at their feet. Despite the
rain, the floor was more or less dry, but the air was cold and
clammy and smelled strongly of mold and the contents of the
covered bucket in the corner. Antigua was crying while Sophie
tried to think of something to say that didn't sound stupid.

Finally, Antigua blew her nose on her apron and wiped her eyes. She smoothed her skirt into a tent over her drawn-up knees and rested her chin on them. "We better save that candle," she said thickly. "You only brung three."

Sophie lifted the shutter and blew out the candle. Darkness rushed in like water.

"I 'spect you leaving directly," said Antigua.

"I'll stay a bit," Sophie said. "Just until I get warmer."

"You got to stay more than a bit for that. It mighty cold down here."

"It's warmer with two."

For reply, Antigua shivered; Sophie worked an arm around her shoulders under the blanket. Antigua stiffened, then put her legs across Sophie's lap. They were about the same size (when, Sophie wondered, had that happened?), and it was a little awkward, but Sophie felt a thin warmth begin to creep up her legs and into her chest.

"How Popi going to get me away?" Antigua asked.

"Mr. Akins is keeping your pa and Poland and Flanders in the sugarhouse. We haven't seen them since yesterday morning."

"Did he whup them?"

"Old Missy wouldn't let him. I heard they're advertising for you in *The Planter*."

Antigua moved irritably. "Ain't you the fount of knowledge?"

Sophie shrugged. "Plenty of gossip in the sugarhouse."

"Bad news travel fast."

She sounded like she might cry again. Sophie said hurriedly, "Where are you planning to go when you get up North?"

"Jane in the kitchen always talking 'bout a place called New York."

The name stirred something in Sophie's mind, faint as the memory of a dream. "I've heard of it. Biggest city in the world, they say."

"Well, that's where I going," Antigua said. "And I going get me a job that pay good money, and find me a free man to marry, with his own house and his own mule and maybe a little shop so he don't have to answer to anybody and can hold his head up like a white man."

Sophie had a vague idea of New York as a big city where people lived in apartments, not houses, and all the black folk lived in a place called Harlem, where it wasn't safe to go after dark. But she didn't know how she knew it, or even if she'd made it up. So she said nothing.

"I know what you thinking," Antigua said. "You thinking I ain't going to make it up North. You thinking I'm a scarlet woman no decent free man with a shop would want for a wife." She drew away, dragging the blanket with her. "Well, I tell you this," she went on, her voice rising, "I every bit as good as you. You think you something special, Mr. Robert Fairchild's daughter? Well, my daddy was Old Massa, Mr. Patrick Fairchild, who was Mr. Robert's Daddy. And that make me you auntie."

She stopped short, took a long breath and said more quietly, "So you have some respect, you hear?"

"Yes, ma'am," said Sophie, startled. If Mr. Patrick Fairchild was Antigua's daddy, that meant that Africa had been meddled with, as Aunt Winney put it, by Old Missy's husband. "Did Old Missy know?"

There was a little pause while Antigua seemed to be regretting having said anything, then settled against Sophie again.

"Yes. She know. She and Mammy, they bring me into the world, and when the cord cut, Old Missy she tell Momi she ain't angry, but it better if she go away for a spell. Soon's she on her feet again, Old Missy send her to New Orleans to learn fancy cooking. 'Don't you fret 'bout you baby girl, neither,' she say to Momi. 'We take extra-good care of her until you come back.' When Momi come back, she marry Popi and have Flandy."

Sophie found Antigua's hand and held it while they sat and listened to the rain drumming on the summerhouse roof.

"Does Mrs. Charles know Old Massa was your father?"

"I don't know." Antigua sounded sleepy. "I 'spect not."

"Do you think—" began Sophie, then stopped.

"What?"

"That you'll like it up North," finished Sophie lamely. She couldn't ask Antigua if she was going to have a baby. A baby who would be the property of Dr. Charles, no matter how pale its skin was or how sandy its hair. Just as Dr. Charles had assumed that Sophie was the property of Mr. Robert Fairchild, who'd fathered Sophie on his slave wench Louisette.

Antigua was still talking. ". . . but at least I be free. Soph? You awake?"

Sophie started guiltily. "I'm sorry, Anti. What were you saying?"

Antigua gave Sophie a squeeze. "Don't matter. I just running my mouth 'cause I don't want you going off and leaving me by my lonesome in the dark. You run along home. I be fine."

Sophie collected herself. "You sure, now? Why don't you light the candle, at least, so you won't be in the dark?"

"Maybe I needs it more some other time and don't have it because I burn it now. You scoot. You want Mr. Akins to send the dogs after you?"

Sophie scrambled to her feet, found the ladder, and climbed out of the pit. "I'll be back when I can," she whispered, "but maybe not for a day or two."

"I'll be fine." Antigua's voice was firm. "I'm beholden to you, Soph."

"It's no more than any girl would do for her auntie," said Sophie and crawled away as fast as she could, leaving Antigua sputtering softly behind her.

Chapter 20

It wasn't yet dawn when Sophie got back to Africa's cabin, but the air was beginning to stir and Rhodes's old rooster was crowing. As she slipped in the door, Africa swatted her hard across the seat.

"I was near out of my mind fretting over you. What are you thinking of, staying out so late? You want Mr. Akins looking for you, too? Use your *head*, girl!"

Sophie blinked. "Nobody saw me." She gave a jaw-cracking yawn. "We got to talking, and I didn't know how late it was getting."

"Huh. How's my baby keeping?"

"She's fine, except for being cold and lonely."

"She'll be a lot more cold and lonely before she gets North," said Africa wearily. "Take off that muddy dress, sugar, and wash your face and arms. It's bad enough for you to be asleep on your feet without looking like you've been chasing 'gators through the swamp all night."

The morning seemed endless. Betty kicked Sophie awake twice as she dozed, propped on her paddle. "Look lively, girl," she hissed the second time. "You want Mr. Akins wondering why you so wore out?"

After the midday break, it was all Sophie could do to stand up and go back to work. Back aching, eyes scratchy, arms weighted as much by fatigue as by the paddle, she almost envied Antigua, curled up in her earthy den with nothing to do but sleep the day away. Almost.

Just before the end of the shift, Sophie heard a commotion of horses and shouting and dogs barking. It was all she could do to keep skimming the blanket like she wasn't scared to death they'd found Antigua and hauled her to the sugarhouse for Mr. Akins to deal with. She saw Young Guam trot by, watched with a beating heart as he climbed the platform where Mr. Akins hovered over the evaporator like a hen with one chick. Young Guam spoke, Mr. Akins threw a response over his shoulder, and Young Guam ran outside again, looking grim.

Phronsie squinted out to the yard. "They ain't got her. I sees dogs and horses and big bucks with sticks. But I don't see Antigua."

Which might have been a relief if Betty's man George hadn't come by to say McCormick the slave hunter had arrived.

Phronsie clicked her tongue. "They say McCormick the best hunter there is. They say he feed them dogs on black meat to give 'em the taste."

"And if'n the dogs don't get you," George said gloomily, "there the 'gators and the injuns and the poor white trash. North's a long ways away, with winter coming and all. That Antigua got grit. Lord bless her, I say."

"Amen," murmured Sophie and "Amen," echoed Betty, and they were all quiet, thinking of the dangers on the road to freedom.

Walking back home, Sophie could hear McCormick's dogs yammering out in the swamp, distant and dismal.

That evening, China came around to see how Canny was coming on and ask when Africa was returning to the kitchen. "Nobody can make velouté smooth as you. And Young Missy, she say my etouffée give her bellyache."

Africa shrugged. "My baby need me, China. I'm sorry as I can be, but you just have to put up with Young Missy's ructions a while longer."

China sighed and nodded. "They saying Antigua probably lost in the swamp, got ate by a 'gator, maybe. I sure sorry for your trouble, Africa."

"I've got a peck of it, China, and that's the truth. It's been preying on my mind so I can hardly remember my own name. I promised Sally a *gris-gris* last week, and I clean forgot it until this very minute." Africa fished around on the mantel among the jars and twists of dried herbs and produced out a little scarlet bag tied with white thread.

"You want me to give it to her?" asked China.

"I have to put it into her hand myself. But if you tell her the *gris-gris* is ready, I'll be mighty grateful."

China looked from the scarlet bag to Africa's face. "Be my pleasure," she said. "I tells her tonight."

Africa closed her fingers on the bag. "Thank you."

The two women hugged, and China hurried off faster than she'd come.

This whole exchange had mystified Sophie. "Why didn't you just tell China that Antigua was safe? And why do you want Sally down here? What can Sally do that China can't?"

Africa put the *gris-gris* back on the mantel. "Sally works in the Big House. She hears things China doesn't. And China knows everything 'bout Antigua she needs to know right now. I wish Ned was here, but he ain't, so we have to get Antigua out without him. We need a plan, Sophie. And we need a friend in the Big House to tell us what the white folks are saying. Sally's not so bad. She's silly, is all, and she likes an easy life. She'll help if we put it to her right."

Next morning, everybody knew that Mr. McCormick's dogs had followed a trail into the bayou and promptly lost it, which wasn't surprising, given the rain and all. However, McCormick had told Dr. Charles he was pretty sure the wench had run into the swamp: round about sunset, he'd found a petticoat snagged on a cypress root. That evening, Sophie heard about Sally's visit from Canny.

"I thought she faint dead away when Momi tell her what she want."

"What did she say?"

"Momi or Sally?"

"Both."

Canny scratched carefully at the edge of the bandage around her chest, watched by the stitched black eyes of her doll. "Momi say we gots Antigua hid, never mind where, and we studying to get her away North before frost. And Sally say she don't want to hear nothing 'bout it, that she got her a good mistress and regular food and nice clothes to wear, and dances and Samson talking 'bout marriage, and she ain't got no mind to go courting trouble."

Sophie could just hear her saying it, too. "And what did your mama say to that?"

"Momi say in that case, she tell Mammy who order up the hoodoo from Aunt Pearl gave her bellyache last spring, and Sally, she say she willing to keep her ear out and tell Momi what she hear, and Momi say that good for now, and can Sally

Delia Sherman

come back tomorrow evening after supper, and Sally say yes. And then she go away and Momi cry."

Africa came in with a steaming bowl. "What you two talking 'bout in here?"

"Sally," said Canny.

"Sally." Africa shook her head ruefully. "Stupid wench bought a hoodoo from old Aunt Pearl over to Doucette. Mammy came down here holding her belly and groaning like a bull 'gator, wanting to know if I did it. I said I didn't know anything 'bout it, gave her a *gris-gris* and some chamomile tea. Just goes to show everything comes in useful in the end."

"Momi," said Canny. "What we going to do about Anti?"

It wasn't just a matter of getting Antigua out of Oak River, but of getting her North. She was a young girl, a house servant, not used to fending for herself. On the road, she'd be in constant danger of being turned in or pressed into the fields of some small farmer with a little land and not enough slaves to work it. At worst, she'd be shot for trespassing or found by some man who'd hurt her worse than Mr. Beau.

They talked until Canny fell asleep without getting any further than deciding that Antigua should go to New Orleans first. "Best place to hide a hen," Africa said, "is in a henhouse. Nobody going to find one runaway slave girl in New Orleans."

"But how's she going to get there?" Sophie asked.

"We talk about that later. You sleep now."

But when Sophie came off her shift next afternoon, Africa just sent her to hoe the weeds out of the pea patch and gather greens for supper. Africa herself took advantage of the bright weather to wash Canny's bandages and blankets and her menfolks' clothes. Ducking under the line where their shirts and pants flapped in the wind, Sophie wondered when Ned and Poland and Flanders would be free to wear them.

208

Sally showed up after supper, looking nervous and sulky. Old Missy was beside herself over Antigua's disappearance, she said, and Miss Liza was fit to be tied. "She weeping and wailing and carrying on like Antigua was her own sister, when everybody know how ugly she treat her. Siberia down to Oak Cottage say Miss Liza just sorry she ain't got nobody to chuck her boots at anymore. Young Missy, she the one sent for Mist' McCormick. She say she find your girl come hell or high water, and then she going to sell her downriver for a field hand."

Africa slapped her aproned thighs. "Well, we better get planning, then. Sophie, fetch me that tin from the back room. You know the one."

Sophie did. It was where the family kept their savings, the money they'd earned selling dried moss and Ned's whittled toys and Africa's jams and pickles. Hoping Canny was asleep, she groped for it in the dark.

Canny stirred restlessly. "Soph? What you doing? Is that Sally I hear out there?"

"I'm fetching something for your mama. You hush now, and go back to sleep."

"I tired of sleeping. I wants to hear what Sally saying 'bout Anti."

"If you lie real still, you can listen from here. Sally's voice isn't exactly soft."

The box was heavy. When Africa counted the money out on the table beside the half-eaten spoon bread, it came to over two hundred dollars. Sally stretched her eyes and whistled.

"We thought we'd buy our freedom by and by," Africa said. "But Anti got her life in front of her." Counting out a hundred dollars, she swept the rest back into the tin. "And so do Poland and Flanders. A hundred dollars should be enough to buy a passage on a paddle-wheel boat to Ohio, maybe further."

Sally shook her head doubtfully. "Ain't nobody going sell Antigua no passage 'less she gots free papers or a travel pass. And that ain't happening 'less you got something on Mammy like you got on me."

"Why Mammy?" Sophie asked.

"Mammy can write," Africa said. "Old Missy taught her when she was a girl."

"So can I write," said Sophie. "As well as Mammy, I bet. You tell me what to say, and I'll write it."

Sally looked at Sophie as if she'd announced she could flap her arms and fly to Ohio. "Naw," she said scornfully. "You never."

Sophie gave her a look. "You wait and see."

Africa got up, went into the back room, returning with a yellow, much-folded paper in her hand. "Can you write like this?"

Sophie unfolded the paper. Scratchy, spidery words sprawled elegantly—and illegibly—across the heavy, expensive paper. Sophie's heart sank.

"Lookit her face," said Sally with mournful satisfaction. "She can't do it."

Sophie ignored her. "What is this, Africa?"

"She lying 'bout knowing how to read, too!"

"You hush up, Sally," Africa said. "It's my travel pass from New Orleans."

Sophie squinted at the loops and curves. Yes, that was *Africa*, and that was *New Orleans*, and that was definitely *August 15, 1845*.

"I see," she said slowly. "It says, *The slave Africa, property of Mr. Patrick Fairchild of Oak River Plantation in the parish of St. Mary's, has my permission to travel by steamboat or wagon between New Orleans to Oak River.* Then the date. I still can't read the signature."

"Maître Jacques Dumont," said Africa. "He taught me pastry-making and fancy sauces. He said I was a fine cook and he wanted to buy me from Old Missy. But I told him I had to go home to my baby girl, and he said babies were why women would never amount to anything."

"Can you write like that?" Sally demanded.

Sophie studied the old-fashioned hand. "It's not what my writing generally looks like," she said carefully. "But I might copy it. With practice."

"What you going to practice on?" Sally wanted to know. "You ain't got no paper nor ink."

"We got soot and rags," Africa said. "For the pass, well, we have to steal some paper, is all, and a pen and some of that fancy ink Old Missy writes her letters with."

"We?" Sally asked, alarmed. "Who *we*? I the only one of us got any business in the Big House, and I ain't stealing nothing, no, ma'am. Not a thing."

"You are, Sally," said Africa. "You're stealing a pen and a bottle of ink and two-three sheets of heavy paper, and you're doing it right smart. You know you're bound to say yes, so you might as well say it now."

Sally didn't see it that way, but when Africa threatened her with Mammy again, she gave in. She went off looking mighty put-out and saying it might be a day or two.

"A day or two is fine," Africa said. "Sophie has her some practicing to do.

As soon as Sally had gone, Africa sent Sophie out to the maze.

"Just tell my baby girl things are going fine, she'll be out in three-four days, and she's going to ride a steamboat, just like a fine lady." Africa pressed a bundle into Sophie's hands. "There's more candles. The soup's cold, but it'll put heart in her. And a comb. She's got to look respectable when she escapes, you tell her that."

Sophie thought of the muddy crawl under the summerhouse. One more thing to plan—a change of clothes for Antigua. There were other things to think about, too. She counted them as she hurried through the dark. Something to carry her things in. A false name for the travel pass, something not so particular to Oak River as Antigua. Sue-Ellen? Ann?

By this time, Sophie hardly had to look for the white stone markers. Her feet knew the way to the central garden all by themselves. She slithered under the camellia and called out softly. "Light the lantern, will you, so I can see where I'm going? I've got more candles."

A pause, a scrape, and then a faint glow seeped up from the pit.

Antigua was hollow-eyed and filthy, but she perked up as Sophie outlined the plan for her escape,

"Better say that I a cook," she said. "They'll be looking for a house slave, and ain't no field hand going anywheres this time of year. Ask Asia can she find me something to wear—Momi might not think to ask her."

"All right," said Sophie. "You can change in the summerhouse. We'll pack your old dress in a basket or something. It'll look suspicious if you're not carrying anything. It's bad enough you're traveling alone."

"Come with me, then." Antigua turned to her, eyes glinting in the lamplight. "Come take the boat with me, we be free together."

Panic swept over Sophie at the thought of leaving Oak River. "I can't," she said shakily. "There's only enough money for one."

Antigua shrugged. After an uncomfortable pause, Sophie said, "I've got to get back, or your Mama'll have my hide. I need a name for the travel pass. Who do you want to be?"

Antigua huffed in surprise. "You asking *me?*"

"It's going to be your name."

Antigua laughed. "I ain't going to be an island no more! I have a *real* name!" She propped her chin on her drawn-up knees to think. She'd taken off her head-rag and unraveled her hair with the comb Sophie had brought so that it lay in a fleecy cloud around her shoulders. She looked more peaceful than Sophie had ever seen her.

"Aren't you scared?" asked Sophie curiously.

"Oh, I plenty scared. I going out somewheres I never been, amongst folk I don't even know they names. But I going be free. Free woman got gumption. Free woman can learn to read and find work and get *paid* for it. Free woman leave if she don't like where she be. Free woman got the world before her."

"Like Adam and Eve."

Antigua frowned. "Oak River a long way from Paradise, Sophie."

"I know."

They sat quiet for a little longer, Antigua thinking over names, Sophie thinking about Antigua's offer. Oak River wasn't her home, after all. She'd been sad to leave New Orleans, and remembered clearly how miserable and lost she'd felt when she arrived, was it only six months ago? But now the thought of leaving felt more dangerous than facing Mr. McCormick's flesh-eating dogs, and she didn't for the life of her know why.

The plantation bell rang for the night shift. "I've got to go," Sophie said. "What name shall I put on your travel pass?"

"Omi Saide," said Antigua.

"Omi Saide? What kind of a name is Omi Saide?" Sophie was in too much of a hurry to be diplomatic. "That's not going to make you disappear into the crowd. Anyone who reads that is going to remember it for sure, and you, too."

"You said whatever I wants."

"Yes, but—"

"Anybody running away not so big a fool as take an African name, make her stand out and be remembered. So I ain't running away." She paused. "It my great-grandma's name, Sophie. And you promised."

Sophie stood up. "So I did. All right, then. Omi Saide."

Antigua stood, too. To Sophie's surprise, she hugged her tightly.

"Next week, you'll be on your way North," said Sophie.

"Good," Antigua said, releasing her. "I mighty sick of this hole in the ground. Now get along, or Momi'll be fretting."

Chapter 21

Antigua was only under the summerhouse two more days.

It was Friday evening. Sophie was practicing writing *Omi Saide, slave of Mr. Franklin Preston of Rich Meadow Plantation, Georgia,* with a half-burned stick on a bit of rag. It didn't look much like Maître Jacques's scrawl, but it didn't look like her usual writing, either, and she was feeling pretty pleased with herself. She was trying a masculine flourish on the signature when Sally came tumbling breathlessly into the cabin.

"Lord 'a mercy, Sophie, where Africa at?"

Africa poked her head out of the back room. "What is it, Sally? What's gone wrong?" Her skin went ashy. "They found her, didn't they? They found my little girl."

Sally shook her head. "No, they ain't found her, not yet. But they will tomorrow, sure's Judgment Day."

"Tell me." Africa sat down in Ned's chair. Sally had launched into her story when Canny called out that she wanted to hear, too, which woke Saxony, who started screaming. Africa disappeared into the back and returned a few minutes later with Saxony hiccoughing on her hip and Canny hanging on to her arm. She settled Canny into Ned's chair and herself and Saxony under Yemaya's vévé.

"You'd oblige me, Sally, if you start again."

Sally sniffed, but told the whole thing over again from the beginning.

Before supper, the slave-hunter had come knocking on the door of the Big House, insisting he had to talk to Dr. Charles. Samson had shown him into the parlor where the doctor was sitting with Old Missy, closed the door, and put his ear to the crack.

Mr. McCormick, he said he'd been thinking, and he thought the runaway wench hadn't gone into the swamp at all. He thought she was maybe laying low somewheres near Oak River—maybe even on Oak River land—waiting for the hue and cry to die down.

Old Missy, she said that didn't sound likely to her, but Dr. Charles wasn't so sure. Mr. McCormick said he had his best tracker tied up under the gallery, a blue hound with a nose could sniff out a baby in a barrel of polecats. Unless Antigua grew wings and flew away, that hound would find her. He asked Dr. Charles for permission to take the hound all over every inch of the plantation and see if they could flush her out.

Sally took a deep breath. "Old Missy, she say this *her* plantation, Mr. McCormick need *her* permission, and he ain't got it. Dr. Charles say Antigua *his* property, and he got a good mind to give Mr. McCormick and his blue hound free rein. They still jawing it over when the supper bell ring, but it got to come round Dr. Charles's way in the end, he being the man of the house. Soon's he could, Samson run find me and I run here. I don't know no more than a sucking child where Antigua be, but it ain't going to be safe much longer, and Lord, O Lord, what we going do?"

The more Sally talked, the more excited she got, and the more excited she got, the quieter Africa was. Watching her rock Saxony, Sophie couldn't say what she herself was thinking, which was that the blue hound would find Antigua sure as little green apples, and then there would be whippings and disgrace, with the slave market at the end of it, inescapable as Fate.

"Now's not the time for losing hope," Africa said. "Now's the time for thinking. If I can get anywhere near that blue hound, I got a powder will fix him so he don't know what he's smelling. But I can't stop Mr. McCormick poking around in every hole and corner big enough to hide a chigger. We got to keep him away from that summerhouse."

"So *that* where she be!" Sally exclaimed.

Africa glared. "So now you know all about it, I'll know who to blame if anybody finds out."

"I ain't telling, no, not me," Sally protested. "I keeping right out of this sorry mess. 'Sides, you aiming to move her, ain't you?"

"You propose to smuggle her into the Big House and put her under Old Missy's bed?" snapped Africa. "Because that's the only place Mr. McCormick's blue hound won't stick his nose."

"Start her off North tonight, then."

Africa shook her head. "We're not ready. We'll do it if we have to, but it'd be better if she went by day. I threw the bones over it," she said unsteadily. "They said she'd go by day."

A silence fell, broken only by the crackle of the flames. Then Canny said, "Sophie, take off them spectacles and looky here at me."

Sophie couldn't imagine what Canny was getting at, but removed her glasses obediently. Out of the fog of nearsightedness, she heard Africa say, "I don't know, Canny. She's like, but she ain't the *same*, not by a long shot."

"We gussies her up, Mr. McCormick won't know the difference. I bet he never even seen Miss Liza."

It took a minute for Sophie to figure out what Canny was suggesting and another to find her voice. "But Miss Liza's sixteen!"

"What do you think, Sally?" asked Africa.

Hard fingers turned Sophie's face from the white-and-black blur that was Canny to the red-and-cream blur that was Sally. The housemaid pulled the tignon off Sophie's head, undid her braids, and combed out her hair, testing the texture of it between her fingers.

"Might could do," she said. "*With* the right dress, and rice powder and hair oil, and gloves for them hands and a bonnet and a shawl and a reticule. But ain't nobody going to believe Miss Liza lazing 'round the summerhouse at dawn, in the middle of the winter, all by her lonesome."

"Oh, yes, they would," said Sophie. "If they thought she was waiting for Mr. Beau."

Sally shook her head. "Old Missy, she tell Mr. Beau not to come 'round here till Christmas."

"All the better," said Sophie. "It's just the fool sort of thing Miss Liza would think was romantic."

"May be," said Sally doubtfully. "But where the clothes coming from? You ain't got no fancy walking dress here, I suppose? Nor no poke bonnet?"

Africa shook her head. "Nothing that would fool a blind mule. Not anywhere in the Quarters." She turned to Sally.

"Oh, no." Sally let go Sophie's hair. "Oh, no. I ain't stealing a hairpin, let alone a walking dress, and you can tell Mammy whatever you wants."

Africa moaned. "This is my baby girl, Sally. She's facing a life of suffering and pain if you don't help her now."

"She ain't my baby girl, and I ain't studying to catch no suffering and pain my own self. I ain't doing it, and that's that."

The baby started to cry again as Africa's arms tightened. "I swear you won't know a peaceful minute, Sally, not from dawn to dawn. Your feet'll be on fire, your eyes'll jump out of your head . . ."

Sally shook her head mulishly. Sophie got an inspiration. "Asia mends Miss Liza's clothes. I'm sure she'd help."

Sally clapped her hands in relief. "Asia! Now, why didn't I think of her? I go gets her now, brings her here, she take care of everything, you see. I gets Asia and dresses Sophie here up like a white lady, then you won't hoodoo me, will you, Africa?"

"No." Africa sounded very tired. "I won't hoodoo you."

Sally hurried off into the night, and Africa set herself to soothing Saxony. When the baby was asleep on her shoulder, she turned to Sophie. "Sally's right. This is craziness. If you get caught, Antigua isn't the only one going to get whipped bloody. We have to think of something else."

"There ain't nothing else," said Canny. "Sophie ain't afraid. Is you, Soph?"

Sophie sighed. "I'm plenty afraid. But it doesn't matter. There's nobody else can do this."

Africa got up. "Then we'll chance it. I surely can't think of a better plan. You got grit and you got a cool head, sugar. We're counting on them both." She laid the sleeping baby in Sophie's arms. "Now, put Saxy to bed and fetch in a bucket of water. You going to be a lady, you have to be clean."

The rest of the night passed in a furtive bustle of preparation. Folk kept dropping by the cabin. Sally sent Samson from the House with pen, paper, and ink. A couple of stable hands volunteered to keep an eye on Mr. McCormick's progress through the plantation. Uncle Italy said he'd drive Antigua to the steamboat landing and buy her passage to New Orleans. Finally Sally showed up with Asia, toting a bundle wrapped up in a paisley shawl—body linen, a mustard-yellow serge walk-ing-dress with a standing collar, and a pair of brown button boots Mrs. Charles had given her. The boots were too narrow, but the dress fit pretty well. Sophie had grown taller and thin-ner since she'd come to Oak River, but not thin enough to do without a corset.

"A lady always wear a corset," said Asia firmly. So she and Sally hooked and laced her into one, with a corset cover on top, and tied some lace-trimmed drawers and a hoop and a petticoat over it all. They threw the heavy skirt over her head, hooked it snug around her waist, and eased her arms into a tight-fitting jacket that buttoned up to her chin, hiding her worn *gris-gris*.

Asia looked Sophie over critically, tsked, unbuttoned the jacket, stuffed some rags into the top of her chemise, adjusted them, and buttoned her up again. Sally brushed Sophie's hair mercilessly, oiled it, rolled it over a rag into a crescent at the nape of her neck, and skewered it in place with a pair of shell combs. The final touch was a dusting of rice powder to lighten her skin.

"Don't squinch up you eyes like that," Sally scolded. "Miss Liza don't never squinch up her eyes."

Sophie tried to stop squinting and prayed she wouldn't do it when she was talking to McCormick. Her body felt strange. The corset held her straight and still. The high collar made her hold her chin high. Her hands were encased in tight tan leather gloves, buttoned at the wrist. A deep poke bonnet shaded her face—Sally's Sunday pride-and-joy, covered in stolen brown velvet hastily tacked on to hide the red cloth. A reticule dan-gled from her wrist for her spectacles and Antigua's travel pass, which she had written out in a quiet moment. Everything was as ready as it was going to be, and it was almost dawn.

Sally draped the paisley shawl across Sophie's elbows.

"You a right picture," she said approvingly. "I hardly knows you from Miss Liza, and I done dressed you."

Sophie wished Africa had a mirror. If she was going to be this uncomfortable, she'd like to know how she looked.

"One more thing." Africa tipped a small mound of dark powder from a little pouch and brushed it onto Sophie's skirts, then put the pouch into her hand. "Sprinkle a little of this in the garden—four-five piles in different places."

Sophie tucked the pouch in her reticule and looked over at Canny, propped in her father's chair, a healing *gris-gris* tied around her waist, her face dotted with healing scabs and pink scars, blinking furiously. She ran back and knelt down beside her in a rustle of petticoats. "Wish us luck, Canny. I'll tell Antigua you were the one thought up this plan, so she knows what a clever little sister she has."

"What if it don't work? What if you all gets caught and whupped and . . . "

Sophie kissed the little girl on the forehead. "Hush now. It'll work just fine."

"I ain't never going see Anti again," Canny said mournfully.

"You don't know that," Sophie said. "Maybe you'll go up North yourself some day, find her living in New York as fine and comfortable as you please."

"You think so?"

"Time to go, sugar," Africa said. "You all can talk later, when Antigua is free."

It was a dark, cold walk to the maze. The boots pinched Sophie's feet, and the tight corset made her breathless. The maze was quiet as death, except for the swish of her mustard-colored skirts over the grass. When they got to the summerhouse, Sophie called softly to Antigua that it was time.

A moment later, Antigua was out of the hidey-hole and hanging onto Africa like a leech. Mother and daughter disappeared into the summerhouse and Sophie busied herself depositing neat little piles of Africa's powder here and there in the garden. Her heart was beating so hard she felt sick. What if she forgot to take off her glasses? What if she took one look at Mr. McCormick and froze like a possum in torchlight? What if she couldn't keep him out of the summerhouse? She remembered the stories she'd heard from the visiting servants, of runaways whipped and fettered and collared with bells. She remembered the tale of Ole One-Eye.

A wave of nausea swept up from her pinched-in belly. Frightened she'd throw up and ruin all Sally's work, Sophie gulped cold air. *I can do this,* she told herself sternly. *It's just playacting. I do it all the time. I pretend to be stupid, I pretend not to mind when I'm treated like a little dog. I pretend to be a yard child. All I have to do now is pretend to be a white girl.* A white girl raised to think that the whole world exists to polish her boots. A white girl who thinks people can be property.

The sky paled to sunrise. An owl hooted, late home from his night's hunting. It was the signal. McCormick was heading towards the maze.

Sophie heard shouting. The sharp bark of a dog insisting loudly that it smelled something interesting circled closer through the maze. She removed her glasses, folded them, and put them in her reticule. Her mind felt as blurred as the garden seen through her naked eyes. The barking and shouting came nearer. One of the men sounded horribly familiar.

A blur of motion by the garden entrance told her that the hunters had arrived.

"Mr. Akins!" she exclaimed in what she hoped was Miss Liza's high-bred whine. "What on earth are you doing here?"

There was an awkward pause. The blurry mass moved close enough so that Sophie could make out that it was made up of several man, some of them black, and a dog straining against a rope. "Miss Fairchild?" said Mr. Akins uncertainly.

Sophie's heart beat so hard, she was sure Mr. Akins could hear it. She licked her lips, then cocked her head like she'd seen Miss Liza do, careful to keep her eyes wide. "You're looking for Antigua, aren't you? Tiresome wench. I hope she drowned in the swamp."

"Begging your pardon, miss," said another man—Mr. McCormick, she guessed. "Crusher's mighty interested in this here garden. How long you been here?"

Sophie shrugged her shoulders daintily. "I don't know. Not long."

"Beats me why you're here at all," Mr. Akins said. "Pardon me for asking, but does Mrs. Charles know where you're at?"

The blue hound began snuffling energetically at Sophie's skirts. She gave a ladylike scream. "Take it away!"

"Could I trouble you to answer me, Miss Fairchild?" asked Mr. Akins. "A runaway slave ain't no small matter."

"I'm not answering anything until you get this horrid thing away from me." It was all too easy to sound hysterical. "Please, Mr. Akins?"

The overseer sighed. "You heard the young lady, McCormick. She don't like your blue hound. Let him sniff 'round, see what he find." The blue hound disappeared. "Well, Miss Fairchild?"

Sophie shivered with cold and nerves. She didn't know what to say next, just that she had to keep him talking and away from the summerhouse. What would Miss Liza do?

"I do believe," she said, "that I'm feeling a bit faint. If you give me your arm as far as that bench over there under the arbor, Mr. Akins, I'd like to sit down."

She slipped her hand through his arm and leaned on him, glancing up around the deep brim of her bonnet.

He frowned down at her. "Wouldn't you be more comfortable in the summerhouse?"

"No, *indeed*," said Sophie petulantly. "I've *been* in the summerhouse. There aren't any chairs, and I'm certain I heard *rats*. I'll just sit out here."

Akins shrugged and led her to the bench. Sophie sank down gracefully, pulled Miss Liza's lace-edged handkerchief from her reticule, and pressed it to her mouth.

"Better, Miss Fairchild?"

"Yes, thank you, Mr. Akins. I can't abide dogs."

The blue hound had stopped barking and seemed to be rushing from place to place, whining.

"Miss Fairchild." Mr. Akins was clearly holding on to his temper with difficulty. "Mr. McCormick here thinks your slave wench is still somewheres on Oak River land. His dog led us here. And you'll forgive me saying you seem mighty anxious to keep me out of that summerhouse."

Reminding herself that Miss Liza Fairchild would naturally be a little nervous, Sophie allowed her lips to tremble. "I declare, Mr. Akins, there's no call to be ugly. It's perfectly simple why I'm here, but you must promise not to tell, because I'd get in terrible trouble, and so would"—she paused dramatically—"Someone Else."

"Who would get in trouble, miss? Antigua? I promise you, that girl'll be in more trouble the longer it takes to catch up with her."

Why was the man so *stupid*? "Why do you keep going on about Antigua? I don't give two pins about Antigua. I hope you do find her, and whip her raw." Sophie fidgeted with her hand-kerchief. "If you *must* know, it's my fiancé, Mr. Beau Waters. You see, Grandmama and Papa think I'm distracting him from his duties, so they've forbidden me to see him until after harvest." She widened her eyes at him. "Have you ever been in love, Mr. Akins?"

Mr. Akins laughed unpleasantly. "I see. Don't you fret, miss. I'll keep your secret."

"Thank you."

But Mr. Akins wasn't quite through with her yet. "In return, Miss Fairchild, I want you to let Crusher here take a sniff around the summerhouse. Just so we can say we done our duty."

"Must you?"

"Yes, Miss Fairchild. Or I'll march right on into that sum-merhouse and take whoever I find there straight to Dr. Charles."

"Oh, very well. But do hurry. I have to get back to Oak Cottage directly."

She held her breath as McCormick led the blue hound up to the summerhouse. She couldn't see that far, but she heard Crusher's ears flap as he shook his head impatiently.

"He don't smell nothing here, Akins. Let's us move along. C'mon," McCormick shouted to the slaves grouped by the entrance. "We got us a nigger to catch."

Mr. Akins lifted his hat, and Sophie gave him a little nod. He faded into the hedge. A moment later, she heard McCormick's voice, startlingly close. "I would've bet a chaw of 'baccy the wench was there."

"May be she was," Mr. Akins said. "But she ain't there now." They passed around to the far side of the maze; when Sophie could hear their voices again, they were too far away for her to make out words. She counted slowly to one hundred, then she put on her glasses and tapped on the summerhouse door. "They're gone."

"Better make sure," Africa said.

Sophie ran through the maze and peered out cautiously, saw a ragged figure behind a tree wave and point off toward Oak Cottage. She ran back to the garden as fast as her tight boots would let her.

"Africa! Antigua! You got to leave, right now! They're headed up to Oak Cottage, and if they see Miss Liza, it won't take long for Mr. Akins to put it all together."

Africa burst out of the summerhouse, her arm around Antigua, who was almost unrecognizable in a gray dress, a black shawl, and an unbecoming fawn headwrap. She was carrying a straw basket and quivering with excitement.

Sophie handed Antigua the reticule with the travel pass. Antigua hugged Sophie, Africa said, "There ain't time enough for that," and then they were all hurrying through the maze and Sophie was wondering whether Uncle Italy was waiting where he'd said and whether she and Africa could get back to where they were supposed to be before anybody missed them. The boots pinched, the corset made her breath come short, and her glasses were so smudged nothing looked quite the way it should.

She ran into a dead end. It was one of the room-like ones, decorated with a classical statue, a plump lady with a sheet around her hips and a smirk on her marble lips. The name Belle Watling popped into Sophie's mind.

Who on earth was Belle Watling?

Sophie shook her head angrily, and turned to lead Africa and Antigua back to the right path.

There was no one behind her.

Heart pounding, Sophie ran back along her track. Her skirts dragged on the grass, and the hoop caught in the raggedy hedges. The morning smelled of recent rain, and very faintly, of roses. A wet breeze blew her the calling of bobwhites and a faint, angry buzzing.

"Hey there, Miss Sophie," said a voice, and a fat, piebald animal-like thing appeared in the air in front of her, grinning toothlessly.

Sophie gaped at it.

"How you like the magical adventure I done give you?"

"What are you talking about? What are you? Where are Antigua and Africa?"

"They gone to they just reward. That other question, I done answer before. You recollect, don't you?"

Sophie felt the world tilt and spin around her, as if she was about to faint. Then everything settled again, and she remembered. She remembered everything: what the Creature was and what it had done, where she had been and when and who.

Her knees folded, and she sat down hard in the wet grass, her skirts mushrooming around her. The angry buzzing grew louder, and a small airplane bustled across the sky overhead.

"It a lot to recollect, all to once," the Creature said.

Disconnected names bounced in Sophie's head—Mr. Akins and Mama, *The Time Garden* and Antigua. Antigua! "I have to know, does Antigua get away? And does Africa get in trouble? What about Sally and Asia? And Canny. Does Canny get over her burns all right? Was she upset when I didn't come back?"

The Creature rolled its amber eyes. "You think I gots nothing to do but hang around here all day granting you wishes?

"They're not wishes," Sophie said. "They're questions."

"Either way, I ain't going to answer 'em. You ain't got no part in that story no more."

"Story?" Sophie was furious. "That wasn't a story! It was real!"

"Of course it real." The Creature was impatient. "Still a story, though."

"I remember now. You said I had to finish a story so I could come home. It doesn't feel finished, though."

The Creature shrugged. "Well, you part finished, anyways."

Sophie looked around, trying to make sense of where and when she was. The air was hot and close—summer, then—and the grass she sat in was wet. It might still be the day she left, or another just like it. Had she been gone for hours or days? Were the police looking for her? How much trouble was she in, anyway? "Creature," she said. "Would you please tell me how long I've been gone?"

It cocked an eye at the cloudy sky. "Twenty minutes? Half an hour? Long enough. You better scoot on home." And then it disappeared.

It would have taken Mr. Akins and his knotted whip to make Sophie scoot just then. She sat in the wet grass, trying to think. She'd wished so hard to come home, and now she was here, she hardly knew how she felt. She was hot and sad—oh, yes, and very tired. Which wasn't so very different from how she'd been feeling for the last week. At least now she wasn't scared half to death as well.

Chapter 22

"Sophie? Sophie! I know you're hiding in here somewhere! It's dinner-time!"

Someone was calling her from the center of the maze. Sophie hauled herself to her feet and walked slowly back, lifting her skirts free of the unmown grass. When she reached the garden, she had to steady herself against one of the moss-covered urns. It was one thing to travel forward a hundred years; it was another to see the changes that a hundred years could make. Everything was overgrown with thistles and weeds; the summerhouse was a shapeless mound of Virginia creeper and climbing roses.

A sturdy white woman stood beside the broken sundial. She looked as run to seed as the garden, with an untidy bun and a faded cotton dress that showed her legs almost to the knee. Still, she was a white woman, and potentially dangerous. Sophie's pulse beat nervously.

The woman, turned, saw Sophie, and went still. *Like a muskrat caught raiding the bean patch*, Sophie thought. "Hello, Aunt Enid."

"Jesus have mercy," Aunt Enid said shakily. "It called me Aunt. And in broad daylight, too." She closed her eyes and clasped her hands. *"Our Father, which art in Heaven—"*

Fighting an unholy desire to giggle, Sophie removed the bonnet. "I'm not a ghost, Aunt Enid. I'm Sophie. I'm back."

Aunt Enid's eyes sprang open. She looked Sophie up and down, only half-convinced. "Sophie? Why are you dressed up like the Girl in Yellow?"

"Not the Girl in Yellow. Miss Elizabeth Fairchild."

"Who is Miss Elizabeth Fairchild? And how did you come by that dress? Not to mention the shawl and bonnet?"

"The bonnet was a present. I stole the dress and the shawl."

Aunt Enid's face was a study. "You stole them! Sophie Martineau, you tell me what's going on here, or I swear I'll—I don't know what I'll do. Bust, I expect."

Sophie sighed. "You won't believe me."

"I don't expect I will," said Aunt Enid. "But, with the help of the Good Lord, I aim to try. There can't be any easy explanation for you to be a good three inches taller than you were an hour ago."

"Three inches taller?" Sophie said. "Really?"

"At least. And you've filled out in the bosom, too."

"Oh, that's rags," said Sophie, but she knew it wasn't, not entirely. "Miss Liza's seventeen, nearly."

"Miss Liza?" Aunt Enid's voice was grim, and her face was pale under her tan. "That would be the Miss Elizabeth Fairchild you mentioned earlier?"

Sophie took pity on her. "I'll tell you all about it, Aunt Enid, I promise. But let's sit down. It's a long story."

They went to the stone bench under the rose arbor. Or rather, where the arbor had been—it had long since rotted and collapsed. The bench was still there, though it was cracked and dirty and thick with rain-wet moss. It would stain her dress, Sophie thought, and pulled the shawl from her shoulders to sit on.

Aunt Enid settled herself on the far end of the bench, propped her hands on her knees, and watched as Sophie stripped off the tan gloves and laid them in her bonnet.

"Well," said Aunt Enid tartly. "I'm waiting."

"I don't know where to start."

"You can start with Miss Elizabeth Fairchild."

Sophie had heard that tone before, from Old Missy. It made her want to invent a soothing lie that would make her aunt stop looking at her like that. But this was 1960. Aunt Enid wasn't Old Missy, and Sophie had no soothing lie to tell. "Elizabeth Fairchild lived here, Aunt Enid, on Oak River Plantation, in Oak Cottage. A hundred years ago, in 1860."

"And just what does that have to do with you?"

"I was there. I went back in time."

Aunt Enid's hands clenched on her shamefully skimpy skirt. "Do you really expect me to believe that?"

"No." For the first time, Sophie dared look up from her lap and straight into her aunt's eyes. "But it's the truth."

"My land," said Aunt Enid.

Sophie closed her eyes. She was so tired she felt dizzy—or maybe it was because she hadn't eaten in a hundred years.

A hundred years. That was funny. Sophie giggled.

"I'm glad you find the situation so amusing." Aunt Enid's voice was dry.

Sophie bit her lip. "I don't. At least, I guess I won't, once I really understand I'm back. It's been almost six months for me."

"Almost six months," said Aunt Enid. "I declare. And where did you spend those six months, exactly?"

"In the Big House, at first. But I got sent to the sugarhouse after Old Missy thought I'd stolen Miss Liza's hairbrush."

Aunt Enid looked, if possible, even more spooked than she had before. "Do you mean to tell me, Sophie Martineau, that you imagine that you've spent the last six months as a *slave*?"

"Yes, ma'am. Except I didn't imagine it. It was the shirt-waist and the tan and being barefoot, I think. And looking like a Fairchild." Sophie looked at the bonnet on her lap. "Turned out to be a blessing in the end."

"Lord have mercy."

Silence fell. Sophie wasn't inclined to break it. It was pleasant just to sit still, though she wished she could get out of the corset and the boots, take off the heavy skirt and jacket and be comfortable in her homespun dress again. How white ladies stood all this paraphernalia was a mystery to her. Even in summer, they wore petticoats and crinolines and long drawers and heavy cotton stockings.

A woman was calling her. Sounded like Old Missy.

"Coming, ma'am," Sophie muttered, and pried her eyes open to see Aunt Enid peering into her face.

"Don't you fall asleep on me, Sophie Martineau. I don't know what to make of your story, and that's a fact. But I can see with my own eyes that *something* out of the way has happened to you. Not even a nearly fourteen-year-old girl can turn into a young woman between 10 o'clock Eucharist and Sunday dinner. So let's say, for the sake of a quiet life, that you haven't run mad and you're not lying—"

"Thank you for believing me," Sophie said.

"I'm not saying I believe you. I'm saying . . . Well, I don't quite know what I'm saying. What I do know is what Sister would say. She'd say you've lost your mind, and have you in some godforsaken hospital or other before you could say Jack Robinson."

"Oh, Lordy." Panic kicked Sophie's brain awake. "I've got to change!" She looked at Aunt Enid uncertainly. "I don't suppose you'd mind bringing me some clothes."

With the subject of slaves and time travel safely behind them, Aunt Enid seemed to relax. "Don't be silly, child. Of course I'll bring your clothes. If you've got anything that'll fit."

Sophie considered. "A skirt, maybe? A short-sleeve shirt? I need underwear, too. And I'll make a start getting out of all this. I might need help with the corset, though. It took Asia and Sally both to get me into it." Tears prickled the back of her nose. Were they all right? Had Antigua got away? She'd never know.

She wished she'd been able to say good-bye to Canny.

Aunt Enid stood. "Asia? Never mind; I don't want to hear. I'll bring an old sheet to wrap that dress in."

By the time her aunt returned, Sophie was down to corset and drawers. She had rubbed the powder off her face with her petticoat, taken the combs out of her hair, and ruthlessly twisted it into her usual braids.

"My land," said Aunt Enid. "What have you done to your hair? You look like a—" She stopped dead, spread the sheet on the bench, transferred Miss Liza's walking dress onto it, motioned for Sophie to turn around, and untied her laces.

"You can't wear your hair like that," she said carefully. "Two braids are fine, or one, now that you're almost grown-up. But six is too—old-fashioned."

"You mean only black folks wear lots of braids," Sophie said.

"Negroes," said Aunt Enid, working the laces loose. "The polite term is Negroes."

The corset joined the other clothes, and Aunt Enid turned her back while Sophie took off the chemise and drawers and put on cotton underpants, the skirt to her seersucker suit, and a sleeveless cotton blouse. The blouse was too tight across her chest, and the skirt barely reached her knees. Feeling half-naked, Sophie tugged at the hem self-consciously.

Aunt Enid tsked fretfully. "You look a sight. Sister may be in the devil's own temper, but she's not stone blind. Come on in the kitchen and I'll think what to do."

Oak Cottage was like a house remembered from a dream. The kitchen, once the storeroom where Mr. Beau had cornered Antigua, was fitted with luxuries Africa couldn't have imagined. Sophie thought she would have loved the icebox and the running water in the sink, but wasn't sure what she'd make of the electric stove.

"Here." Aunt Enid thrust an old denim gardening shirt into her hands. "Put this on. I need to get dinner while I'm thinking. It's the blessing of God that Sister's too put out to come down until I call her."

She opened the oven to baste the roasting chicken. Noticing a bunch of greens in the sink, Sophie got a knife and a cutting board and chopped them up. When she went to look for a bowl to put them in, she saw Aunt Enid staring at her like she'd sprouted wings. "It's getting a little wearing, being astonished every whipstitch. I suppose you miraculously know how to cook, too."

"Just gumbo and such—nothing fancy. I watched Miss Liza make jelly once."

Aunt Enid got her cornered muskrat look. "That's as may be. Now sit down and be still."

Obediently, Sophie sat and let her heavy eyelids drift shut. Next thing she knew, she was smelling something delicious and Aunt Enid was telling her to wake up. "You take this right on up to your room and don't come down to dinner. I'll tell Sister you took sick. It's not even a fib. You look terrible."

Sophie looked from her aunt to the tray in front of her. The heaped plate of chicken and greens was more food than she'd eaten at one meal for six months. The ice tea had a sprig of mint in it. She got up and put her arms around her aunt. "Thank you, Aunt Enid. I'm glad to be home. I missed you."

Aunt Enid was shorter than she remembered, and smelled of lavender and garden soil. She patted Sophie on the back.

"There, there," she said. "There's no need to take on. Run on upstairs now, and don't worry about a thing. Sister will be driving back to New Orleans directly after dinner."

Sophie ate her chicken and greens without tasting them; going to sleep was like falling off a cliff. She woke at dawn, convinced she'd overslept, that she'd be late getting to the sugarhouse and Mr. Akins would be mad.

It took her a minute to remember that she was back in 1960, where slavery was against the law, and Mr. Akins was dust. She also remembered that Mama had left without saying good-bye. Whatever had been changed by Sophie's time in the past, it wasn't Mama.

Feeling odd, Sophie went into the bathroom and rediscovered the glories of modern plumbing. She ran herself a scalding bath, scrubbed her skin with scented soap that didn't sting, and washed the dirt and tangles out of her hair with shampoo and cream rinse. Aunt Enid's threadbare towels seemed impossibly luxurious and fluffy, but Sophie couldn't find a thing to wear that didn't look downright indecent on her. She finally settled on Aunt Enid's shirt and a cotton skirt, then braided her hair in two tails and went down to breakfast.

"You look like a charity child," Aunt Enid said. " We'll have to buy you some new clothes. Eat up and we'll drive into Lafayette."

Sophie would rather have stayed home, but it never occurred to her to say so. As soon as Ofelia's rattletrap Chevy pulled up at Oak Cottage, Aunt Enid bundled Sophie into her old pink Thunderbird and headed for the road to Lafayette. Hanging on to the door, Sophie gritted her teeth against the

Delia Sherman

noise and stink and wished horse-drawn carriages hadn't gone out of fashion.

She'd completely forgotten about traffic. The first time a truck roared past the Thunderbird, she almost jumped out of her skin. Aunt Enid shot her a worried look, and she smiled reassuringly back. She didn't want her aunt thinking she'd gone crazy.

In Lafayette, Aunt Enid took her to a dress shop. The salesladies clucked and exclaimed just like Asia and Hepzibah when they saw her gingham shirtwaist back in 1860, except that the salesladies were white and Sophie was a customer, so they had to be polite. It all made Sophie feel horribly uncomfortable. But by the time the purchases were paid for and wrapped, she'd recovered a little more of her balance. She knew she was back in the twentieth century, where there were cars and dress shops, and the black woman who brought her fried catfish at the Cajun Café belonged to nobody but herself.

It was very odd, though, to see the waitress lower her gaze when she put down Sophie's plate and to hear her speak in a soft "white folks" voice, as if she was talking to Miss Liza. Odd and unpleasant. Even painful.

"Quit staring at that girl," Aunt Enid said when the waitress had gone back into the kitchen. "You'll embarrass her."

Sophie felt a flash of anger. "She's not a girl," she said. "She's a grown woman."

Aunt Enid glanced around nervously, then leaned forward. "You are Mrs. Charles Fairchild's granddaughter," she said, very low. "Her *white* granddaughter. And Mrs. Fairchild's granddaughter knows better than to talk about things she doesn't understand in a public place where folk might hear her."

Sophie opened her mouth and shut it again. There wasn't any point in arguing with a Fairchild, even a nice one.

236

When they got back to Oak Cottage, it was late enough that Ofelia, who liked to get home before dark, was waiting on the gallery with her hat on. Aunt Enid hadn't even stopped the Thunderbird before she was down the steps and in her own car. So she didn't really see Sophie until she came into the kitchen next morning to see her frying up an egg for breakfast.

Ofelia took one look, threw up her hands, and ran out of the kitchen.

Pausing to take the pan off the burner, Sophie followed and found her backed up against the gallery steps, her hand to her chest. "Uh-uh," she said. "Whatever you're fixing to tell me, I don't want to hear it. This place haunted with all kinds of strange goings-on and sadness. Only way I can do my work is to pay none of it no mind. And I got to work, or my babies don't eat. I'm just the hired help. You need someone to talk to, you talk to God."

Six months ago, Sophie might have cried or sulked, and Ofelia might have given in. Today, she said, "You're right, Ofelia. I'll do that," and went back inside. She was disappointed, and a little hurt, but the last thing she wanted was to be like Old Missy and make folks mind her just because she was white and rich and free and they weren't.

What had become of Old Missy, anyway? And what had happened to Oak River when the war started? Aunt Enid just looked at Sophie wall-eyed when she brought the subject up, so she turned to Grandmama, who just naturally assumed everyone was as interested in Oak River's history as she was.

The first time Sophie took the coffee tray up to Grandmama, she was greeted with a scowl. "What are you doing here? Where's Ofelia?"

"Ofelia's busy, Grandmama. Here's your coffee, just like you like it."

At first, Grandmama kept wondering aloud what Enid was thinking of to leave her own mother at the mercy of a gawky girl. But by the time Sophie had found her favorite handkerchief and her fancy work, she'd calmed down some.

"Thank you, child," she said at last. "I'm glad someone has thought to teach you manners since last week."

Sophie smiled. Dealing with Grandmama wasn't all that different from dealing with Old Missy, really. Both of them believed in their God-given right to run everybody's life for them. Old Missy was just a little nicer about it. Had she ended up crotchety and bedridden, Sophie wondered. Or had she died before she'd gotten as old as her descendant? No, her descendant's wife. Despite her family pride, Grandmama was only a Fairchild by marriage.

"Grandmama, I'd purely love to hear more about Oak River in the old days. Did you and Grandpa live in the Big House?"

Grandmama glared. "How old do you think I am, miss? Mr. Fairchild—your grandpa, that is—never lived in the Big House. His father, Stephen Fairchild, was raised there, but he brought his bride home to Oak Cottage. Your grandpa boarded the old place up after his mother passed on in 1926. I remember because I was expecting your mother." She frowned, as if at unpleasant memories. "There wasn't much left after the war. Things got lost and burned and sold to pay the high taxes the Yankees put on everything. Except for these old doodads." She waved her hand at the crowding tables and chairs.

"What happened to the Big House?"

"The Yankees looted it," said Grandmama. "Took every last piece of silver and jewelry in the house, down to Mrs. Fairchild's pearl and gold ear-bobs, so the story goes. One of the proudest families in the parish, eight hundred acres of cane and nearly two hundred slaves to work them, and overnight, just about, they came down to nothing but a handful of servants and a load of debt."

Who had stayed, Sophie wondered. Mammy, for certain, and Aunt Winney, and maybe Uncle Germany and Aunt Europe and Uncle Italy—the old ones who'd have a hard time making a new life away from Oak River. But what about Africa and Ned, Asia and Hepzibah and Sally and Samson? What about Poland and Flanders? What had happened to Canny?

But Grandmama wouldn't know the answer to any of these questions.

"What happened then?" Sophie asked.

"I disremember," said Grandmama. "There was a son, I know, worked like a slave to save the place. Had to sell off everything but the Big House and Oak Cottage and maybe a hundred acres, but they got along pretty well until the Depression. That's when Grandpa's daddy had to sell the rest of the cane fields."

Sophie tried and failed to imagine Dr. Charles cutting cane or Mrs. Charles scrubbing floors. Sophie shuddered. If she'd been a terror to live with when life was good, what must she have been like when life was hard?

Grandmama was nodding to herself. "It used to gall Grandpa like a stone in his shoe. He was so proud of his family and all they'd had. He knew all about them. Sometimes I thought he was more interested in folks who'd been dead and buried a hundred years than his own children. He was always playing with those papers."

Sophie came to full attention. "Papers?"

"Letters and plantation books and such. He showed me a letter written by Mr. Patrick Fairchild II, your great-great-great-great-great-grandfather, he'd be, to his wife, Caroline. I never did see such hen-tracks; I couldn't make head or tail of them."

Sophie leaned forward. "Are the papers still here?"

"Of course they are. They're important historical documents."

"Would you mind if I looked at them?"

Grandmama looked pleased. "I don't suppose it would do any harm. As long as you were careful."

Next morning, Sophie went to the office to look for Grandpa Fairchild's papers.

If Dr. Charles or Young Missy and her rawhide strap had left their shadows in the room, Sophie couldn't feel it. She opened a window and rummaged through cardboard boxes and antique trunks in a breeze scented by roses and magnolia. She unearthed dress patterns from the 1920's, thirty years' worth of seed catalogues, an old dress box from La Maison Blanche full of old photographs, and a dozen lace handkerchiefs wrapped in tissue. Finally, in a cabinet behind the sofa, she found what she was looking for.

Like Aunt Enid, the antebellum Fairchilds had been of a saving disposition. They'd kept the plantation books, of course—heavy, leather-bound books full of lists and columns of numbers representing barrels of sugar sold and slaves bought, sold, born, injured, dead. There were also numerous manila envelopes tied with tape and carefully labeled: *Bills of Sale—Clothing, Machinery, Household Goods, Slaves; Letters—Business—1825-1830; Letters—Personal—1850-1851; Advertisements—Slaves Wanted; Advertisements—Runaways.*

The file on runaway slaves was thinner than the others. Inside, Sophie found yellow, brittle clippings, offering rewards for the return, "alive and unharmed," of missing Fairchild human property. The runaways were mostly men, often purchased in

New Orleans. The advertisements were arranged in roughly chronological order, beginning with the oldest. Familiar names caught Sophie's eye: *Germany, known as Old One-Eye; Flanders; Betty.* And then, at the very bottom of the pile:

Two female slaves, ran from Oak River Plantation, St. Mary's Parish, Louisiana, November 1860. May be traveling as mistress and maid. Antigua, 18 years, 5'6", medium skin, good teeth, comely. Sophie, 14 years, 5'6", brown hair and eyes, fair skin, can read and write. Could pass for white. Reward for their return: $500 for either, $800 for both. Reward for information as to their whereabouts: $200 for either, $300 for both.

Sophie read it over twice. *Reward, $500.* A lot of money, though not, of course, as much as the rewards for healthy field hands. Old Missy must have really wanted them back. Slightly dazed, Sophie went in search of Aunt Enid, found her in the garden, weeding tomatoes.

"Look at this," she said, holding out the yellowed scrap.

Aunt Enid wiped her earthy hands on her shirttail, fished her reading glasses out of her pocket, and stared at the advertisement until Sophie couldn't contain herself any longer. "It's me and Antigua, see? 'Sophie, 14 years, 5'6'"? She offered a $500 reward."

Aunt Enid looked at Sophie over the top of her glasses. It was a cold look, a Fairchild look. "Yes. I see. Could pass for white. Well." She handed the paper to Sophie. "You better put this back where you found it."

The trees in the old oak grove were swagged with enough Spanish moss to buy both Poland and Flanders their freedom. Sophie followed a faint and weedy path through the grove to what was left of the Quarters. Most of the cabins had been swallowed by the commercial cane fields, but Africa's was still there, first cabin on the right, next to the trees.

Even ignoring the boarded-up windows and the rotting porch and the planks nailed across the front door, it didn't look the way Sophie remembered. The shake roof had been replaced with tin, and the wooden foundation repaired with cement blocks. The fence and cistern barrel were gone, and an electrical wire dangled from a hole in the wall.

Sophie sat on the porch steps and closed her eyes, trying to imagine Canny beside her, shucking black-eyed peas. It didn't help. The Quarters Canny had lived in had been loud with folks calling to each other, the squawking of chickens and the squealing of pigs. They had smelled of cooking and wood smoke and animals. All Sophie could hear now was the swelling roar of cicadas and the rustle of the cane. All she could smell was dust.

It was like sitting in a graveyard.

Sophie cried, and wished that the Creature would come take her back to the past, and then was mad at herself for wishing something so stupid. The past had been horrible—full of germs and cruelty and folks who thought it was good and moral to own other folks as if they were dogs or horses. She wouldn't want that back again, not for any reason.

When Sophie was all cried out, she watched the shadows creep over the cane field and thought about masters and overseers and slaves and slave hunters. It was hard to believe, now that she didn't have them right in front of her, that such folk had ever really existed. But it was even harder to believe that she had lived in this ruin, had hoed and watered and picked beans in that weed patch, a slave among other slaves, the property of Mrs. Patrick Fairchild II of Oak River Plantation.

Chapter 23

Next morning, Sophie asked Aunt Enid for permission to work on the ruined garden at the center of the maze.

Aunt Enid looked startled. "What do you know about gardening?"

"I know the difference between a rose cane and a bramble," Sophie said. "I know how to use a hoe. Most important, I know what that garden's supposed to look like. Please?"

The muskrat look grew more pronounced. "I don't know, Sophie. It's awful hot. It wouldn't do to have you keeling over from heatstroke."

"It's not as hot as the sugarhouse."

Aunt Enid threw her hands up in surrender. "The tools are in the shed. Help yourself—just put them away when you're done. And wear gloves, for gracious' sakes. Sister's purely going to create when she sees your hands."

"She's going to create anyway," Sophie said. "Did she say when's she coming down to visit?"

"The weekend after your birthday, don't you remember?" Aunt Enid sighed. "There's bound to be ructions, one way or another. If we're lucky, she'll be so exercised over the state of your extremities that she won't notice what's happened in the middle."

❧

Delia Sherman

Over the next week, Sophie pruned and cleared and weeded and hoed and scrubbed the moss from the stone benches. She found the sundial half-buried in the ground, set it back on its column, and planted zinnias from the Piggly-Wiggly under it. If she could have found a way to replace its motto with "Papa Legba throw the rock tomorrow that kill the chicken yesterday," she would have. Aunt Enid gave her advice when she asked for it and some peonies she'd lifted from her own garden, but otherwise left her alone. Sophie was grateful. The maze garden was hers, and she didn't want anybody else meddling with it.

In the afternoons, she encouraged Grandmama to talk about the Fairchilds' proud past. One day, she brought up the dress-box of old photographs from the office.

Grandmama was very excited. "My land, child, don't put that dirty thing down on the bed! You don't know where it's been. Drag that little table over, yes, right up by the bed, and go get a sheet to spread over the coverlet. Didn't your mama teach you anything?"

Sophie got the sheet and the table, opened the box, and laid out the photographs in rows. Soon dozen of Fairchilds were staring up at her: men in suits and ties and the uniforms of three wars, women in big hats and flowery dresses of various lengths and styles, solemn-eyed children dressed in their Sunday best.

Grandmama tapped one flyspecked picture with a bent forefinger. "This was taken after the war."

Sophie didn't need to ask which war—for Grandmama, it was always the War Of Northern Aggression. She took up the photo and examined it. A tall, handsome, harried-looking man Sophie didn't recognize was standing on the front gallery of the Big House, his left hand on the shoulder of an old woman in a rocking chair, wearing a frilly white cap just like Old Missy's.

Sophie looked closer. It was Old Missy, grown thin and bent. And that was Mrs. Charles beside her, scowling fit to curdle milk. Miss Liza sat at their feet, dressed in black and holding a moon-faced baby in her lap. Sophie didn't recognize the fourth woman in the picture. She stood in the circle of the man's arm, dark-haired and beautiful, her hands resting on the shoulders of a sturdy little boy.

Sophie turned the picture over and squinted at the thin, scratchy writing. "Oak River," she read aloud. "1866 or 1867. Mrs. Patrick Fairchild II, Elizabeth Fairchild Waters and her son Beaufort Sinclair Waters III, Frederick Andrew Fairchild, Robert Andrew Fairchild, Louisette Fairchild."

Robert Andrew Fairchild? Louisette?

Sophie studied the faded faces. Mr. Robert didn't look like the kind of man who would run away from his debts to her. And what was he doing at Oak River anyway? Where was Dr. Charles?

She handed the photo to Grandmama.

"If that's Mrs. Charles Fairchild, where's Mr. Charles?"

Grandmama considered. "Her husband was a Doctor Fairchild, if I remember correctly, and he died in the war, along with his son-in-law. The younger brother inherited. Robert, that would be. They had to call him home from France with his wife and child." She smiled at the faded sepia faces. "Pretty thing, isn't she? Foreign, of course."

It was a good thing that Grandmama was hard of hearing, because Sophie couldn't for the life of her have explained why she was laughing. She hadn't lied to Dr. Charles after all. Mr. Robert must have married Louisette in France, then forced the family to accept her as white when he came back after the war.

Sophie studied her ancestress' proud, beautiful face. She looked happy, Sophie thought. She also looked a little like Mama.

A few days later, Aunt Enid found Sophie in the office, going through the plantation files again.

"You're going to wear those old papers right out, looking for what's not there," she said. "I'm going to drive you into Oakwood, introduce you to Mrs. Robinson at the Parish Museum. She's got things in that back room of hers nobody's set eyes on since Grant was president."

Twenty minutes later, Sophie was standing in the dank, neon-lit exhibition area of the Parish Museum, shaking hands with a plump little woman in pale green rhinestone glasses and a print cotton housedress.

"A school project!" Mrs. Robinson burbled. "How exciting! It's so important for young people to understand their heritage, I always think. And Mrs. Fairchild's granddaughter, too! Our papers are a terrible mess, I'm afraid—most folks come in here are more interested in the artifacts." She gestured at dusty glass cases stuffed with sewing baskets, knitted cotton stockings, hair receivers, buttonhooks, and shaving mugs.

Sophie smiled at her patiently. "My assignment is to find out more about the slaves."

Puzzled wrinkles gathered behind the rhinestone glasses. "Can't recall anybody asking about the servants before. You won't find any papers—they couldn't write, you know. And so many things got lost." She shook her head. "We have a few artifacts—cane knives and wooden plates and so on, from the Oak River Quarters, mostly. And an old stool from Doucette. Oh, and a trunk Ned Roberts brought in after his mama passed. Been in his family since the war, he said, but Ofelia was bound and determined to get it out of the house. Can't imagine there's much in it, but you're welcome to look."

Excitement leapt in Sophie, but she kept her voice even. "Thank you, ma'am. I'd like that."

The trunk was in a back room piled high with cartons and boxes. "That's it over there," Mrs. Robinson said, "under the quilt. It's a lady's trunk, pre-war, I'm pretty sure, and I didn't want any harm to come to it. You call me if you need anything, now."

As Mrs. Robinson left the room, Sophie whipped the quilt off the trunk and opened its domed lid. To her joy, it was filled with papers, tied neatly into bundles, each one labeled with its contents and their dates. Sophie took them out gently, one by one, until she came to a thin bundle tied with a faded yellow ribbon. The label read: *Aunt Omi to Grandma, 1861–1870*.

Aunt Omi. Omi Saide. Antigua. Antigua had survived.

Sophie blinked back tears, then took the bundle to the desk under the window, untied the ribbon, and carefully unfolded the first letter.

Dear Momi:

My friend Sue Potter is writing this for me because my writing ain't all that good yet. I am in New York City now. I won't say everything that happened to me on the way here, because it too long a story and maybe it might make trouble for the people who help me. Although I guess the war is trouble enough for everybody.

Don't worry about me. I have a job making shoes in a factory. It pay enough to live on and a little left over. New York is dirtier than a pigsty and I never knew there could be so many folks in one place, but I got good friends. Sue is teaching me reading and writing. You will like Sue. She is dark as Popi and she born free.

I miss you all, Momi, and worry and pray for you every day. When the war over, maybe you all can get away from Oak River, come up to New York, live with me. Tell Sophie she should come too.

The handwriting of the signature was different from the rest of the letter—firm and round.

Omi Saide, was Antigua.

Because Sophie's birthday fell on a work day, Mama had decided they would celebrate it the weekend after. On July 6, the day of her actual birthday, Ofelia presented her with a cake—chocolate with white icing, Sophie's favorite. When Sophie thanked her shyly, she said, "Least I can do, with all the help you've been, keeping your grandmama company and all."

Sophie blew out her fourteen candles and Ofelia sat down and had coffee and cake with her and Aunt Enid. Then they all got down to the serious business of cleaning the house before Mama came. Aunt Enid even made an effort to tidy up the office, but it didn't come to much.

Friday, after lunch, Sophie took a long bath. She slathered cream on her work-roughened hands and feet, braided her hair in a tail, put on the crispest of her new blouses and the fullest of her new skirts, and examined the result in the armoire's mirrored door. A Fairchild woman stared back at her—long-faced, eagle-nosed, worried-looking, and a lot older than fourteen. Grimly, Sophie undid the braid and pulled her hair into two frizzy bunches below her ears, like Dorothy in *The Wizard of Oz*. It helped a little.

When she got down to the kitchen, Mama was sitting at the table with Aunt Enid, chatting and sipping a glass of ice tea. When she saw Sophie, her eyes widened with shock.

"What on *earth* have you done to your hair?"

She sounded so exactly like Young Missy that Sophie had to smile.

"Hello, Mama," she said. "Did you have a nice trip?"

"Don't try and change the subject. Why are you wearing your aunt's clothes?"

"They're mine, actually. We got them in Lafayette. I—had a growth spurt."

At this, Aunt Enid's muskrat look came on so strong that Sophie had to clamp her lips together to keep from laughing.

Mama heaved a martyred sigh. "I expect that means a whole new fall wardrobe," she said. "Thank heaven for uniforms, is all I have to say."

And that was that. Mama hardly looked at Sophie the rest of the evening, but kept up a lively stream of stories about someone called "Lou," who took her out to dinner at Commander's Palace and Galatoire's and had a house on Lake Ponchartrain. School was going well and her boss had given her a raise—not enough to make keeping the Metairie house an option, but something. The only time she took any notice of Sophie was when she cleared the supper dishes and served up Ofelia's chess pie and coffee.

"Gracious, darling!" Mama said. "How housewifely you've grown! I declare, I hardly recognize my lazy little daughter!"

Sophie slid into her seat and poked at her pie. It was going to be a long weekend.

❧

During breakfast the next morning, Henry the yardman brought a parcel for Sophie. The return address was New York City.

It was a good-sized package, bundled up in brown paper and lots of twine, not nearly as neat as the packages Papa's secretary usually sent. The handwriting on the label was unfamiliar, too.

"I can't imagine what Rand was thinking, sending your present here," Mama said. "We're just going to have to carry it back home at the end of the summer."

"Better open it," Aunt Enid said. "There might be a letter."

Sophie got the kitchen scissors and attacked the twine. She opened the box, took out an envelope addressed to her in the same writing as on the package, and laid it aside. Underneath were magazines: a half-dozen *New Yorkers*, a Sunday *New York Times* and a *Herald Tribune*. And books, four of them—two obviously kids' books and two equally obviously for adults.

Sophie picked up *A Tree Grows in Brooklyn* and opened it curiously.

"Put that back in the box, Sophie," Mama said. "We're sending them right back where they came from. The very idea!"

Sophie looked up to see the envelope open on the table and Mama holding a typed page. Furious, she snatched it out of her mother's hand.

"That was addressed to me." She was surprised how calm she sounded. "So are the books. I get to decide what happens to them. Not you."

Mama's lips pinched to invisibility, and her eyes narrowed. Sophie glared back.

After a tense moment, Mama shrugged. "I'd hope a daughter of mine would have too much pride to allow herself to be bribed with a few books."

Too angry to speak, Sophie tumbled everything into the box and carried it out to the garden shed, where she hid it under an upturned wheelbarrow. Grabbing the letter and a handful of *New Yorkers*, she ran out into the field.

After three weeks of hard work, the maze was starting to look more the way it should. Henry had scythed the grass, and was helping Sophie trim back the hedges. The path to the center was clear, as well as the little side-room where Belle Watling simpered above a freshly painted bench. By the time Sophie got to the central garden, she could read her letter in relative calm.

Dear Sophie, it said.

> *Your father has told me so much about you, I feel like I must know you. But I don't, not really. So when it came time to send you a birthday present, I had to take my best guess.*
>
> *Your father said you read everything, even the backs of cereal boxes, but mostly make-believe and kids' books. This makes perfect sense to me.* Stuart Little *and* The Princess and the Goblin *are among my favorite books in the world.*
>
> *But fathers don't always realize that daughters grow up. Now you're fourteen, your tastes may have changed. So I'm also sending some books that don't have magic in them, except the magic of taking you to a place you've never been before.*
>
> *Also, I'm sending some magazines.* The New Yorker *has some funny cartoons (Charles Addams is my favorite), and there are theatre and movie reviews and lists of museums.*
>
> *The reason almost everything I've sent is about New York is that it's my hometown and I love it. It's also because*

your father and I would like you to come and visit us before school starts. I know how annoying it can be to have adults plan everything over your head, so we haven't said anything to your mother yet, in case you'd rather not come. But if you would, just drop us a line or give us a call, and we'll take it from there.

I only had brothers, growing up, and always wanted a little sister to share books and my favorite exhibits at the Metropolitan Museum with and shopping and ice-cream soda at Schrafft's. And your father is full of plans about going to Horn & Hardart's Automat and rowing on Central Park Lake.

Do come and visit, Sophie. It'll be fun.

The letter was signed "Judith H. Martineau."

Sophie read the letter twice. It was obvious that Judith H. Martineau really wanted Sophie to like her, but didn't expect it to happen right away. Which was a good thing, because the name Martineau attached to the unfamiliar Judith H. made Sophie queasy. So did the fact that it contained no word from Papa—not even a P.S.

She glanced at *The New Yorker*. The cover was a drawing of two shadowy children chasing a flock of butterflies with nets. The children were tiny, the butterflies were giants loosely sketched in colored chalk. She'd never seen anything like it. The articles inside were all about people and places she'd never heard of. Most of the cartoons were incomprehensible, but an Addams cartoon, featuring a skinny lady with long black hair and a black dress that rippled around her feet like an octopus's tentacles, made her laugh. Judith H. had a good sense of humor. Too bad Mama would never let them meet.

Mama appeared the garden entrance, looking hot and bothered. Her high heels were smeared with dirt from crossing the field, and the curls of her permanent wave clung wetly to her forehead and neck. She'd never have lasted a minute in the sugarhouse.

"Enid said you'd be here," Mama said. "I can't imagine why."

"I like it." Sophie stood up. "Why don't you sit here in the shade, and I'll go fetch some lemonade."

"You stay right where you are, Miss. You've been avoiding me ever since I arrived. If this is about that silly disagreement we had last time I was here, all I have to say is that I'm surprised at you."

She didn't look surprised. Although Mama was dark where Mrs. Charles was fair, curved where Mrs. Charles was flat, Mama looked just like Mrs. Charles confronting an errant slave: disgusted, impatient, and ready to pull out her rawhide.

Mama took a handkerchief out of her belt and patted her sweating forehead. "It's hormones, I expect. Thinking you're all grown up and able to decide things on your own when you've no more sense than a rabbit. I suppose now you're going to tell me that you want me to let you visit your father and that woman in New York City. Well, you can't. You're much too young to travel alone. I wouldn't sleep a wink for worrying you'd lose your money or your luggage or your ticket, or get yourself kidnapped. Besides, I can't afford a ticket."

As her mother talked, a familiar feeling of hopelessness crept over Sophie. She could argue or she could beg, but the outcome would be the same. Mama would fuss until Sophie gave in, and that was how it would be until the end of time. Unless she ran away. Maybe she could dye her hair blond, dress up like she was older, borrow some money from Aunt Enid, and travel up to New York on her own. Antigua had done it. So could she.

And Mama would just come after her, or call the police.

And then the world spun around, just as it had when she came back from the past, and Sophie realized that Mama didn't actually own her—not the way Dr. Charles owned Antigua. She couldn't keep Sophie from visiting her own father if Sophie wanted to. She could make an almighty fuss, but a fuss wasn't a whipping. A whipping was the least of what Antigua would have suffered if Mr. Akins had caught her, and she'd chosen freedom anyway.

Sophie raised her head and looked her mother straight in the eye. "You don't need to pay for it. If I write Papa and tell him I'd like to visit, I'm sure he'll fix it so I can."

Mama stared at her. "How can you talk so ugly to me, after everything I've done for you? Why, I took that horrible job so you could have the life you're used to."

"You like your job," Sophie pointed out. "And I think I might want a different kind of life than the one I'm used to."

"Ingratitude," Mama said, "is very unattractive in a young lady."

"I'm going to New York."

Mama turned on her high heel and stalked out of the garden.

Sophie pressed her fingers to her eyes. She'd write Judith H. and Papa tonight. No matter what Mama said or did, she wouldn't back down and she wouldn't change her mind. Maybe Mama would come around in the end and maybe she wouldn't. Maybe Papa wouldn't like having her there, maybe she wouldn't get along with Judith H. Maybe Sophie would be sorry, just like Mama said, and come running home again with her tail between her legs. Maybe she'd be happy and learn to do for herself. She'd never know unless she tried.

Sophie Fairchild Martineau got up from the stone bench, shook out her skirts and, walking in Antigua's footsteps, left the maze.

Acknowledgements

Over the eighteen years I worked on this book, I had a lot of help from a lot of people. If I were to write a proper thank-you here to everyone who has inspired me, supported me, helped me with my research, listened to me agonize over a plot point, or asked just the question I needed to get me to the next scene or the next draft, this Acknowledgment would be as long as the book itself, so maybe it's a good thing I've lost track. Okay, it's not. But I hope the people I've inadvertently left out will forgive me; I'm sure I thanked you profusely at least once.

Much of my primary research took place during two trips to Louisiana, in 1994 and in 1996. The librarians of Loyola University library guided me to a manila folder full of advertisements for escaped slaves, one of which read "blond and blue-eyed, could pass for white." The library of the Baton Rouge Rural Life Museum was full of useful volumes on plantation life. Madewood, Tezcuco, Alice, and Laura Plantations contributed gardens, layouts, floorplans, and useful details to my invented houses at Oak River. I pestered their docents—and the docents of Destrahan, the Port Allen Museum, and the Jeanerette Sugar Museum—with as many questions about life on a sugar plantation as Sophie had, and these amazingly dedicated historians, volunteers, and enthusiasts managed to answer them all. If I didn't always ask the right questions, it's not their fault.

For seeing this novel through the painful first draft and reading subsequent drafts at (approximately) five-year intervals, I would like to thank the Genrettes: Laurie J. Marks, Rosemary Kirstein, and Didi Stewart. Linda Post and Mimi Panitch helped me talk through the plot. Ellen Klages, Caroline Stevermer, and Eve Sweetser patiently read several drafts and provided encouragement. The Massachusetts All-Stars—Kelly Link, Gavin Grant, Cassandra Clare, Joshua Lewis, Holly Black, Sarah Smith, and Ellen Kushner—put their fingers on all the weak points and gave excellent suggestions for strengthening them.

N. K. Jemisin, Alaya Dawn Johnson, Nisi Shawl, K. Tempest Bradford, and Nalo Hopkinson were kind enough to discuss white privilege, class and race, cultural appropriation, and Writing the Other with me, and to read the manuscript for howlers. Helen and Tim Atkinson kindly lent me their house as a retreat when I wrote my last draft. Doselle Young spent hours with me on Skype, working out the frame story. Donnard Sturgis (a.k.a. Sophie's godfather) has answered many questions about Voudon, Yemaya, and Papa Legba. Silvana Siddali, Associate Professor of American History at St. Louis University, helped me with details of antebellum politics, fashion, and culture. Insofar as *The Freedom Maze* is accurate, it's due to all of them. Any mistakes and glitches, of course, are entirely my own work.

Great thanks are due to Kelly Link and Gavin J. Grant of Big Mouth House. They read this book as friends and writing-group members and approached me, years later, as editors and publishers. I am more grateful than I can say for their faith in me and for giving Sophie and her friends a chance to tell their story to a wider audience.

Thanks, too, to Jane Yolen (a.k.a. Sophie's godmother) who encouraged me to write the book in the first place.

Finally, I thank Ellen Kushner, partner of my joys and sorrows. She drove around Southern Louisiana with me, wandering through cane fields, peering in the windows of ruined slave cabins and moldering plantation houses, going through envelopes of yellowing clippings from 19th century newspapers, and visiting endless plantations and museums. She listened to me agonize over the characters, the plot, the setting, the pacing, and the style of this book, and read it almost as many times as I did. Without her support—and the occasional stern pep talk—I doubt I would have finished it.